Hobbs, Valerie.
How far would you have
gotten if I hadn't called
you back? : a novel
c1995.

S

8/02

How Far Would You Have Gotten If I Hadn't Called You Back?

A Richard Jackson Book

How Far Would You Have Gotten If I Hadn't Called You Back?

a novel by
VALERIE HOBBS

Orchard Books   New York

Permission to quote from the following works is gratefully
acknowledged. Page 126: "The Road Not Taken" from *The
Poetry of Robert Frost* edited by Edward Connery Lathem.
Reprinted with permission of the Estate of Robert Frost and
Jonathan Cape, London, England. Public Domain in the
United States. Page 305: "Night" from *Selected Poetry of
Robinson Jeffers* by Robinson Jeffers. Copyright © 1925 by
Robinson Jeffers and renewed 1953 by Robinson Jeffers.
Reprinted by permission of Random House, Inc.

Orchard Books, 95 Madison Avenue, New York, NY 10016

Manufactured in the United States of America
Book design by Mina Greenstein
The text of this book is set in 11 point Fournier.
10 9 8 7 6 5 4 3 2

Library of Congress Cataloging-in-Publication Data
Hobbs, Valerie.
How far would you have gotten if I hadn't called you
back? : a novel / by Valerie Hobbs.
p. cm. "A Richard Jackson book"—Half t.p.
Summary: After moving with her family from New Jersey to
California in 1960, sixteen-year-old Bron discovers the world
of drag racing.
ISBN 0-531-09480-4. ISBN 0-531-08780-8 (lib. bdg.)
[1. Moving, Household—Fiction. 2. Drag racing—Fiction.
3. California—Fiction.] I. Title.
PZ7.H65237Ho 1995 [Fic]—dc20 94-48799

FOR JACK

How Far Would You Have Gotten If I Hadn't Called You Back?

1

OJALA WAS, still is, a small dusty town twenty miles inland from the California everybody knows, the California of postcards. We got there by mistake, a wrong turn off the freeway. "A happy accident," my mother said. Already she had fallen for the dusty red tile and pseudo-Spanish arches of the town.

All we owned was packed in the trunk of the car, a gull gray '49 Plymouth, and in a plywood box roped to the top. "California or Bust" said the box in bright orange letters across one side, Buddy's idea. Crossing the country was a thrill of a lifetime for my brother. For me, it was agony. Indiana was a cornfield, Utah had some mountains. All the rest was gas stops and cheap motels.

Sometimes, if he was really tired and the road was flat and empty, my father let me drive. But that was rare. Mostly I slept in the back, hogging the seat, leaving Buddy just a corner. Buddy never complained. He counted cows, sang to himself, mashing his nose against the window, watching,

watching. He was ten. He didn't even smell like a person yet and most of the time I didn't treat him like one. I was six years older. Around my neck on a shoelace stiff with dried spit and tears was Joe Panucci's senior ring, all I had left of my real life. In New Jersey. A place nobody would leave unless their mother was crazy and their father unreliable and they had no other choice.

We stood in the shade of the arches squinting out at the street like prospectors, each seeing something different. There wasn't that much to see. Drugstore, pool parlor, Bailey's Market, city hall, Flying A station with a single pump. You could turn your head once from left to right and you wouldn't miss a thing. One hundred and three, the drugstore thermometer read. But a "dry" heat, said my mother.

She had this way of seeing the good side of everything that could drive you crazy. Look at the *bright* side, she'd say. Every cloud has a silver lining! Every wrong turn off the highway was the start of an exciting adventure.

Ten past two in the afternoon and there was no one around. Not a single living soul. Just this eerie glare, this violation of light and color: a vine with horrid purple flowers that had swallowed up the post office; a pickup truck painted to mimic the glassy surface of a candied apple, with chrome so highly polished you could see the perfect reflection of your dusty toes and worn-out sandals in it. All this against a hazy, bombed-out background of hacienda beige.

My mother had begun to glow and hum like a heater left on too long. It was the way she often got in church at the end of a rousing sermon. "It's perfect, isn't it, Tom? Just look at all this *history*!" My father looked wary, but I knew he'd stop anywhere she said. He had never been a healthy man, and by then, three thousand four hundred and fifty-three miles from home—according to Bess's odometer, which, if you couldn't trust the radiator not to boil or the hoses not to blow, you probably couldn't trust—by that time he was exhausted. Only Mother's promises and a cold washrag plastered to the back of his neck kept him going. "Let's get a local paper," Mom said. "I'm sure we'll find the perfect spot for the restaurant, I just know it."

We'd sampled a dozen cities by then, meandering up the coast as if for once there was an unlimited supply of time and money. But nothing felt "right." "Too big," my mother would say. "No charm, no *joie de vivre!*" She'd sigh as if each beachside town or glitzy dress store had gone clear out of its way to personally disappoint her. "Gauche!" she'd cry. "I simply don't under*stand* this."

My father would shake his head, cluck his tongue, look back over the seat, and roll his eyes at Buddy and me. Our mother was a little crazy, the look said, and didn't we love her for it? But now he was tired. He didn't care where we settled. One place was as good as another. I thought, If that isn't crazy, what is?

It was cool inside Ojala Pharmacy and dark when you first stepped in. "Howdy, folks," a voice called out from somewhere in the back, beyond the racks of cough remedies and bedpans.

I headed right for the magazine rack, Buddy in tow. "No more magazines," my father warned. He'd said the same thing clear across the country, every place we stopped. But I knew he'd shell out. It was a small price to pay for having ruined my life.

The magazines were on one long rack that led to a soda fountain where a single person sat, a girl about my age, twirling her right foot and the straw in her Coke. She was dressed all in white—sandals, sundress, white satin ribbon trailing the length of a silver blond ponytail. Her skin was the honeyed gold of Sunday morning waffles, her lips and fingernails a perfectly executed, perfectly matched bright crimson. I caught myself staring, but you could see she was used to that.

Behind the counter was a woman with a gummy smile and hips like my mother's. What my father called the "hubba hubba" kind. From a leopard-print scarf tied around her head, a mop of red curls sprang like an explosion of copper wires. "Hot enough for ya?"

"Sure is!" my father said.

"It's a dry heat, though, isn't it?" said my mother.

"Dry your wash in twenty minutes," said the waitress. "Towels and all. What can I getcha?"

Buddy leaped up on one of the stools and began spinning in furious circles. "I wanna Coke. No, I wanna malt! A chocolate malt!" Buddy yelled everything in those days. Until we had him checked, we thought he might be hard of hearing, but he was normal enough for a ten-year-old. Yelling was just his way of making sure we knew he was still around. Clear across the country we'd left things behind—the car keys in a half-dozen restaurants, Mom's purse in an Esso rest room on the Pennsylvania Turnpike, the AAA Triptik (our Bible)—and Buddy wasn't about to get left behind. He was having too much fun.

My mother took the seat beside him, dabbing daintily at her face with a paper napkin. Her yellow checkered sundress looked wrung out and stuck on to dry. Tendrils of damp hair clung to her neck. Everything about her was pretty except her earlobes, which were made for hanging bones from. But I would never tell her that. Even at my

(4)

worst I had a little sense. "I believe I'll have something very tall and very cool . . . lemonade! Perfect."

My father stood behind Buddy and Mother like a loony old man rustling the change in his pocket. Handing over his money, no matter how little, made him very nervous. Already we'd spent twice what was budgeted on motels with swimming pools, endless bottles of Coca-Cola, comic books, and movie magazines, not to mention the new generator for Bess, who broke our hearts in Cheyenne. What would be left to open the restaurant? There were deep wet rings beneath the arms of my father's faded plaid sportshirt. He took the seat on the other side of Buddy, rumpling Buddy's already rumpled head.

I didn't know whether to sit or to run, so I stood behind, with them but not with them, somewhere in the middle. The girl in white looked over in the long, lazy way movie stars do (I knew because I'd tried so hard to perfect that gaze myself) and I could see in her eyes all that we were: Gypsies, transients, poor people. I hated Ojala from that moment.

"Chocolate malt for the young man, one lemonade . . ." my father said, following up with his standard "coffee, hot and black, like my women." The redheaded waitress looked like she was biting her tongue.

"I don't want anything," I said. Leafing through *Photoplay*, I could hear my parents chatting away to the redhead, telling her our life history. Not everything, of course, just what they considered all the good parts, all the great things that had happened on the road. It was meant to be spontaneous and zany, but it never was. My father laughed too long at his own jokes. My mother could never get straight what it meant to be his "straight man." Buddy yelled his lines in all the wrong places. "Remember the rattlesnake, Dad? Remember the dinosaur turds?" I wanted to melt, evaporate. The girl in white was watching them, laughing at them. Couldn't they tell?

AFTER, we piled back into Bess. "Hot as a blast furnace," my father grumbled. "Hot as blazes," my mother said. Buddy and I mouthed their lines along with them. It was what they said every time, but they didn't seem to know that. Buddy thought they were funny; I thought them pathetic, senile, decrepit. Whenever I needed another word with which to indict them, I'd pull out the thesaurus I won in the eighth grade spell-off. *Rueful, opprobrious, ignoble . . .*

"Let's ride out toward the mountains," my mother suggested.

"Get a lay of the land," Buddy and I said simultaneously. My father chuckled.

Any direction was mountains, so huge you couldn't see where they left off in the air, huge and covered with a gray-green furlike vegetation, in patches like the backside of a mangy dog. Ojala was ringed all around by these mountains. I wondered how losers like us had managed to find our way in.

We passed a few more businesses, poking out of dirt lots like a string of broken teeth—Ojala Bowl, Ojala Liquor, and a tiny Mexican restaurant, Carlito's, with a single car in the parking lot. "Looks like they could use some competition," my father said dryly. But my mother was lost in the scenery as we began to climb the winding road east out of town. The wind came at us through her window, carrying her excitement. "Look at all the orange trees! I promised you orange trees, didn't I, children?" Then, with a horrorstruck look at my father, "Those aren't orange trees, Tom. What do you suppose they are?" Stuck to the sides of the hills were bushy green trees in neat rows like connect-the-dots. "Alligator pears," my father pronounced.

"Oh," my mother said, a little uncertainly.

Bess began steaming before we got very far. My father pulled into a lookout to let her cool down and we all got out. "Don't go too close!" my mother warned. A gust of hot wind hit Buddy first and tried to blow him back. We held hands (Buddy would do that then) and stuck our toes over the edge, just like we always did.

In the gray haze below was the tiny city of Ojala that my mother had already taken to her easy heart, a handful of red-roofed yellow mud huts and a half-dozen roads leading nowhere. Ahead was gray space, a cloudless sky, mountain ridges as far as you could see in outlines fading whiter as they went. A hawk floated in on an updraft, then dropped out of sight like a downed jet.

My father stood behind my mother, arms around her waist. They were the same height, not much taller than I. He could rest his chin on her shoulder. "So this is it, is it, lass?" he said.

"Mmmmm . . ." she murmured, smiling like the winner on *Queen for a Day*.

That same afternoon we found a house and rented it for what Mother called its "possibilities." It was yellow, faded almost to white, with a wide front porch gaping open like a toothless mouth. "Neat!" Buddy yelled, racing up the sagging front steps. "A porch!"

"Nine forty-six," my mother read aloud from a number handpainted on the door. "A lucky number!"

"Why?" I asked. She had clasped her hands under her chin, as if in prayer.

"Hmmm?" You could see she was already transforming the place from the paint buckets in her mind.

"Why is it lucky? Why is 946 lucky, Ma?" I knew she didn't have an answer. She never did.

She gave me a puzzled look, as if my ability to reason had been impaired at birth. "It just is," she said.

Buddy raced across the porch from window to window, peering into the darkness and yelling, "Here's a bedroom! Here's a living room!" The front steps were worn to a trough in the center. "I can take care of this," my father said, prying the top step loose with the toe of his shoe. "Nothing I can't handle."

Mother gave him one of her adoring smiles and took his arm as if they were honeymooners. I thought for a minute that he'd whisk her up and carry her over the threshold. They did the craziest things sometimes, kissed in the supermarket, sang songs they didn't know the words to. They didn't care who might be watching. I had to explain them to my friends, as if they were from some foreign country where the customs were different. Of course, my friends all thought they were great.

My father worked the key into the lock, rattling the door till it dropped open like a yawn. The smell hit first. "There's something dead in here," I said. Scattered across the bare wood floor were broken dishes, beer bottles, pizza boxes—*Angelo's, A Cut Above. We Deliver*—a naked Barbie with her head on backward.

"It'll take a little work," Mom said. She shuffled aside a pair of men's boxer shorts with the toe of her Wedgie.

"It'll take a whole army! *Ma!*" I cried, but she was not in the place where you could reason with her.

"Whatever stinks," cried Buddy, "is down there." He pointed to a dark space under the heater grate.

I peered down, pinching my nose. "Can we get our deposit back?" Buddy and Dad went in search of the stench, while Mom and I "explored," me clumping along at her heels offering a running commentary. Each room was a different color, pea green, yellow ocher, cotton candy—all the worst Crayola colors, the ones that stayed new till you threw out the box. One bedroom reminded me of the liner in my grandmother Lewis's coffin, that same suffocating deep rose. "Nothing a gallon of off-white won't fix," she said. Off-white was her cure for everything. "A piano could go here," she said. "Or even here."

"What piano?" I said.

"Your father will find one, don't worry," she said.

I poked along, pointing out broken door hinges, falling plaster. "This place sure stinks. No telling what they'll find down there! Rats probably." Mother's jaw locked down, but she didn't answer. "Rats carry typhoid, don't they? Well, *don't* they?"

The kitchen was the same muddy yellow as the first bedroom and attached like an afterthought to the back of the house. Rusty red linoleum made to resemble bricks groaned underfoot as if you were breaking its back.

"Just look at the light in this room," Mother exclaimed, ignoring a cracked, mud-spattered window, busted pipes under the sink dripping water onto buckled linoleum.

"Check *this* out," I said. "There must be ten years of caked crud on this stove."

"Plenty of windows," she said. "That's important when you're cooking all day. Nice deep sink! Those stains will come right out with Clorox."

"It's a dump, Ma," I said. "Face it. It's a righteous dump."

In the hard light of the empty kitchen, my mother's face

was pale and soft-looking. There were lines intersecting lines I'd never noticed before. "Bron," she said. "Please, *please* stop this. . . ."

THE MOON was full that first night in Ojala, an enormous, mottled white eye. For dinner, we had Frostee burgers on the porch, staring up at the moon like cave people. "A picnic," Mother said, gathering her skirt to squat on the top step. She always wore anklets with her flats even though I said she shouldn't, that no one else did, that she looked really dumb. "Perfect! Just feel that wonderful warm air! In Plainfield we'd have our sweaters on."

"But we'd be inside the house," I pointed out. "At our table. Sitting in our chairs, eating off our plates." Buddy's eyes went round, seeing what I was seeing, the house we'd both been born in with its wedding-cake porch rail and weeping willow tree. I wanted to tell him how we'd been conned. How all your life they let you believe that no matter what happened outside in the world, no matter what anyone said or had or thought, there'd always be dinner on the chipped Formica table (now precious in memory as a shrine), an updated Rexall calendar hanging over the stove, the worn place in the floor in front of the sink, the old upright piano. I could smell it still, that house.

"Bron," Mother said sadly. "You have no sense of ad-*ven*ture."

A hot almost constant breeze, a strange otherworldly presence, carried the sounds of traffic from the other end of the Avenue: engines gunned and whipped to a howling pitch, tires squealing onto asphalt, a sharp curse followed by the careening waterfall of a girl's laughter.

"I wonder if it ever rains," my father said. He and Buddy had unearthed the source of the stench, a dead cat so dry that it broke apart in their hands. Buddy saved the head in a cigar box along with all his other treasures from across the country, half an arrowhead, a bunch of wooden nickels, assorted bird's feathers, the "genuine" dinosaur turd he'd found in a cave somewhere in Utah. All he'd brought from home was his baseball cards. It was different for me. I'd cried for days over what I'd had to leave behind, hugging my ice skates as if they were my soon-to-be abandoned children.

WE MOVED into the old yellow house when it was as clean as anyone could get it, not downstairs where the two "dining rooms" would be, but upstairs into a single room in the attic. My mother hung sheets to partition off the "bedrooms" and said I could hang all my posters on the slanted ceiling, James Dean and Elvis hanging from the rafters, and wasn't that nice? I said it looked like a hospital for the criminally insane. Buddy doubled over with laughter, clutching his stomach. He thought I was the funniest person in the world. Half of what I said was to see myself in his eyes. The other half was for revenge.

Like a hostage, I began plotting escape. No way would I live in a town with a single theater showing last year's movies. I'd get a job, save every penny, catch a ride with some nice truck driver like my Uncle Jack, who drove big rigs for a living. Then one day, when no one was expecting such a terrific surprise, I'd show up at Plainfield High, just as if I'd never left, wearing a dyed-to-match outfit and brand-new white bucks, Joe's ring on a clean shoelace.

In version one of the daydream, the good version, all my friends would gasp as if they'd seen a ghost. Then they'd shriek and run toward me, falling all over each other to see who'd get to me first. We'd hug in a big heap and cry and laugh and it would be just like always, chocolate

Cokes at Swingler's, Bill Haley on the jukebox, Friday night sock hops in the gym, slumber parties, new cheers for the football games.

In version two, I was invisible, already forgotten. I'd stand somewhere in the backfield, white bucks frozen to the earth. "Hey, guys! I'm back!" But no one would turn, no one would hear me. Or if they did, someone would invariably say, "Hey, isn't that the girl whose father tried to, you know, *off* himself?"

2

THE WELSH KITCHEN was either ahead of its time or behind it, charming or an embarrassment, I never knew which. Mom and Dad seemed unconcerned about that. They were far too busy to care about such things as reputation, particularly before we really had one. They simply had to make it all work or we'd be out on the street.

How I hated those words. As a child I'd lie awake at night worrying about where we'd hang our clothes *out on the street*, whether we would take the refrigerator to keep the milk cold, and where *out on the street* we would put our complete set of the Great Books. I'd seen the old men who slept in boxes outside the Salvation Army. I'd smelled their horrid odor, seen them fumble with their pants to pee against the sides of buildings. My heart would race at the thought of living near them on the street, sleeping in four cardboard boxes like turtle people.

Now I had more important things to worry about. I

knew what happened at school to kids who didn't have the right clothes or lived in the wrong neighborhoods, who had physical disabilities or dark skins, whose parents drove buses or pumped gas. In the wink of an eye or a sideways glance, less than that, you could be ostracized forever, made to wander the edges of the known world like a leper.

I decided not to tell anyone who I was or where I lived. But people were friendly and inquisitive in Ojala, or maybe just nosy. Shopkeepers would ask if I was visiting with family and I'd say yes, that we had driven all the way from Florida to spend a week at the Ojala Inn, that Florida was too humid and crowded in the summer, that we'd closed our summer home and driven the whole way, just to see the country. I saw their willingness to believe as naïve and pitiful. What would they say if they knew that we slept like a family of rats in the attic?

The restaurant was a salvage operation, an invention. My father bore home, like a triumphant hunter, mismatched tables from thrift stores in three counties. Some were round, some had fat intricately carved legs, most of them wobbled. Mother covered them with yards and yards of blue-and-white checkered fabric sewn by hand into tablecloths. All the chairs, some with stiff high backs, some as spindly thin as old women, she painted a "cheerful" blue. There were lace café curtains in the windows and travel posters thumbtacked to the walls: *Great Britain Welcomes You!* with apple-cheeked children herding cows . . . *The Brecon Beacons, more than just a few sheep.* . . . A map of Wales covered with indecipherable words, cities like Cumsyfiog and Abergavenny, had been framed and hung just inside the door to give the impression that our customers would be entering a new and exciting country. They would be having, like it or not, one of my mother's adventures.

We'd have fresh flowers on the tables, Mother said, always fresh, fresh flowers. "Somebody better fix the front steps or what we'll have is a lawsuit," I said.

Dad began to sing again, old songs from the mines and hymns I hadn't heard since I was a child, "Men of Harlech," "Cwm Pennant." . . . I'd awaken in the morning with a lump already in my throat, remembering times when life was predictable and ordinary, before his "accident," before Mother promised him his restaurant. I'd awaken and remember, heart sinking, where I was now, my father singing in the kitchen, "experimenting," stewing things in enormous pots salvaged from who knew where, leeks and onions, roast lamb spitting and sizzling. "Here," he'd say, offering a steaming wooden spoon. "Try the Sicilian Spaghetti. Try my Sumptuous Shepherd's Pie!" He'd be decked all in white, "chef's clothes" delivered by the laundry, but by noon he'd be covered like a mad artist in stripes of red and green, splotches of gravy and mustard. Steam would rise from the pots and gather on the windows and on my father, drenching him.

He was happy. My father was a happy man. Still, he had to be watched.

Buddy began to run with a pack of dark-eyed, dark-skinned boys from the neighborhood, kids with names like Luis and Hector. His fair skin darkened, and with his brown eyes and hair, you could hardly tell him after a while from the others, except that he was always the loudest. He began to speak a strange language, half English, half Spanish, and rode horses bareback, leaping into the saddle from the ground like a quick brown monkey. I was happy for him but lonelier than ever.

My father repaired the front steps, bending dozens of nails, slamming his thumb blue, swearing in two languages.

He'd never been handy with tools, but he worked with a resolve we'd never seen in him. "It's because it's his own place," Mother said. "All he needed was his own place."

But she worried. Worry was her middle name, my father said. Helen Worry Lewis. She worried that we'd open for business and no one would show up. Or, worse, that they'd show up once and never come back. What if it was all— the sale of Great-grandmother's house, the exhausting trip across the country at the peril of my father's health, our break with lifelong friends and family—what if it was all One Big Mistake?

A week before our intended Grand Opening a woman appeared at the door. She wore a blond wig and a polyester three-piece suit the color of a frog. "I do a column for the *Sun*," she said. "Club news, local color, that sort of thing. . . ." She slithered past me at the door, sticking her nose into the smaller of the two dining rooms, peering into the bathroom. When she came upon my father and his dented soup pots, her nose crinkled up. "Smells divine!" she said, ducking quickly back into the dining room. On the day the sign went up, *Welsh Kitchen* in golden Gothic script, her column "What's New under the Sun" appeared with this postscript: "A family from New Jersey has just settled in town with grand plans to open a Welsh restaurant in the very near future. Mr. and Mrs. Lewis and their two children, Ernest (Buddy) and Bronwyn, promise fine food at reasonable prices. Do stop by. The ambience is highly unusual."

"Well, that's nice," my mother said. "Isn't it?"

The lines in her forehead deepened. You could always read the direction of her mind by the depth of those lines. But, I told myself, it was her way to worry. It was the way she did things. If she didn't have anything to worry about, she'd make something up. Sometimes in the night, long after my father's snoring began, I'd hear her sigh, turn over, sigh, plump her pillow, turn over again. Sometimes she'd creep downstairs and smoke a cigarette, a rare indiscretion. I had no sympathy. It had been her idea to yank us from our home and drag us clear across the country. Her fault that I would never be a Varsity cheerleader and potential (though not probable) Homecoming Queen. It was her fault that Joe Panucci probably had another girlfriend. (I'd sent him twenty-two letters SWAK but what was paper to real live flesh?) Her fault that we were living in a converted garbage dump like mental patients. No matter that it was my father's dream we were pursuing, it was her fault we were pursuing it. She trusted him. That was her problem: She still trusted him.

UNTIL SCHOOL BEGAN that fall, I read three-inch dollar-fifty trash novels, *Love's Sweet Sorrow*, *Mandingo*, or walked the back streets kicking dust through my sandals, crying. There was nothing I could do, nothing to turn my parents around, nothing I could say to make them understand how completely they'd ruined my life. They'd stopped hearing me.

For an Easterner, walking those back streets was like exploring a strange planet or a movie set left standing long after the film had been made, *The Grapes of Wrath*, *High Noon*. There were no lawns—I supposed, wrongly, that Ojalans were simply too lazy to tend them—and no side-walks. None of the flowers I knew, the white tulips Mom planted and replanted each fall (had she brought them with her?), the wild narcissus and clouds of yellow forsythia we kids would pass each spring on the way to the bus stop, none of these grew here.

Here, exotic ugly plants grew in globular or spiny profusion with red or yellow prickly blossoms sticking to their hides. Enormous trees that smelled of menthol dwarfed single-story mud huts (the adobe I had no name for then), so that they appeared even smaller than they were and less substantial. Beneath the trees and clear across the roads lay curls of dried bark that cracked when you stepped on it, releasing puffs of dusty brown smoke into the air.

Here, everything—houses, cars, sleeping dogs—wore a coat of fine reddish brown dust. It got in your eyes and your hair as you walked, so that after a while you could taste it.

I walked every back street, muttering to myself like someone old and half-mad. And then one afternoon I glanced up from my sandals and saw for the first time a small church I'd passed a dozen times. It was badly in need of paint, but its gold cross shone as if someone climbed the steeple every morning to polish it. *The Lord giveth, The Lord taketh away* said the weekly message board. I could not have agreed more. In the attached building, used, I guessed, for Sunday school classes, a door stood open, and just inside the door was an upright piano. Glancing around and finding no one to stop me, I stepped inside.

The room was mostly bare. Chairs had been folded and stacked along one wall. There was only one picture, the one I thought Jesus would have liked best, with all the children and animals. Beneath the picture was the piano.

I lifted the lid. Not a key was chipped or scarred, just yellowed with age like a set of strong old teeth. Middle C sent a rippling reverberation through the room. When no one came, I slid out the bench and sat down. The room was cool and dim. The one door leading into the church was closed. I played a scale, then a simple sonata. It was like releasing rusty water from a pump.

I never walked the main street, the other end of the Avenue, where "the kids" were. They owned the town, these teenagers, and everyone seemed to know it—shopkeepers, gas station attendants, even the police chief, who smiled and waved as if granting approval of everything they did.

From late afternoon until long past midnight, the kids would cruise Ojala Avenue, all three miles of it, back and forth, back and forth, in their spectacular cars. After a while I knew all the cars and would watch for them: the candy-apple pickup, the deep purple Chevy with the silver fins, the blue Olds convertible. The drivers, always boys, would honk their horns, wave, call out to each other, or make obscene hand gestures. Sometimes one of the more daring would leap from the backseat of one convertible (the blue Olds) into another (a white Ford with skinny stripes of red and gold), flat into the laps of his friends in the back. I'd sit on my father's new steps (we'd had to make a terrific fuss over them, how straight and even they were, what a magnificent job my father had done) and I'd watch the cars and all the waving arms shimmering and dancing through the heat waves like a nonstop Gidget movie. These were California kids. *Everybody* had heard of them. They were as famous as the movie stars they imitated.

At noon they would gather at the Frostee, sprawl on the hoods of their cars or all over the blue Olds convertible, drinking Cokes, laughing, always laughing. They all had perfect teeth. This was hard not to notice. Perfectly straight, perfectly white teeth. From Bailey's Market across the way as I helped my father load bagfuls of food into Bess's trunk,

I'd watch these kids and study what they wore, how the girls did their hair. They were all very tan with impossibly long legs, boys and girls alike, California Barbies and Kens. They terrified me with their confidence, with their seeming hold on the world.

3

ON THE SATURDAY before school began, I sneaked up the road to get a closer look at Ojala High (*Conquistadors, Class of 1955* said a brass plaque stuck in a rock at the entrance). Until then I'd surveyed it only from a distance. Expect nothing, I told myself, and you won't be disappointed. What could rival Plainfield High, a ninety-year-old redbrick fortress whose graduates were senators and rocket scientists? Ojala High was just a scattering of outbuildings, like army barracks, all with that same squat mud hut look as the rest of Ojala, dingy yellowed concrete with dusty sunburned orange tile.

I walked past the front entrance, double wooden doors held fast with a padlock and rusted chain. Candy wrappers and bits of newspaper clung to spiny bushes leading to a center courtyard. Scattered through it were picnic tables, their surfaces carved with names and dates, hearts alongside swastikas. I traced my finger through the rough furrows of

Monica + Brad 1954. Where was Monica now? Did she ever have a single lonely day here at Ojala High?

Kicking my way through curled bark, seed pods, piles of stiff dead leaves, I circled the courtyard wondering which room I'd be assigned to (no doubt the one with EAT SHIT scrawled across it), whether there were homerooms. At PHS we'd been corralled each morning in homerooms to hear announcements and salute the flag, but that was where we found our friends. Where would I find friends here? Where would I sit at lunch? At one of these picnic tables? Or were they for the seniors? And how would I know? Plainfield High had senior benches, a senior parking lot, senior steps. If you touched the sacred steps, they made you scrub them down with a toothbrush. Would I learn the Ojala High rules in time, or would I break one and ruin my whole year before it even started?

For nights I lay awake like a zombie, and finally school began. I wasn't ready, but I never would have been, so what did it matter? From the first day, I was the one in dyed-to-match gray, my one new outfit, a shadow who could slide into a back-row seat while every head was turned away. Once there, I'd bury my head in a book, looking neither left nor right nor up, unless I absolutely had to. In the hallways I skirted walls and prayed I wouldn't bump into anyone. Locker doors opened and shut with the clang and rattle of prison bars. I held my breath and floated somewhere above it all, invisible.

Anonymity ended abruptly one sixth-period American history class. "Bronwyn Lewis, let's hear from you. Why don't you read from the first full paragraph on page 153." Mr. Demski looked expectantly over his half glasses, bald head gleaming in the hard-edged fluorescent light. My heart began to hammer. A thought like an arrow shot through my mind: What if I throw up? "Louder, please," the teacher called, as I fumbled my way through the first few sentences of a passage long as my trembling arm.

"General Sherman," I began again, "alawng with fawty of his ablest commandiz . . ." The room grew suddenly still, ominously quiet. As in waiting. As in snakes in the sun. Not a paper rustled. Not a foot skimmed the floor. Then a snort, an exploded giggle, whispers traveling at the speed of light. Head down, hair shielding my flaming face, I fought with Sherman to the sea and finished the passage just as the bell rang. I fled to the girls' room, twin hearts beating in my ears. Dumb shit dumb shit dumb shit.

I laid my forehead on the cold tile next to the Modess machine, fighting nausea. Someone came in. I heard a purse and books hit the rim of a sink.

"So where ya from anyway?" When I turned, she was putting on mascara, touching the tiny brush to the tips of her lashes, giving each lash the attention of a microbiologist. I wasn't sure she had spoken to me, but there was no one else in the room. Just me and what *Seventeen* would have put on a cover and called the quintessential California girl. Wide-set mischievous green eyes, blond pageboy kissing the curve of tanned half-bare shoulders. I thought for a minute she might be the drugstore girl, but her lipstick was a soft pink, her nails buffed to a natural gloss, and I couldn't be sure.

"New Jersey," I said. "Plainfield."

"Well, Jersey," she said, slinging her purse over her shoulder, gathering up her books. "You'd better do something about that hair."

I watched the door swing behind her and turned, as if ordered, to look in the mirror. Red-rimmed eyes of indeterminate color, not blue, but not really green, not small but not wide either, or exotic, or even very memorable. Just eyes. With eyelashes. The thin and spiky kind. My nose I'd hated since I knew what noses were and what they could be. Mine was the pug variety, spattered with thirty-seven freckles (documented). I grimaced to show my teeth, straight enough, except for the one I'd chipped roller-skating. And what could I do with my hair? with the failed dishwater pageboy that took an hour to curl and half an hour to fall?

I knew right then that I wasn't going to make it. I would never be one of them. The way they walked, the things they said. They were different from eastern kids. Slicker, cleverer. They knew things I would never know. Always a step behind, I would be lost forever in the labyrinth of a language, an entire way of life, created long before I came along, in girls' rooms where California girls spawn.

4

WHEN I WAS A CHILD, six or seven, waiting in the night for my father to come home, I would replay in my mind the story of how I came to be. It was a talisman, half truth, half myth, that I took comfort in until I heard the stones crunch beneath the tires of the old Plymouth, heard the door slam, my mother's muffled words, the creak and give of the steps as my father achieved them one by one, swaying to a faraway rhythm none of us knew, of pubs and the camaraderie of men, of a rich vein struck, and drinks all around. I would marvel at how my father, from a tiny country called Wales, halfway across the world, managed to find my mother in Metuchen, New Jersey, how it was that she came to love him (he loved her all along), and how, as a result, I was born. In my mind, it was nothing less than a miracle.

She was seventeen when they met and her life had never been easy. Always she'd had to diaper and feed and chase and swat someone smaller than herself. She didn't complain.

She wasn't the type. Besides, what good would it have done? Grandfather had salted himself away in the basement and Grandmother had returned, in spirit, to Copenhagen. There were things that her body did, cooked cabbage soup, for instance, endless pots of cabbage soup, but her mind free-floated. She would tell the children marvelous stories of her childhood, of the night her father lit up all of Copenhagen with electric lights, of debutante balls, of beaux in horse-drawn carriages. Only then would she come to life, and in such a marvelous way that they would not dare to ask how their father (by his own reckoning a "peasant") had come into the picture.

It was not a good time to be living in America. The bottom had dropped out and no one had work. There were soup lines and lots of empty promises. Grandfather, a photographer by trade, found nothing a grown man could do to feed eight hungry mouths. What work there was went to younger men with stronger backs. So, like everyone else, the family went on relief. Grandfather, his pride shattered, went down into the basement to saw away on an ancient violin. The children survived, Mother said, by "catch as catch can."

My father was thirty-two, the youngest of four sons, the one his mother called for on her deathbed, the favored one. In a photograph taken sometime before he left the Old Country for good, he is standing with his brothers in front of the row house in which they were born. They are four short men dressed in baggy pants and woolen sweaters who have threaded their arms over and around each other, waiting for the shutter to release. Their smiles are identical, brash and overconfident. They have dusted their hands, their hair, their lungs of the mines; they are leaving for America to make their fortune.

June 1937. My mother has managed somehow to graduate. (The eldest boys, Bill and Magnus, have had to quit school, have gone to work on the docks. They are tall as men now, and are as silent as men.) She applies for a summer job as counselor at a camp in the Watchung Mountains. She can hardly believe her luck when she gets it.

My father cannot find a job, nor can his "next-to" brother, Taffy. They trudge the streets of New York, a city that looks less and less like a place in which to make one's fortune and more and more like the mines. A knocking-heads-in-the-dark, senseless kind of place. Down to their last two bucks, they land jobs at an Italian restaurant. They learn to cook. Manicotti, minestrone. *Rigoletto!* Taffy says. *Caruso! Mussolini!* They get canned for drinking the profits, but now they have a trade. They apply for jobs as cooks at a summer camp in the Watchung Mountains.

My mother had a musical laugh when she was a girl that actually stopped people in the streets. She had an hourglass figure (she's always hated it) and a Garbo profile; Father had a nose for garlic and an eye for women. As the story goes, he spotted her across a room crowded with crying children, harried parents, stacked luggage, teenage counselors in their middy blouses, and said to his brother, "Taffy, that's the girl I'm going to marry."

She does not like him. He is foreign. His pants bag down over his brogans like old men's. He is a lot older than she is, than the other boys who work as counselors (not in the kitchen slinging hash), who wear bright white tennies and play baseball. But she is full of herself, of her newfound power that can make a man send flowers, write her poetry. He *is* a man after all, and even if she will have nothing whatever to do with him, she has attracted the attentions of a grown-up man. She gives the poems he slides under her door to her roommate, Ethel, who sticks them all around the mirror, like petals of a flower turned in upon itself.

He is crazy in love. Taffy cannot shut him up, cannot make him understand about American girls, how they laugh at him, think he's a fool. Taffy takes this personally, as if it is himself they toy with; he wants to fight them with his bare fists as he might have done in the Old Country, but you cannot fight girls, American girls with their long legs and their donkey laughter. But there is only one American girl his brother will look at, the one with the sharp nose, the one who covers her mouth when she laughs, who blushes bright as a peony.

She is having the time of her life. She is wonderful with the children, which comes naturally as rain, but they are not her children. They are hers only for a time, after which she is free to be the carefree girl she never was, to take long walks in the hills, to lie on her back in a meadow full of buttercups, to dream of the future when she will be a famous artist. Even so, there is a tug somewhere inside from time to time, as if she knows this is just a borrowed life.

He is relentless as a landlord. Everywhere she goes, he manages to be. He has friends now, is, in a certain way, a center of things. He and Taffy tell stories of the Old Country, of their hazardous passage across the Atlantic, of the night the ship nearly went down, of how they'd sung the passengers calm with their Welsh hymns, and of how they'd been honored by the captain afterward. They are coaxed, with little effort, into singing at the Saturday night socials. My father sings "All through the Night." My mother dabs at her eyes.

There are other girls who like him now. She concedes

that he has a certain rough charm. And anyway, it is nearing the end of the summer. It is almost time to go home. He begs her for a walk, just a walk to the lake, and at last she relents.

It is the night he has been dreaming of. He shaves before dinner. He shaves again after dinner. He changes his clothes, three outfits, three times. He kisses Taffy on both cheeks for luck. He takes off on a run in his new white tennies, and is at her cabin too soon. He hides behind a tree, catching his breath. The bark is rough and real under his fingertips, like coal. He will make the moment last, the moment before she comes to him, a moment 'that sits delicious on the tongue. At last he knocks and she answers.

For a moment, he's afraid she's changed her mind. There's that little frown between her lovely eyes. He has seen that frown before. It stops his heart. But she throws a light sweater over her shoulders and steps into the night with him. At the dock, they sit side by side staring out into the dark water. She has slipped off her sandals and dangles her toes in the water. He cannot speak. She does all the talking, easily, fills in all the spaces as he gazes at her. She has this confidence that fills him with something he has no name for.

The water feels lovely, she says. He should put his feet in. He has spent half a paycheck on his tennies and is terrified of letting them out of his sight, but he wants to be like everyone else, carefree like all the Americans, and so he slips out of the new white shoes and lays them carefully on the solid center of the dock. To him they represent more than he could have explained, or would have explained to her. They represent all he believes about and feels for America, which he cannot explain either.

The moon is full. It bobs inches above the horizon;

pieces break off and skitter across the surface of the lake. It is as perfect a moment as any he has dreamed, but he cannot bank it, save it up for later when she is gone. He announces that he is going to kiss her. The words bubble out of him with no preamble, no warning, a geyser of feeling.

She is horrified. It is the worst moment of her life, worse than anything she could have imagined. She grabs the first thing she finds, his left shoe. She tells him that if he does the thing he said, she will throw his shoe into the lake. But he is beyond the sound of ordinary human speech. Already he can taste the sweetness of her lips; he is guided there by something outside himself. In an ache and a breath, he has pulled her toward him. He has found those lips. His juices rise in celebration.

In a gasp, she breaks free. She scrambles to her feet and, with a mighty heave (she is the pitcher on the girls' softball team), tosses his left tennie clear out into the middle of the lake. They watch it float for a moment like a child's toy boat, and they watch it sink. They watch the place in which it was. There are no words, no sounds in the night. Maybe crickets.

He is stricken. He wants to cry but cannot, being a man. She is panting. Her eyes are very wide. There is a film of sweat across her upper lip. She has turned away. She is seeing how the lights twinkle in the windows of the cabins, of her cabin, how they seem to dance in the heavy summer air. They are caught like that in the moonlight, neither knowing what to do next, he on the dock staring at the water, she turned away.

As a child, I never tired of that story and would ask that it be retold exactly as I'd first heard it, over and over again. If a word was omitted or changed, I would correct it. His *left* shoe, not *the* lake, *Watchung* Lake. I suppose now that it explained something I could not otherwise understand, the reason for my being, the product of two people who fell in love and who, no matter the state of their ordinary lives, my father's problems with the bottle, chose very deliberately to add me to their lives.

There were two versions of the story, actually. My mother's, which ended on the dock, and my father's, which went on from there. "What happened then?" I'd ask my mother, but she'd put me off with vague half answers as if she no longer remembered. But my father was always willing to carry on.

"Well, she wouldn't leave me alone," he'd say. "I wouldn't have a thing to do with her after that night, not a thing. Taffy, I said, that's one mean-spirited woman. So, on the last day of summer, we packed our bags and headed for the train. . . ."

"But then what? What happened then?" I'd cry, afraid that if he boarded the train I'd never get born.

"Well, just as the conductor cried, *All aboard!* what do you know! There she was, running for the train, crying her eyes out, yelling and waving. And what did she have under her arm but a brand-new pair of tennies. My size, too."

"Tom . . ." my mother would say, shaking her head. My father loved a story, but the stories were never necessarily true.

"And what could I do? Who knows when the next size-ten fella would come along and love your mother the way I do?"

"And then I got born, right?"

"And then you got born," my father would say.

(31)

"And then what?"

"Well, what do you think?" He'd make his bushy eyebrows wriggle like Groucho Marx's.

"We all lived happily ever after!"

"That's right," my father would say, patting my mother's fanny as she passed. "That's exactly right."

5

BY LATE SEPTEMBER the heat had begun to lift and with it some of the haze that clung to the hills. Now and then a cool breeze blew in from the north and bounced a ball of tumbleweed down the middle of the Avenue, or a cloud drifted through an otherwise cloudless gray sky, doors slammed shut of their own accord, sweaters came out of storage boxes, and, at last, it rained.

When we lived in the East, like most Easterners we complained about the rain. Now our parched souls longed for it. Even my mother, who had championed California from the first, grew weary of the endless dry days. She'd gaze longingly out the window at the sky, and when the first drops fell, she was the first to race from the house. "Rain!" she cried. "Good Lord, it's finally raining!" Swooping her arms, she danced in circles on the dead yellow grass of the lawn. "Come out and see! It's raining. Tom! Children!" I hung back, waiting for the straitjackets. But

Buddy and Dad ran out and, grabbing hands, they all danced together, mouths open to the rain like geese waiting to drown.

The restaurant opened that day, the day of the rain. Not another drop fell until February. My mother pronounced the rain a particularly good omen. I didn't ask why.

Everything within reason had been done to make the place presentable. Appealing. Warm. Cozy. Understated. Unique. Most of all, a place you'd bring your family for (as we so cleverly advertised in the *Ojala Sun*) "a good home-cooked meal."

"If they want a home-cooked meal, won't they stay home and eat?" I said in a voice grown vinegarish.

I would not have admitted it to anyone, not even to myself, but I was proud of all we'd accomplished. The floor had been stripped and varnished and now gleamed a soft dark gold, every wall was "off-white" with, as my mother put it, "just a whisper of lavender." The tables with their bright blue-and-white checks looked inviting, jaunty, as if they were floating free of the knock-knees and bowed legs that had pinned them to the earth. Next to the front door was the cashier's stand, an upended blue box more or less, where I, the hostess-cashier, would collect the money and make change.

None of this had been easy. Along with the many hours of hard labor (over which I had whined and been bribed), there had been a number of altercations ("discussions," my mother said) over critical issues of decorum. The last one had gone on the longest. This was a matter of whether or not catsup bottles belonged on the tables.

Each day before my mother came down, hair wrapped in toilet-paper curlers, my father like Santa on an evil mission would place a catsup bottle in the center of each table. Sleep caught in the corners of her eyes, my mother would wander into the dining room, spot the catsup bottles, sniff disdainfully (awake now), and remove them, one by one. My father, hiding in the kitchen, would giggle like a girl.

This went on for weeks until at last my father gave up. Now in the center of each table was a small clear glass vase of daisies, a Hanukkah candle ("But they're just the right size!" my mother insisted), and one of my laboriously handprinted menus. Also on each table, over my mother's objections, was a set of standard-issue restaurant salt and pepper shakers, glass with a chrome top.

"Déclassé!" my mother cried. "Gauche!" But my father, citing "over twenty-five years in the service industry," insisted. "You'll thank me for it," he said. "At the end of the evening, when your feet are aching, you'll say, 'I sure am glad I didn't have to run and fetch the salt, Tom!' You'll see." My mother, who had not thought much about what would happen when there were *people* in the room, deferred to his greater experience.

The rain stopped abruptly, as if recalled. For five minutes the sun shone fiercely through the clear air; then it, too, disappeared, and a light, steady drizzle set in. We began the countdown. Rain or no rain, customers or no customers, the doors would open at five.

As if they'd been posed for a publicity photo, my father and mother stood side by side just inside the swinging door that separated the larger of the two dining rooms from the kitchen. My father had changed into a clean apron and looked like a prosperous businessman, palms on his buttocks to ease his aching back, belly extended. He was gaining weight, a good sign. On his feet were a pair of combat boots purchased in an Army-Navy store, heavy well-worn black boots with turned-up toes. Buddy, our busboy, was dressed like my father in miniature, apron dragging the floor.

My mother was giddy with nervous excitement. She fiddled with the hem of her apron, one of the frilly white jobs she'd made for herself and for Frieda, our "professional waitress." A perk for Frieda turned out to be the fact that beneath the apron was the same black uniform she wore for her counter job at Ojala Pharmacy. "This way, I won't even have to change," she said. "I'll just run on over and switch aprons!" My parents, standing in the doorway of their dining room, steam billowing through the hole my father had cut to pass dinner plates through, were beaming. Everything was perfect. Nothing, it seemed, could ruin a perfect moment of self-congratulation.

"Time for a little celebration!" my father cried. The swinging doors whap-whapped and he was gone. I caught my mother's eye. We knew what celebration meant. I waited for her to say something, to intercept him. Her right hand was raised as if a thought had made it just that far into action or as if she'd gone somewhere else, back in time, and decided to stay there.

My father swung back through the doors, a tray balanced on his right shoulder. On the tray was a chilled bottle of champagne and four water glasses. There was color in his cheeks and a too familiar sparkle in his eye. "By God, we've earned it, haven't we?"

"I'll say!" agreed Frieda, releasing a long plume of cigarette smoke toward the ceiling. "You guys did a great job . . . considering. Did I tell you my brother-in-law used to own this place? Back in '52, '53 . . ."

"Well, can you believe it? It's almost time to open!" my mother cried, coming to life, clapping her hands like a dance teacher at a recital. "We'll save this for later." She reached for the bottle and would have whipped it out of sight (now you see it, now you don't!) when my father's hand came down upon hers. I hated what came between them then. It froze the air and everything around, so that we four became, for a time, statues in the child's game at which I'd played my heart out once. There was history in that look, memories of a night we'd all worked so hard to pretend hadn't happened.

And then the spell got broken. "Hey, let's save it, what the hell," said Frieda, and my father dropped his hand. There was sweat on his upper lip and surprise on his face. I thought my mother might cry but she smiled instead, a smile pieced together like a broken dish. Frieda lit another cigarette with the one she'd smoked to a nub, squinting through a mascara-laden eyelid. Suddenly she looked up and winked at me. Or at least I think she winked. She was quick. Everything she did was quick and all her movements were efficient, as if she were constantly in training for her profession.

My father checked the clock. "Five o'clock!" he announced. "Open the gates!" Then he and my mother did this after-you-Alphonse thing about who would flip over the CLOSED sign and open the door. "It's *your* place!" "Ah, but I couldn't have done it without you!" At last he reached for the sign, but then did something anyone but us kids would have seen as strange. He turned suddenly and, as if there were no one in the place but the two of them, took my mother in his arms, whispering something fond and ardent in her ear. She purred back, blushing, hiding her face against his neck.

Over my mother's shoulder, my father caught my eye. He'd hooked me before like that and I hated it. I couldn't wriggle away, couldn't give him what he wanted. Either

(37)

way, I'd be losing something, my father or my own self-respect. Forgive me, his eyes said, or something else, something infinitely more complicated that I wasn't ready, wasn't able if I had been ready, to decipher. Then he closed his eyes, rocking my mother, humming into her shoulder, and they began a slow waltz. Frieda laughed the gravelly laugh of a chain smoker and hummed along, *The Blue Danube*, duh duh duh duh *duh*—duh *duh* duh *duh*! I stomped off into the kitchen and stared at the solemn predictable face of the wall clock with the busted-off second hand we'd hauled for some reason all the way from home.

At five-fifteen the first customers stepped tentatively onto the porch. Like timid deer, they sniffed their way to the door and peered inside. They were dressed in their Sunday best, the woman in a beige pillbox hat with a bright red feather, the man in a pin-striped suit. His umbrella had dancing ducks imprinted on it. The ducks wore red rubber boots and appeared to be very happy.

My father gave my mother a little shove and she stumbled forward like she'd been wound up from behind. "Well!" she cried. "Hello! Have you come for dinner? Well, of *course* you've—" She began again. "Lovely evening, isn't it?"

The couple smiled a little uncertainly, standing side by side as if on review, waiting for my mother to seat them. Suddenly her face dropped. "The candles!" she cried. "We've forgotten to light the candles. Tom?" She turned, but my father had gone back into the kitchen. "Bron? Light the candles, will you, darling?" Then she took hold of herself. "Right this way," she said. "We have a lovely table for you right by the window." She handed our first live customers their menus and scurried away into the kitchen.

I stood at my podium holding my breath, as if I were expected any moment to present a speech on the psychological effects of the Cold War. "Chilly in here," the man said, then, realizing how his voice carried, leaned toward his wife and hissed, "Isn't it?" She turned toward me. I looked out the door. A short fat man in a pale blue leisure suit was climbing out of his car. Customer number two.

By five-thirty-five every table was full. I'd done my job, seated all the people, and watched while my mother streaked past, racing from my father's window to one dining room or the other, like a horse sensing fire, terror in her eyes. Half the time she had nothing in her hands but the edge of her apron that she'd screwed into damp wrinkles.

Frieda, calm as a fire captain, took most of the tables herself and was attempting to train my mother at the same time. "Aw, tell them to keep their shirts on," she'd say. "Tell 'em you're sorry they had to wait. Give 'em a cup of coffee on the house. . . . Here, take this to five and I'll get that new table."

My mother, tearily grateful, grabbed Frieda's elbows each time and thanked her over and over. Meanwhile, someone would call for a check or wave an empty coffee cup or want to know if there was anything chocolate for dessert. At my post by the door, I maintained an air of dignified invisibility, answering polite inquiries about why there was nothing "Welsh" on the menu with an equally polite answer, my father's: They only eat mutton in Wales, I'd say, stewed mutton and boiled potatoes. The customer would turn away with a look of mild revulsion every time. It really never occurred to me until Frieda pushed a coffeepot into my hand that I might help my mother.

In some ways, looking back, it was an enchanted night. The mayor's wife endured a plate of spaghetti in the lap of her beige linen skirt with battlefield grace; when the coffeepots went dry, no one seemed to need another cup; when my father ran out of pot roast, one table after another began ordering the Chicken Marengo. And when my father, having lost his temper because a steak had been sent back for more cooking, yelled, "Tell them to go to the other Greek!" there was momentary confusion among the diners and then they began to laugh, as if we were all together at a marvelous and wacky wedding banquet.

At ten-fifteen we closed the doors behind the last couple, who'd brought their own bottle of wine and tripped out arm in arm, calling over their shoulders that they'd be back the next night. My mother turned over the OPEN sign, put her face in her hands, and began to sob. Frieda lit a cigarette with one hand (bending a match over and striking it, a neat trick) and patted my mother on the shoulder with the other. "You did just fine for a new girl," she said. "You'll get the hang of it." Then she untied her apron and slipped into her sweater. "Same time tomorrow?"

"Not so fast!" my father said. Like a trick rabbit, the champagne magically reappeared. "It's time for our toast!" The cork popped like a gunshot and my father began pouring bubbles into the four water glasses. My mother blew her nose, wiped the mascara from beneath her eyes. She looked like she'd been dragged half-drowned from the surf. My father handed Frieda a glass nearly full and then held one out to my mother, who hesitated as if she might say something, then closed her fingers around it. I accepted mine with a smirk. "To the Welsh Kitchen!" my father cried. "And to the Queen. Long live the Queen!"

Frieda looked at my mother to see what she would do, and when my mother did nothing, said, "I'll drink to that," and drained her glass in a straight swallow. My father did the same and poured another. My mother had taken a single small sip and set her glass on the table. She would not meet my eyes.

I swirled the yellowish bubbles in the bottom of my glass, throat thick with things that couldn't be said. I was the holdout. I was the one who wouldn't forgive, who wouldn't give him another chance, the one who wouldn't trust him. What was so wrong with a little champagne? And wasn't Frieda right? Didn't he deserve it? At last I looked up and met my father's eyes, the sorrow and the hope, with eyes that gave nothing in return. "I'll drink to that," I said. I swallowed and held my glass for a refill. My father, with just a moment's hesitation, tipped the lip of the bottle into my empty glass.

6

For MANY YEARS, until I pretended to forget, my father and I would play a game that began as he, humming some tune from the Old Country, got ready for his morning shave. Each of us had our lines, but the first was always his: the "handsome devil" opening. He loved that line. Said it man to man, into the bathroom mirror, without any trace of the self-doubt that always rode in his back pocket like a empty wallet. "Ah, there you are, you handsome devil," he'd say. He and his reflection would smile in perfect agreement.

The next line was mine, but I had to hug it close until the appropriate time. I'd hold on while my father, solemn as a priest, opened the medicine cabinet, took his Queen Mary shaving cup from the shelf, then the soft fragrant brush, and laid them on the edge of the sink. Then came the razor, sterling silver, given to him by his father, who came as close as a crusty Welsh miner could to passing on his manhood. After his shave my father would always take the razor apart, polishing it carefully before placing it on the glass shelf, where it perched like a silver grasshopper.

When steam rose in clouds from the bowl of the sink, he'd wet the brush and work up a cupful of foam. At last he would begin to brush his face, covering his cheeks and chin in broad, sure strokes. Three dabs under the nose and his face was half-submerged in dense white bubbles.

That was the time for my line.

"Do you know what?" I'd shriek.

His eyes would sparkle as he pulled the foam in a clean line across his lips. "No, what?"

The world, my father—there was no difference then—balanced on a breath. With a word I could hold them still. Until the last possible second I could cup a small world of time in my hands, thinking it was all time, and then at last surrender. "I *adore* you!" I'd yell, and fall face first into outstretched arms and sticky foam.

My mind has tried to connect this with what came later, but in truth there were years before he had his "accident." Always it was an "accident," something that "happened" to him, to all of us, like God twisting Job's arm for no apparent reason except to test the mettle of an otherwise perfect man. No one saw it coming.

It was Thanksgiving and my father, working at Max's Steak and Ribs for the fourth or fifth time, pulled the dinner shift. That meant good tips. Even so, he went off as if cast into hell. He'd always hated being a waiter. It was worse than the mines, he said. In the mines at least you were a man. Ma, Buddy, and I went to Grandma's for dinner. My mother was always so happy with her family. She'd laugh like a kid, holding a hand over her mouth to hide her "crooked" tooth.

After dinner, as always, Uncle Bill told the story of

Uncle Ernie falling backward out of Mrs. Burbridge's bedroom window, arms pumping backward, grabbing air, Mr. Burbridge below waving a pitchfork. I was fourteen and finally understood why everybody laughed, why Uncle Ernie was in the Burbridges' bedroom. Uncle Bill put all he had into a dramatic re-creation. His timing was perfect, his gestures wonderfully exaggerated. Still, everyone watched my mother reacting. She had that rare quality of attention that made you feel, while you had it, very special. Bigger than you thought you were. Funnier, more generous. Years of experience with my father had made her like that: the one person in the audience who makes the production come alive.

And then suddenly, as if a signal had been activated that only she could hear, she rose from the table and said we had to go.

We left in a flurry of good-byes. Mother turned the key and Bess roared into life. Revving the engine a half-dozen times, she jammed the gearshift into low and lurched off. She drove always with silent, grim concentration.

At first it looked as if a carnival had come to town and settled, for some strange reason, on our lawn. There were lights on in every room of the house, and red revolving lights on the police car and the ambulance, a slow red wash across expectant faces gazing at the open front door.

"Oh, my God," my mother said, but quietly, as if she had lived this before and knew all her lines. Her foot hit the brake, the car bucked to a stop, and she was gone. Hands clasped, back straight, I sat on the edge of the seat, as if awaiting my turn at a piano recital.

A huge black bird hopped across the lawn toward the car, heavy dark wings flapping. Mrs. Jackson, the pastor's wife, breathless in her husband's black winter coat, reached inside the car to draw me out, eyes wide and glittering, secretive. "Wait," she said, and reached inside for Buddy, asleep in the backseat. "Now," she said, and then stopped as if awaiting a cue. "Well," she said. "Well, then." Turning, she laid Buddy back in the car. Then she looked down at me, back at the house, down at me, and decided. "Let us pray," she said and, holding my hands inside hers, drew me down on the sharp stones. Her prayer was all of a piece, strung-together phrases I remembered from Pastor Jackson's Sunday sermons, pleas to a merciful Jesus, my father's name. The cold night came up through my knees and settled in the pit of my stomach. "Forgive and bless our brother Tom. . . ." A siren screamed and I watched the long, white ambulance slide like a wave of a hand into the night. "Amen," she said quickly. "We can go in now." Buddy, still asleep and drooling on his hand, stayed behind in the car.

We threaded through a thin dispersing cloud of sympathetic murmurs, dark whispers. "Poor lambs . . . how could a man . . . ?"

The house was cold. "Wait right here," Mrs. Jackson said, her hand on my shoulder as if to push me into that one spot on the living room rug. "Everything is going to be fine," she said. Then, in answer to all the questions she was afraid I might ask, soft chins trembling, she shook her head. One vigorous shake, a blanket answer for the unanswerable. She left, and I looked around the room—at the shabby, plaid couch, the heavy maple china closet, my father's listing recliner—saw it all in a different kind of light, a cold clear light as if the weight of all our lives had been willed somehow to me.

I found Mrs. Jackson in the bathroom. She had taken off her husband's coat and, kneeling in her flannel nightgown, scrubbed angrily at something on the tile floor. "Mrs. Jackson?" Her head turned. Her face tried several things, then stuck in an expression of baffled concern. Her hands lifted and reached out to push me back into the hall, but I had already seen the silver razor on the floor and the blood dripping like bright red poster paint from the edge of the sink.

THINGS LOOKED the same in the morning, the way they always did. My mother came into the kitchen, tucking the ends of her fine brown hair into a roll at the back of her neck. She wore an everyday dress. She smiled. She said what she always said. She set an upside-down box of cornflakes on the table. Forgetting the milk and the cereal bowls, she sat down and waited for us to have our breakfast.

At last she said, "Your daddy has had an accident."

DRIVING ACROSS TOWN, we passed Grandmother's house. My mother's eyes seared holes in the windshield, her hands gripping the wheel as if some outside force might tear it away. Her head never turned. Not at Grandmother's, not even when she came to the cross street where she could have found Uncle Bill.

We lurched to a stop beneath the smooth gray face of Muhlenberg Hospital. Mother turned off the key. We watched a boy about my age limp out on crutches. Then came a smiling new mother hugging a small blanket-wrapped bundle. Then an old man with dull, gray hair appeared and raised a hand in a wave. I saw the bright white bandage on the wrist before I knew who he was. He had shrunk. His pants bagged down over his shoes. His fingers trembled at the buttons of his sweater. He had not shaved. Coming toward us, he shuffled like an old beggar, like one of the bums at the Salvation Army. When he got to the car, my mother would not turn her face. She did something I never saw her do: She pretended he wasn't there. "Lass?" he said.

All time stopped then. There was not time and there never again would be. If my mother did not turn, if she did not take him in, the earth would crack open and my father would fall away. Birds listened. Traffic stopped dead. Dogs slept. There was no music. There was no sound. Not even breathing. I had given that up the night before and lived like a blind fish in a swamp. Buddy's thumb, after a six-month layoff, had found his mouth and plugged it.

And then, because he knew she would, that she always would, my mother turned his way. What she thought crossed her face like swift, fierce rain, then rose up in equal ferocity, hawklike from some deep wound in an all-forgiving earth. "Tom?"

Superficial wounds, the report said. Scratches. I found a folded copy in the drawer next to my father's side of the bed. Later on, there was only the most fragile of scars, like a thin white snake or a bracelet made of thread.

Things were different in the neighborhood after that. We were the Family with the Father Who Tried to Kill Himself. Two years later, we sold the house and headed West. "A new start," my mother said, clapping her hands.

7

"What's New Under the Sun," October 3: If you haven't stopped by the Welsh Kitchen for one of Tom Lewis's Chicken Marengo specials, you're about the only one in town who hasn't. Harriet Dunn took her Readers' Club there on Friday night and pronounced the food "sumptuous." We hear there's a movement afoot to try to get the Lewises to open for lunch. By the by, there is no such thing as Welsh food, according to Lewis, a native of Wales. All they eat in that old country, he says, is boiled sheep. I, for one, will take the chicken, thank you.

WITH FRIEDA'S HELP, my mother's waitressing skills improved. But no matter how hard she tried to keep a steady hand, she could not get the hang of it. Each time she hefted a plate, *au jus* slopped over the side. "Never look at 'em and you won't spill 'em," my father would remind her, but this was something my mother could not reconcile with what she called "good common sense." There was always as much coffee in her saucers as in the cups, for which she would abjectly apologize. I began serving coffee for her. I could do it without spilling a drop. I began to plot.

Each evening at shift's end, Frieda and my mother would count their tips, smoothing out crumpled dollar bills, stacking the silver and pennies to exchange for bills. I loved the musty, metallic smell of the money. Stuffing coins into the appropriate rollers, I would sit at a nearby table and listen to their end-of-the-night talk. Frieda always had some great story to relate, though I began to wonder if she hadn't imported them from some other place, like the Roundup, where she sometimes worked a weekend shift. Would I have missed "that old fart on seven making goo-goo eyes at his sixteen-year-old date"?

Frieda's Winston sent a pale ghost of smoke toward the ceiling, and my mother with a quick glance at the kitchen would sneak an occasional puff. I thought she looked glamorous when she smoked, like Lauren Bacall in *To Have and Have Not*, a lock of her hair falling free like a pull of butterscotch taffy. She smoothed and faced her bills like a blackjack dealer, like someone used to money, though she never had been. Those tips always seemed like a fortune to me, and to my mother, too. She counted them down to the last greasy penny even though her "booty," as she called it, went straight back into the business.

She would pay my dollar twenty-five an hour out of her tips.

I began to hint, first to my mother—"Homework comes first"—and then to my father—"one of these days"—that I'd make a great waitress. I'd carry coffee to my father on a dead run without spilling a drop and then stand there waiting, like Lassie, wagging all over for praise. I offered to work for tips. "It's up to your mother," he'd say, but he'd already painted an OPEN FOR WEEKEND LUNCH sign. Frieda worked days at the pharmacy; my mother was "still getting her sea legs." That left me.

By November I had three shifts, two weekday evenings and a Saturday lunch. My mother worried about my school-work, but there was nothing to worry about. No one did homework at Ojala High. School was something you did between parties, or if you weren't popular. A week or two after classes began, when I turned in the only history home-work, the looks I got could have pickled my father's herring. After that, unwilling to capitulate entirely (weren't these kids going to college?), I gave it to Mr. Demski after school.

He was a nice man, Mr. Demski, who never gave up trying even though no one ever listened to him. Something was always stuck to the back of his mossy green corduroy jacket—Chiquita banana labels, pieces of wadded-up tape. "How ya doin', Mr. Demski?" somebody would say, and clap him on the back with an eraser full of chalk dust. He must have known what was happening, but he never let on. Behind the smudged lenses of his wire rims his bright blue eyes always seemed to know more than you gave him credit for. I'd drop by his classroom after school, intending to leave my homework and run, but he'd stop me every time with some question he seemed to have ready like the lesson plans stacked in his worn leather briefcase.

"Where did you say you went to school? New Jersey? Well, you got a good education there, young lady," he said. "I hope you appreciated it. Here, I just don't know. . . ."

I was always anxious to leave the room. You didn't want to be seen talking with a teacher, unless you were in trouble. Then it was okay. I'd begun learning the rules.

(50)

They were pretty easy after all, at least the ones having to do with schoolwork. Cool kids didn't do it. Instead, you made "deals" at the end of the semester, promising you'd turn over a new leaf, do a last-minute "extra credit" report on the Globe Theater or the Aztecs.

Everything happened according to rules that nobody wrote down or even talked about. You just had to know them. There were rules for boys, and there were lots of rules for girls. If you were a girl you got out of gym classes any way you could, usually by claiming you had cramps. Girls who played sports were "jocks" or "dykes." Sweat was cool only on guys. Studying for tests was really uncool. Two or three "smart kids" trying to make the cut, usually girls, did all the studying, and the rest copied. It was cool to be a cheerleader, dumb to play in the band; cool to come to school on "wheels" (but never a bicycle), dumb to walk. I learned to whine my way out of gym (though I'd always loved basketball), stopped studying for tests, but still walked to school. There wasn't much I could do about that.

My escape fund grew quarter by quarter, but, with school and my part-time job, I had little time to write to old friends, and when, in a letter from my best friend, I learned that Joe Panucci had been seen at Makeout Peak with Irene Capritto, I stopped writing to him and started saving for a car.

"That's all you want, you kids," Frieda said one Thursday night as we counted our tips. "My Johnny was the same way, before he went into the service. Souped-up car, you should see it! He left it in the garage and told me I'm supposed to dust it off at least once a month, can you beat that? Then he comes home on leave and drives my T-Bird. All grown-up now, big stuff."

I stopped counting my money and stared at her. For a

savvy lady she sure was slow catching on. How long had I talked about getting a car? Was she deaf? "Hey, couldn't I buy it from him? I mean, if he doesn't want it anymore?"

"Oh, you wouldn't want it," she said. "It's not a girl's car."

All my life the things I wanted most were always meant for boys: ice hockey, blue jeans with front zippers, BB guns, bikes with a center bar. "That's not fair," I said, eyelids stinging.

She stopped facing her bills. I could see her figuring. She'd been a lot like me when she was young, she said once. Snot-nosed and full of herself. Then she gave me a smack on the butt to let me know she was kidding. "No, I suppose it's not fair," she said finally. "You can see the car if you want. I don't know if Johnny will let it go, but you can come on over and take a look at it."

She was still in her bathrobe, hair in pink foam rollers, when I showed up at her door the next morning. "Johnny called last night," she said. "Right after you and me talked about the car. Isn't that the damndest thing . . . ?"

"Will he sell it?" I followed her through the tiny house closed up against the heat and out the back door, worried that Johnny might decide to have the car encased in plastic and saved as a living memorial to his teenage years. From what I could see, cars had a way of getting under your skin. Frieda's garage was separated from the house by a square of dead brown grass and a clothesline full of damp clothes. We had to duck under baggy old ladies' undies and black waitress uniforms to reach it.

"You ain't even seen it yet. How do you know you want it?" She was teasing, one hand on the garage handle, holding out. But when she inched open the garage door, my breath caught. It was the most beautiful little car I'd ever seen, midnight blue with perfect strips of chrome trim swept back from the hood like silver cat whiskers. *Ford* it said across its nose. "It's pretty old," Frieda said. "A '47, I think, or '46 maybe, but Johnny says the engine's newer than that, almost brand-new. I should know, I paid for it."

I touched the hood, cool and shiny as a mirror. My sweaty fingers left ghost prints behind. I slipped into the driver's seat. Cool leather hugged my back and the backs of my thighs. I pushed the clutch down, turned the wheel with the special little steering knob. The air inside that car smelled like something I remembered from another time and place: a carnival maybe, on a dark, cold night. It had that same sharp, indefinable edge of thrill to it. "See? It isn't really a girl's car, is it?" Frieda said. "You can hardly push that clutch down."

"It's the most beautiful car in the world," I said. "I'll die if I can't have it."

Frieda backed away from the window where she'd been watching me try all the dials and knobs. She crossed her arms. She snorted. She uncrossed her arms. She tapped her fingernails like machine-gun fire on the hood of the car. "That's such a stupid thing to say," she said. "You don't need a car. You need your head examined!" She stomped off. I leaped from the car and raced after her.

"I didn't mean it!" I cried, hot on her heels. My heart clunked dully, two beats behind. "I didn't really mean that." But it was true. I wanted that car with a kind of crazy raw passion, passion as erratic and short-lived and powerful as lightning.

"Sit down," she said, yanking out a kitchen chair. I fell into it like a dropped stone. "You had breakfast?"

I nodded, picking at the cuticle of my left thumb.

"First of all, a car, *no* car, is that important. It's a machine, pure and simple. It gets you here, it gets you there. . . ." She poured two cups of thick black coffee and set them on the table. "Put some milk in it. Girl your age shouldn't drink black coffee."

I did what she said.

"That's all John did with his life, work on that damned car. It's the reason he's in the Army and not in college." High on each cheek was a perfectly round spot of color and she squinted her eyes, remembering something I knew nothing about. "Maybe if he'd had a dad to talk some sense into him. . . ." She began yanking rollers from her hair, dumping them into her lap. Her hair sprung back in bright orange ringlets. Without her makeup she looked like a different person, flat and weathered. Kind of lonely. She talked about men all the time, about how unreliable they were, how selfish and shortsighted, demanding, violent, whatever her two ex-husbands had been. But she hadn't stopped looking around. Not one what she called "decent" man escaped her notice or a rating on her 99-point scale. "Sixty-seven," she'd mutter, glancing over at someone like the owner of Ojala Theater, one of our regulars.

"I didn't really mean it about dying," I said. "It's just a thing you say."

"Who says? Kids your age? Kids at school?"

I nodded.

"Well, let me tell you something about these 'kids,'" she said. "They haven't got a whole brain between them, Bronwyn. They haven't got your brains, that's for damned sure. And they don't care about anything but themselves, about having fun, about their damned cars. Do you think that's normal?"

I didn't know how to answer that.

"Well, it isn't. It isn't normal to spend an entire day

(54)

driving up and down the Avenue, drinking beer and what all. I'll tell you, much as I wanted my boy to go to college, I was relieved when he finally enlisted in the Army. Some of 'em hanging around here are in their mid-twenties. Still hanging out with the high school kids, racing their damned hot rods. Ojala's a nice little town," she said. "But I'm not so sure it's good for teenagers. There just isn't enough to do, so they invent things. Like chickie races."

"Chickie races?" I knew what she meant—there wasn't a teenager in the whole country who didn't—but I wasn't going to let on.

"You know, like in the James Dean movie, racing their cars till one of them, the 'chicken,' backs down. Guy who runs the pool hall, what's his name, Sam something, Sam Detweiler. His kid sailed straight into that stone wall out on Carne Road. Won the race, though, for what good it did him."

"If I had a car, I could, like, you know, run errands and stuff for my dad," I said.

"Don't you bullshit me, girl," she said. "Just don't you ever dare bullshit me. I don't stand for that stuff."

Frieda let me take the car on a promise, sure that Johnny'd go along. "Anyway, it's my car, most of it," she said. I was to turn over my savings, every penny, and give her so much every week out of my tips. "And don't think I won't take it right back if you get yourself in trouble," she said.

I drove home over eggs, taking all the back roads, stalling the car at every stop sign. The clutch *was* hard to work, but the sun just danced off that hood in a zillion stars, tiny as grains of sand. I couldn't believe my luck. I couldn't believe the car was really mine.

Buddy had been watching at the window ever since I

left for Frieda's, and came running from the house the minute I pulled up. "Take me for a ride," he yelled. I'd begun to get the hang of the clutch by then. Buddy jumped in and I took right off again before my parents could pop out and ask to come along.

It was okay for younger brothers and sisters to be seen with you. It wasn't cool, but it was okay. Buddy wasn't old enough to hang his arm on the edge of the window as I did mine. His crew cut barely cleared the dashboard. He sat on the edge of the seat, listening to the sound of the engine, his eyes wide as they were the first time he sat on a horse. "I think it's a 365," he said solemnly.

"A what?"

"A 365," he repeated. "Cubic inches."

"How do you know about that stuff? About cubic inches and all that?"

"I don't know." He shrugged. "Everybody knows."

We passed the Frostee, my heart banging away in my throat. No matter what time of day, somebody always hung out there, sipping Cokes, watching the street. I didn't dare turn my head. "Who's there?" I asked Buddy. "What cars are there?" He turned. "No! Don't turn! Look in the mirror."

He scooted up on his knees and peered into the rearview mirror. "There's a blue car," he said. "A Chevy, I think."

Chick and Angela.

"And that white one with the pinstripes, White Lightning. That's Tommy Nyro's. He's really cool." Tommy Nyro was one of the guys Frieda talked about. He'd been out of school for years but he'd hang around the Frostee anyway.

We drove the length of Ojala Avenue, turned at the "turning tree," and headed back. "Let's get a Coke," Buddy said.

"I can't."

"Why not?"

"I can't pull in there yet." We watched the Frostee Shop slip by, Chick and Angela, Chick following my car with his nose lifted just a little, like a retriever.

8

WHO KNOWS HOW Ojala got its name?

She asked again: "Doesn't anybody know?"

Not a word in response. Not a single hand in the air. Another rule at Ojala High was never to answer a teacher's question unless put directly to you.

"Do you know, Bronwyn Lewis?" Mrs. Beamis always used full names. "Well, you couldn't really know, now could you? You're a foreigner, ha ha. . . . But make a guess! How do you think Ojala got its name?"

"Well, I don't really know, Mrs. Beamis," I said. This was the appropriate response. On the surface it was both sincere and respectful, but offered nothing in the way of substance.

Mrs. Beamis ("Wide-Body Betty") settled into her "thinking" posture: left arm (horizontal) resting on her ample stomach and supporting her right arm (vertical). In this position, she would chew the vermilion polish off her right thumbnail, eyes narrowed and scheming. She was no dummy. She was one of the few who could read the teenage brain, which made her dangerous. "Well, then," she said. I held my breath in anticipation. "We'll assign that one to you, Bronwyn Lewis." She turned and put a check on her list. I groaned, just loud enough for my classmates to hear. "That one" referred to the articles we were to write in journalism 1, for *Ojala Highlights*, the school newspaper.

Being a *Highlights* reporter afforded some status at the school, however limited. It was a little too close to Brain status, but the kids had to be nice to you or find their names in the *Highlights* in places they didn't want them, like under a picture of "Teddy Twoshoes," the groundskeeper. Or worse, their names would not appear where they were supposed to: in the list of Homecoming nominees or under the photo of a spectacular end run or hook shot.

"Mrs. Beamis?"

"Yes, Lanie McCulsky?"

"Mrs. Beamis, maybe nobody really cares about how the town got its name." Lanie had an edgy plaintive whine that usually worked with teachers.

"Well, I don't know, Lanie McCulsky," Mrs. Beamis said. (Sure you do, I thought. Sure you do. You know everything.) "It seems to me that if you're living in a place, you should know its history. It's almost a citizen's obligation, if you see what I mean."

Lanie shot me a look as if to say, "Well, I tried." My head swam with gratitude. It was the first sign that anyone had noticed me as anything but a freak.

After I'd been assigned the task of finding the origin of the strange word for which the town was named, other students were given such topics as the Litter Campaign and the Scholarship Club's Second Annual Dog Wash.

Mrs. Beamis made her final check on the list and turned to the board. What followed would undoubtedly be another thrilling lesson in the judicious use of the dash or reasons why one should never begin a sentence with a conjunction. Then Sal spoke up, a rare event. In New Jersey, Sal would have been known as a "hood" because of what he wore: black from his shoes right up to the fisherman's cap pulled low on his forehead. He was a loner, though, not a member of any gang. Didn't have a friend in the world or at least at Ojala High, which is all that counted. "I got a idea," he said without raising his hand for permission. Mrs. Beamis turned, frowning. "*Do* you," she said.

"Yeah. This buddy of mine in Ventura? Well, he got knifed Saturday night."

Mrs. Beamis puckered her mouth. It was clear that she was considering several responses. At last she said, "The newspaper is for students at Ojala High School, Sal Lopez. But thank you for sharing that information."

"Well, the thing is, his cousin goes here. Art Lopez. It'd be a good story, blood, guts, a little excitement for a change...."

The class broke into hoots and howls. Somebody in the back row beat his fists on the desk.

"That's enough!" Mrs. Beamis cried. "That's enough of that. Take out your grammar books."

I had no particular affection for Sal or for anyone else in that class, but I understood what he meant. *Highlights* was dull as dogwater. Nobody read it unless their picture or name made one of the pages. All the real news—who was going with who, who might be "pg," who got a new car or died in one—all the real stuff got carried by grapevine faster than spit. That's what we cared about, love and death.

Only Mrs. Beamis cared about the honor roll and how the school board voted on the new proficiency test.

For a small town (pop. 2,896—plus us Lewises and whatever children had been born since the sign went up), Ojala had an unusually high death rate. Premature death. Self-inflicted death, according to Frieda, though there weren't all that many suicides. Accidents mostly, with cars or with guns. People took guns for granted in Ojala, pretty much like they did in the old West. Ranchers wore .45s slung in holsters from their dusty Levi's or hung two or three rifles in racks across the rear window of their pickup trucks. With that many guns, you had to accept a certain number of hunting accidents, or even sometimes the tragedy of a child's playing cowboy with his daddy's gun and shooting one of his friends.

Cars were another matter. A week after we moved into town, the *Ojala Sun*'s banner read: YOUTH DIES IN RACE WITH TRAIN. "My Lord," my mother said. "What an awful thing." A month or two later, the headline read: TWO DEAD ON WAY TO ALTAR. "Robert Martinez and Tiffany Jean Davis were to be married on Sunday," the story began. "Now their parents will bury them instead." The *Sun* made no distinction between news and editorials, something Mrs. Beamis would never have tolerated. "Three young people in less than three months," my mother said, shaking her head sadly. When a boy named Gary Clemson wrapped his souped-up Chevrolet around an oak tree at the entrance to town, both my parents were horrified. "Can you believe this?" my mother said. "It's like an epidemic."

"It's the alcohol," Frieda said. "They all drink like fish."

"Don't look at *me*," I said.

Frieda was right. Everybody drank. But it was "just

beer," so it didn't really count. Beer didn't taste all that good to me, not at first. But then I noticed that the second beer had a great way of smoothing out the bumps in things and that a third could make you feel the way you *should* feel, but didn't the rest of the time: confident, pretty, smart. Like you always knew just what you were doing. For the first time since his "accident," I stopped spying on my father, searching for hidden bottles. It wasn't that I forgave him—I'd never do that—but drinking to numb things over began to make a grim kind of sense. The more I drank, the more sense it made.

The older guys, Tommy Nyro, Carl Wilson, bought the beer for us, taking a bottle for their trouble—always Olympia because of the black dots on the back of the label. Some sort of company code, we guessed, but we had a code of our own for them. One dot meant you got a kiss, two meant a hand on the boob, three a hand in the panties, four meant you went all the way. It was thrilling to peel off those labels, even if you didn't have a steady boyfriend. Even if you didn't have a chance in the world to date one of the guys in the hot cars. Still, it made your heart race.

Somebody would claim to have sneaked up on a couple getting it on in the back of a car parked in the orange orchards. "Swear to God!" they'd say, but you never believed it, not really. What girl would take the chance of being called a slut or a punchboard? I wouldn't. I knew I never would. My hold on popularity (what little I had) was tenuous at best. I was "Jersey," a foreigner, like Wide-Body Beamis said. Somebody from another planet. Only now I was somebody from another planet who could guzzle three bottles of Olympia and still dance upright.

What you couldn't help thinking about sometimes in

that space between sober and silly, if you had even half a brain, was what Frieda said once after another kid was nearly killed racing Tommy Nyro to the rock wall out on Carne Road: We were playing Russian roulette with our lives. But the more we drank, the less that seemed to matter.

"What time is it, boys and girls?"

"Party time!"

We didn't plan our parties, which weren't really parties at all, but traveling affairs involving cars and plenty of beer and lasting long into the morning. Party time, like Homecoming or the holiday season, was something that happened just because it always happened. Party time began at the Frostee with Chick and Angela, who seemed to have nowhere else to go, or Tommy Nyro. Somebody said he'd been there so long, he owned shares of stock in the Frostee Freeze Corporation. For a while everybody believed that. Why else would he spend his life there? No one seemed to have homes to go to. They lived like nomads on the road.

Party time began sometime after dark when, elbow jutting out the open driver's window, head tilted at the appropriate James Dean angle, Tommy or Carl, sometimes Chick, would start up his engine, rev it a few times, then squeal wildly out onto the asphalt of Ojala Avenue, burning rubber strips halfway down to Our Lady of Sorrows. In the cloud of smoke left in his wake there'd be a shout or two of appreciation, maybe a long low whistle, then everybody would go back to business: "Where's the party?"

"I dunno, Sandy's?"

"Naw, Sandy's mom's back."

"Then where's the party?"

"I dunno. . . ."

Then Tommy or whoever it was would return, as if

from military reconnaissance, park his car, stick his hands in his pockets, and amble up to the rest of the gang. "Where's the party?"

"We dunno."

Sometime later someone else would get up, wander over to his own car, get in, start the engine, rev it up four or five times, coast to the edge of the driveway, and screech out onto the Avenue. There was a ranking for this activity, but nobody ever spelled it out, not in so many words. In the current crowd of contenders, Carl held the unofficial record with a nine-second spin halfway across Ojala Avenue, nearly into an oak tree at the edge of Bailey's Market parking lot.

But J.C. held all the real records.

J.C. ("For J. C. Aga*j*anian," Angela told me, "the race car driver. Not Jesus, for God sakes!") made only occasional appearances. J.C. was a man, but not a boy-man like Tommy Nyro. He had responsibilities, a son, and a divorce before he could vote. But instead of setting him off-limits to the girls, his past gave him a tragic glamour. Poor J.C. was heartbroken, the story went. Susan, his ex, was "such a bitch." Whenever he had the baby for the day, he'd hang around the Frostee, where any number of girls would fawn over them both, finally leaving J.C. free to talk engines while they baby-sat.

I'd seen him only a few times and only from a distance, surrounded by his fans like Buddy Holly on tour. What got me was how neat he always looked in his Pendleton shirt and pressed cords, his hair slicked back with just a bit of a curl pulled forward. He made the others seem like little boys, took them down a peg or two without even trying. Whenever he showed up, driving his black '32 Ford (a "Deuce," Buddy told me, with a Chevy 356 and dual cams under the hood), everybody swarmed around him. "J.C., how ya doin', man? Gettin' any lately?" Someone, some girl, even somebody's steady, would touch the sleeve of his wool shirt, and the boys would act suddenly grown-up and serious, their voices dropping a notch. "How's she runnin', J.C.?" "Oh, keepin' up, keepin' up." Everybody would grin and chuckle, nod their heads as if he'd said something wise and important.

I watched all this from the uncool side of the Frostee, where families sat with squalling children, munching on cold french fries and greasy tacos. Buddy and I would walk down and have our dinner there, chewy overcooked quarter-pound cheeseburgers instead of my father's Pot Roast Siciliano or Shepherd's Pie. "Can't we drive in this one time?" Buddy would whine, but I wasn't ready.

Every Saturday morning, sometimes with Buddy's help, I'd wash and polish my new car, Silver I called her after the Lone Ranger's horse and the bicycle I'd left behind in Plainfield. I'd buff and polish Silver until her midnight blue paint shone like Parker indigo ink. Then I'd shine her mirrors and windows, attack resistant bits of grease with toothpicks and Q-Tips. Silver was ready but I wasn't, not yet.

In daydreams more vivid than real life, I'd drive ever so casually into the Frostee and park Silver at the end of the line. I'd turn off the motor and wait, as if I had all the time in the world, as if I'd just happened into the place on a whim, a tourist on holiday. I'd watch the kids up ahead, gathered around Chick's car or J.C.'s Deuce, absorbed in their little games. They really were children, I'd say to myself. I'd play if they insisted, but really I didn't care one way or the other. If I held my hand straight out, it wouldn't shake a bit. Actually, I didn't even know what I was doing there. Maybe I'd just get a Coke and go home.

Then someone would look my way, maybe Angela. She'd turn to someone else, nod back at me. Then two or three other kids would turn their heads. They'd try to look real casual, but I'd know. Then one of the guys, always a guy, would wander back, dragging his heels, thumbs in his belt loops, looking the car over. Then he'd whistle, a long, low, appreciative whistle. "Cool car," he'd say. (No, he wouldn't say that. That was too uncool.) Probably he'd say, "Your car?" And I'd nod. I wouldn't say anything back. I wouldn't even smile. I'd act as if this happened every day and Silver wasn't anything special.

After a while a few more of the kids would wander back, looking the car over, glancing warily at me. Someone, probably Tommy (I didn't even dare to put J.C. in a daydream), would ask to lift the hood and the guys would stick their heads in, marveling over the thises and the thats, what Buddy called the "goodies." The girls would hang back just a little, jealous, taking their cues from the guys. Girls didn't have cool cars. They drove their fathers' cars, then their boyfriends' cars. No one would know what to make of a girl with a cool car.

Then Tommy or Chick would do something, say something, give some kind of secret signal (I never knew just what this was), and suddenly I'd be one of them. I'd do all the right things, know just the right words to say.

This always happened at night. Silver would be the star. Bathed in the pink neon glow of the Frostee sign, you could almost hear her sing.

THERE WERE two kinds of people in my life: family and "real" people. Lanie was the first real person to ride in my car. She didn't ask to. I just happened to be around one day when she needed a ride home. By that time I'd endured two months of what I believed to be extreme emotional torture, hanging out by myself during recess and lunch in the most appropriate place I could find, the far end of the football field, under a tree that wept dry leaves. I'd write the words to "Mr. Blue" in my notebook or compose maudlin poems about misfits and exiles. In class I'd pretend to be an idiot or claim laryngitis when asked to read aloud.

For two months, I'd done everything right. I refused to do homework, never dressed for PE, but still I was regarded as something of a freak. I could read my status in a stray glance, hear what I was worth in a passing comment. "Hey, isn't that the girl from . . ."

I would always be The Girl From and there was nothing I could do about it.

I'd tell myself it didn't matter. High school wouldn't last forever. And, besides, now that I had a car, I could always drive back to New Jersey, couldn't I?

Lanie was in the nurse's office when I went by one afternoon to apply as a fourth-period student aide. I knew her name, though I doubt she knew mine. Except for the comment in journalism, she didn't seem to know I was even in the class. But I was there all right, and a lot of the time I was staring at her.

She was maybe the prettiest girl in the school, but her status was hard to read. Everywhere at once, she was nowhere for long. You couldn't tell who her best friends were, whether or not her parents had money (which guaranteed a niche in the country club set, no matter what you looked like or how you behaved). I figured she was just like all the others, self-absorbed, and wrote her off. In the pages of my journal, with bitter diatribe and cutting wit, I wrote nearly everybody off one way or another.

The nurse, Call-me-Cynthia Spellman, seemed like

someone you could talk to, who understood things. She didn't look a whole lot older than us kids. I figured that while I worked beside her rolling bandages or whatever, she could tell me what I was doing wrong. But I was too late. "I have three applications already," she said. "And one of these is a young lady who's going to be a nurse one day. I suppose I should let her have the job." She smiled sympathetically, and I could see she wouldn't be budged unless I really pushed. I could have said that I'd craved since the moment of my birth to be a doctor, but it wasn't true. I didn't really want to be a student aide all that much. It was just a lazy option out of a class like biology that I probably needed if I ever wanted to go to college.

"Thanks anyway," I said, and turned to leave.

"Oh . . . Bronwyn," she said, glancing down at my application to confirm my strange name. "Do you drive to school by any chance?" I nodded. Would driving help me get the job after all?

"Could you drive Lanie home? She's got the flu, I'm afraid, and there's no one to pick her up. I hate to ask you. Have you had the flu?"

"Sure," I said. "I mean, sure, I can give her a ride." Call-me-Cynthia Spellman wrote out a yellow off-campus pass and handed it over with a smile.

"I'm sorry you got stuck," Lanie said as we crossed the parking lot. "I don't have the flu, don't worry. I just didn't study for the lit test."

"Oh, sure," I said. "I didn't either, but I don't have the test until sixth period. I probably just won't go back to school."

"Yeah, that's cool. . . . Hey, is this your car?" Lanie had deep brown, almost black eyes and black wisps of hair that framed her face like Audrey Hepburn's. In journalism I'd stare at her profile, her perfect nose, bright red earrings the size of quarters that matched her angora sweater, and I'd wonder why she wasn't snatched up for the movies. But there were lots of beautiful girls at Ojala High. A Hollywood producer could have had his pick of a dozen brunets or blonds, every one of them prettier than Annette Funicello or Sandra Dee. I began to think there was something in the water.

But Lanie was different from all the other girls. She didn't seem to know she was beautiful, or care much about it if she knew. Others would gaze just a little too long into the mirrors of their compacts, run the tip of a lipstick too slowly across their lips, kiss them together, close the compact, then glance around to see who might be watching. Toward the end of class half a dozen compacts got fished out of purses and opened with little powdery clicks. Being seen without makeup was like being caught without underpants.

But Lanie would forget to layer on the eye shadow. Her lipstick wore off before lunch. Never once did I see her fish a hairbrush from her purse. But she was different in other more important ways as well.

Lots of what my father called "the richies" lived in Ojala, in imitation Swiss chalets or Mediterranean villas tucked high in the hills, or nearer town at the end of long, private drives with locked wrought-iron gates. Most of the kids who lived in these fortresses attended local private schools or were boarded out, but enough attended Ojala High to make their presence felt. You could identify the richies by what they wore only if you had an especially critical eye, like Lanie's. "See that?" she'd whisper, nodding her head toward a senior in chinos and what appeared to be an ordinary brown leather belt. "Alligator. Fifty bucks."

Every girl in school, Lanie included, had closets full of the latest clothes, dyed-to-match skirt-and-sweater sets for the girls, spotless white bucks for everyone (which meant you had to clean them with a toothbrush nightly or you had more than one pair). Did money grow on palm trees? There had to be some reason why none of the kids were ever short of cash—why they were so generous with it, "lending" you a buck or two whenever you "forgot" your money. Buying six-packs or a keg for party time was simply a matter of throwing cash hand over fist into a hat. But it was never like that for Lanie. She worked just like I did for every nickel, washing hair and sweeping floors at the Hairem. Her dyed-to-match was earned.

She didn't let me drive her all the way home that first day. "Right here's fine," she said when we got to the end of town where a few failing businesses hung on. I pulled to the side of the road and she hopped out, walking off in the direction of the dry cleaners, turning once to wave. I waved back. Did she think she'd fooled me? Maybe. But I'd pulled that trick a few times myself back in Jersey, ashamed of my shame but willing to live with it, willing to do whatever it took not to stand out.

Lanie lived in the worst section of town, "Felony Flats" some called it. Doubling back that day, I spotted her a good mile or two down Indio Muerto Road headed toward a shabby trailer park. I didn't feel sorry for her. I didn't compare her fortune, or misfortune, to mine and count my blessings. Instead I used what I knew a week later to give me the courage I didn't otherwise have and asked if she'd have lunch with me. "Sometime," I said, giving her an out. "You know, when you're free."

"How about today?" she said, surprising me. "It's spaghetti day in the caf." I thought only kids who got free lunch tickets ate in the cafeteria, but I figured Lanie knew what she was doing. "Great," I said.

The cafeteria was filled with students and dense overlapping layers of noise. Half the tables were full and the room had that stuffy dead-air feeling of a gym on the night of a big game. All four walls were plastered with brightly painted butcher-paper banners announcing the weekend's Homecoming football game. *Conquistadors Are Going to War! Go, OHS!! Two, four, six, eight. Who Do We Appreciate?* I was hit with a sharp jab of homesickness, the first I'd had in a while. Homecoming. Yellow asters, hot chocolate, the sound of the band as it marched onto the field, the first cheer . . .

We joined a line that snaked toward the front, where fat ladies in chef's aprons slopped bloody noodles onto plastic plates.

Lanie turned to me. Her mouth moved but I couldn't hear her. The cinder-block walls seemed to throb and breathe with the noise in the room, slammed trays, catcalls, the kind of laughter that usually comes at somebody's expense. A milk carton hit the wall behind my head and splattered like bird shit down the pale green wall. I turned. The boy behind me had his finger up his nose.

Lanie yelled in my ear. "I used to eat spaghetti all the time. That canned stuff, you know . . . ?"

"Franco-American! I did, too!" It was a beginning, a bond. We liked the same foods. There'd be other things for sure.

We got our trays and slid them along under the waiting ladles of the fat ladies, who were either impatient or bored, depending on their age. I followed Lanie to a table where three girls had huddled in a clump. I figured they were freshmen. "Hi, girls," Lanie said, setting her tray down. "Mind if we join you?" They stared at her with startled expressions, mouths open. Two wore braces. The boldest of the three muttered, "Sure." We dropped onto the wooden bench across from each other and began eating our spaghetti. The freshmen were whispering all three at once, heads low over their trays.

"I'm a pig. I just can't help it," Lanie said, slurping in a fork full of orangy noodles. Two girls at the next table turned. "Gross!" one complained. "Sorry!" Lanie said; then she was giggling and I along with her. It felt so good to have someone to giggle with. I glanced more fondly now at the freshmen. The bold one crossed her eyes at me. The tips of her hair were stained with spaghetti sauce.

I told Lanie all about Silver. She told me about her boyfriend, Jimbo. Jimbo wasn't exactly Mr. Popular, she said, but she was sure I'd like him. Which meant she wanted me to meet him. Which meant we'd spend more time together. Which meant I had a friend. I'd have kissed a rattlesnake if she'd asked me, which turned out to be a closer comparison to her boyfriend than I ever expected.

Lanie spent most of her time with Jimbo, but once in a while I'd get to drive her home, all the way home. The first time we pulled up to the rusted green-and-white metal box, she didn't apologize like I expected, like I would have. She even invited me in.

Lanie's mother was a bona fide, grade A alcoholic, so bad she never even got out of bed except to shuffle to the bathroom. All day long, she just lay there propped up on yellowed sheets, fat as an old sow, smoking Marlboros. She lifted her eyelids for just a second when Lanie introduced us but then looked back at the TV, where some woman was hyperventilating over having won a washer-dryer combination.

Aurelia McCulsky weighed nearly three hundred

pounds and looked like an active volcano ready to blow. But Lanie carried on as if she were just a normal person. She fixed her a tuna sandwich and some chicken noodle soup that day and then helped her eat. The mother could hardly lift her fat arms. Food ran down that old thing's chin, all of her chins, and messed the sheets, but Lanie just kept on, "Here you go, Ma. . . ." It was as if she didn't see the repulsive creature her mother was, the doughy rolls of flesh, the slack moist lips out of which she babbled her nonsense.

Lanie's father wasn't much better. He was a drinker, too, but never drank enough at one time to keep him down. We'd see him cruising the Avenue in his El Camino with the bucking-bronco hood ornament, one arm laid over the steering wheel, Stetson tipped back, looking for all the world like he was somebody. Usually he had a lady with him and half the time they weren't ladies at all, but girls about half his age. Lanie (and I used to think a whole lot about this), somehow Lanie never let any of this get her down. Whenever she saw her daddy in town, she'd walk right up and give him a kiss. She'd look at him like he really was somebody, like all those years acting like he was made it true. I couldn't understand it.

Of course, she thought my life was just great, that the Welsh Kitchen was "fabulous." We'd raid the refrigerators late in the night, stuffing our arms with home-baked rolls and slices of cold roast lamb, leftover rhubarb pie piled high with ice cream. Out on the front porch, we'd watch the last of the partiers cruise the Avenue. When I looked back at my first night in Ojala, at our sad picnic of Frostee Freeze burgers, I could smile because now I had a friend.

But like some of the boys who got close to her now and then, I had Lanie only between the times she and Jimbo went steady, which was almost always. Alone, I never had the nerve to cruise the Avenue, though lots of the guys did. When Lanie went back to Jimbo—and no matter how badly he treated her, she always did—I would sit on my porch alone and long for New Jersey again.

9

LIKE SOMETHING with a will of its own, the Welsh Kitchen began to engulf my parents. Weight dropped from my father's slight frame; I reinstated my search for hidden bottles; my mother gained twenty pounds stuffing continual bits of food into her mouth, "for energy." Their day, except for Tuesday, the one day the restaurant closed, started before the sun. Somewhere almost out of consciousness, like background in a stage play, I'd hear my father banging pots around, my mother sifting flour. Or I'd hear them before that, my father's heavy tread up the stairs, coffee cups clattering in their saucers, one cup laced with cream and sugar for my mother. I'd hear him whisper, hear her stir and sigh. They'd talk quietly in the dark, and on good days my mother would chuckle at something my father said. If they made love (I could barely stand the thought of that), it must have been a quickie under the sheets in the dead of night.

"One of these days," my father promised, we'd move into a proper house, a house with a piano, and Buddy would have his own horse. Sometimes my fingers itched with the need to play and I would sneak, like an addict after a fix, into the church on Acacia Street. The kind of piano my father would have found on one of his excursions into junk land wasn't the kind I wanted to play. There would never be money for a good piano, a real piano, and we'd always live in the attic. That was the way it was. Something was always nibbling away at the profits—a scandalous laundry bill, repairs for the refrigerator, the extra-large slices of pie my mother would serve her favorite old people. "It's the little things that are killing us, sweetheart," my father said. "I know they're all good customers, but business is business."

Now it seemed they argued all the time. "Minor differences of opinion," my mother said, but they were differences with a kind of heat and energy they never had before, and sometimes my mother would cry.

One ongoing disagreement concerned Mitra, a woman my mother met in line at Bailey's and hired on the spot. Mitra was to work part-time, doing what my mother didn't quite know. What she knew, and it was enough for her, was that Mitra's meager pension barely covered her rent.

Mitra had other more serious problems. Her back was terribly bent, both forward and at an angle to the right, so that she seemed always to be moving sideways like a crab. She was "old" in my terms, fifty or sixty, with stringy mouse-colored hair and a sharp thin nose with oversized nostrils. When my mother introduced her, she repeated something remotely resembling my name, *BAWhmn*, full of wind, tunneling out in a kind of snort from the back of the throat and down those awful nostrils. She'd be helping out in the kitchen, my mother said vaguely. My father frowned.

For a while Mitra worked along with my father, cleaning up in his wake. She would hum tunelessly or chatter away in some incomprehensible language that turned out to be English when you knew her long enough. My father began to warm to her in spite of himself. She became his straight man. "I could have been a baker," he'd say.

"Nawgh . . ." said Mitra, rolling her eyes.

"But I couldn't raise the dough!"

"Awghhh!" Mitra cried gleefully.

Then she began to wander out of the kitchen to peer shyly into the dining room. Then she got her hands on a coffeepot and we couldn't get her back in the kitchen again. That was when the trouble started. I could always see it coming; some old lady, usually a lady, always old, would sidle up and draw me aside as if she were about to reveal that my slip was showing. "Dear . . ." she'd say, summoning my ear down to the level of her lips with her finger crooked. "I hate to *say* anything, but that . . . woman, the one who's serving the coffee? Well, like I said, I hate to say anything, but she probably shouldn't be, you know, *talking* to people." I'd thank the lady for her concern and promise to talk with my father about it. But I knew what would happen. My father would blow up, insist my mother keep Mitra out of the dining room ("Business is business!"), and my mother would refuse. "How can I suggest a thing like that?" she'd cry. "You know how much she loves people."

Which was impossible to understand. At Buchenwald, Mitra had been a monstrous experiment, an interesting study in angles and degrees, a math equation for some imaginative fiend. To what degree, he must have wondered, could a human body bend and still not break? Mitra had been tied and twisted chin to hip and left for days, like a discarded child's toy. Then sometime later, for some hideous reason that reason couldn't know, half her palate had been removed. Years later, when she was free and could make sounds again, the words came out against all odds, twisting down a hollow tunnel in an anguish of minor explosions into the startled face of anyone patient enough to wait for them. Or horrified enough. On her arm was a tattoo of smudged blue numbers. Customers would stare at these numbers as she poured their coffee, then, in troubled whispers, give their children some explanation for them. Some customers would leave, making vague excuses about not being as hungry as they'd thought. Then my father would explode again. "This is a *business*," he'd cry. "You have to draw a line between friendship and business."

"You draw your lines," my mother said. "And I'll draw mine."

Finally Mitra, no fool where people were concerned, began to stay in the kitchen, chattering away to my father as he sliced his roast, basted his Chicken Marengo. "I just *love* this man," she'd say (or some mangled version of that), laying her head against his arm. She radiated love like other people radiated caution or apathy or self-righteousness, and by then, I'd begun to love her, too. There was no way to help it if you knew her long enough. "Which woman?" I'd insist when someone would call me over to complain. "The redhead? No? Oh, *that* one. What's the problem?"

My father began sipping coffee laced with something as telling as an old lady's perfume. I told myself that whatever he did couldn't get to me. I was older now and kept my guard up. I was no longer the child who would race home from the school bus stop, terrified of finding a dead man on the bathroom floor. Memory, vivid in the particulars as always, had begun scabbing over. I was now simply ashamed of him. Shame felt better than fear. It distanced me, so that if he ever tried that old trick again and succeeded, I wouldn't miss him, not a bit.

10

*I*N SOME WAYS Lanie was the kind of friend you didn't want to have. She was too pretty, too nice. She didn't seem to have any glaring faults, the kind you could tote up to make yourself feel better. You could get better grades than Lanie, but you always knew who the boys were looking at, and that's all that really mattered.

In Ojala, Lanie was Miss Everything and had been since junior high. Miss Ojala Junior League, Miss Dairy Delight, Miss Ventura County. She won every contest she entered, so it didn't make much sense for anyone else to try. This got to the girls who might have otherwise had a chance. They'd say she was stuck on herself and some of them, behind her back, called her a "hick." But she went out of her way to do things for people and they always came around. Like Mitra, she was just a good person. She was good even to people who didn't earn or deserve that goodness.

Like Jimbo. A year ahead of us, a senior, Jimbo Callahan

looked like Mr. Peanut Man without the top hat. He was shorter than Lanie and shaved his hair so close you could see his shiny scalp sticking through. He was the color of Mr. Peanut Man, too, a sort of yellow-beige. He was descended from Eskimos, he said, but no one believed him. He'd say anything to take you off guard. Then he'd grin with the gold tooth he liked to show off. Leaning back on his heels the way all the guys did, hands stuffed down in the front pockets of his jeans, he'd try his best to be taller and more important than he was. Nobody liked him much.

And nobody, maybe not even his own mother, knew what Lanie saw in him. Crude and tactless, he particularly enjoyed embarrassing girls, the younger the better, going as far out of his way as Lanie would go in the other direction to do someone a favor. Yet he was rarely challenged, only rarely, only when someone got real fed up. Those he called friends more or less put up with him, or egged him on if they were bored. Ole Jimbo knew how to have a good time, they'd say. You had to give him that. They'd tease him a little, but they never pushed him far. Like animals do, they'd long before sensed the mean streak that ran straight through him. But Lanie didn't. She loved the "real" Jimmy, the one "inside," the one only she knew.

And maybe her attachment to Jimbo had more to do with his family than she was willing to admit. She loved the Callahans. Fourth-generation Californians, they were every bit as fine and well mannered as Jimbo was coarse, particularly Saundra, Jimbo's older sister. Lanie idolized Saundra, sleeping overnight in Saundra's attic room at the rambling old Victorian the Callahans had restored. She marveled at the way they "dined," all at the same time, seated around a twelve-foot-long mahogany table that had been in the family for three generations. She loved the way they

(81)

talked and laughed, passing pot roast and mashed potatoes in the "everyday" dishes (white with a simple blue band and tiny forget-me-nots in the center). They were like the people on the cover of *The Saturday Evening Post*, she said, the ones Norman Rockwell painted. They even said grace.

But as much as she loved those dinners, she never felt anything but out of place, worrying about fork selection or having to eat something like artichokes. How did you eat artichokes? At first all she could do was imitate Saundra, smoothing the soft linen napkin over her lap, taking a tiny sip of water, passing a dish to her immediate right. She didn't know if a mutt could ever be anything but a mutt, she said.

And there across that fine old table was Jimbo, belching just for effect, challenging his father at every opportunity, like an adolescent sea lion but with none of a sea lion's grace. How such fine people could conceive a Jimbo was a puzzle. My theory was that he'd been adopted and that if the Callahans hadn't taken pity on him, he'd be out on the tundra hauling blubber where he belonged.

Even though Lanie and Jimbo were a permanent item, there were always other boys around, waiting. Lanie had to be real fed up with Jimbo to call it quits, but the minute she did, someone would step right in. She dated the police chief's son for three weeks or so, a record. He's so *nice*, she'd say, as if there were something terribly wrong with him. Then one day, there she was cruising the Avenue in Jimbo's Chevy pickup again, squashed to his side, smiling that hundred-watt smile. Seeing her with Jimbo always made me want to kick something.

One time I thought she really might be finished with him. That was just after the year officially began, New Year's Eve, with Tommy Nyro's run through town.

We closed the restaurant that night at the usual time. Without a liquor license, we never drew the late crowds, but I figured my father would call for a little end-of-the-year celebration and that Frieda and my mother would go along. He was getting looser all the time, spiking his coffee liberally from a bottle he hid behind the giant cans of chicken broth and stewed tomatoes. Who did he think he was fooling? My mother? Maybe. But I'd been on his trail too long and knew all the signs: the shaky hands, the watery eyes focused somewhere off center, cigarettes left burning two at a time at the edge of his prep table, a tuneless, breathless hum as he went about the usual business of dinner preparation. By then he could make Chicken Marengo in his sleep.

In the early months, before he began hiding bottles again, I'd find him sitting on the back porch peeling carrots or potatoes with a quick sure wrist, whistling a familiar tune. Scrape, scrape, scrape, quick and sure, the peels would fly into a grocery bag, and his silver hair and white chef's clothes could dazzle a morning awake. His back would seem straighter, and I'd think: Maybe it's different now. He'd look up as I approached, clear-eyed, and offer his lopsided, self-defeated grin. The grin never changed. "How's my lass?" he'd say, and I'd crack a little inside. "Give your old dad a kiss." I'd bend and quickly peck the side of his face. Just that easily I could tell how things were going with him. If my lips touched stubble, I'd begin to watch him more closely.

And then, as I've said, I stopped watching.

CHRISTMAS came and went so fast I hardly had time to complain. Where was the snow? The air had some snap to it but there was no drama, no pent-up excitement as the day drew near. A half-dozen strings of lights sagged across the

Avenue from the arcade to palm trees on the opposite side. Santa (Mr. McCulsky high as a kite in his El Camino) cruised up and down calling "Merry Christmas," patting fannies, kissing every girl he could get his mittens on. Donkeys escaped from the crèche at Our Lady of Sorrows and wandered into people's yards looking for plants to chew on. It was pitiful.

And then it was New Year's Eve. Back East, my relatives would be watching Guy Lombardo because that's what everybody did. In Ojala it was different. There were different expectations, an entirely different tradition. After my parents dropped wearily into bed, I crept behind Buddy's partition, put my hand over his mouth, and woke him up. In the darkness I helped him get into his clothes (he'd laid them in a neat pile ready to jump into), and we slid like bandits out of the house.

In the empty lot across from Our Lady of Sorrows a crowd was already gathered. Someone had started a huge bonfire with dried Christmas trees, and sparks leaped into the dark, clear sky strung with stars like bits of floating ice. All the kids were there, cars parked fender to fender as if waiting for a drive-in movie to begin. There were oil drums filled with ice and beer and Coca-Cola, and someone had gone after pizzas. "This is so cool!" Buddy yelled. I shushed him with a poke. Jimbo's pickup was in one of the best spots for viewing.

"Hey, kiddo," Jimbo said, pulling Buddy up over the tailgate. "Come out to see old Tommy, huh? Well, you better hold on to your sissie's hand." He stuck his face right into mine, with a leer and that gold tooth glittering. "She's gonna be *real* scared." Buddy ducked his head in embarrassment at having gotten Jimbo's attention. He inched away from me at the thought of having to hold my hand.

Jimbo popped the cap off an Oly. Foam bubbled up and

ran down over his fingers. "I can just see old Tommy now," he mused. "I know just what he's thinking." Of course, what he wanted was to *be* Tommy, to have Tommy's daring and his reputation. He tipped the Oly for a long, slow pull. Already he was rocky on his feet and his words had begun slipping up against each other. "Old Tom, laughin' his azzoff . . . They'll never get *me*! Countin' down, ten, nine, eight, seven, six, five . . ." Jimbo frowned down at his watch, trying to make out the time. "Eight minutes," he said. "Hey! Go, Tommy!" He punched the air with his fist. Then, almost as an afterthought, he hurled his empty bottle against the trunk of an oak tree. It hit dead on, glass popping and shattering down the base of the trunk.

"Sit down," Lanie said. "Sit down, Jimmy, before you fall down."

He looked at her with a crooked grin, pupils suddenly focused. "You shut your mouth and do what you're supposed to do," he said. "Run get me another beer."

"In a pig's eye," Lanie said. He could never back her down, which was how the trouble usually began.

"In a *what's* eye? You calling me a pig?" He leaned over and pinched the skin between Lanie's neck and shoulder so hard it took her breath away. But then he swayed and let go.

"I'll get you a beer," Buddy said, scrambling over the side.

"Buddy!" I yelled, but he was gone.

"Aw, Lanie," Jimbo said then, sinking to the bed of the truck beside her. "Come here, Lanie girl, Jimbo loves you. . . ." He tried to turn her chin, but she held firm. She could get as angry as anyone I ever knew, but it was a quick showy kind of anger that never held up under fire. "Take your friggin' hands off me," she said.

"I'll do what I want with my friggin' hands," he said. "I'll put 'em wherever I friggin' want to." While she squirmed, he pinned her legs with his knee and pulled her sweater out of her slacks, fumbling for the zipper in her slacks.

"You bastard . . . !" she cried, breaking free just as the sound of an engine winding to a pitch came toward us somewhere out of the darkness. Jimbo leaped up and stumbled out of the truck. "Here he comes!" he yelled. "Here comes Tommy!"

I stood and scanned the crowd for Buddy. I yelled his name. I whistled our secret whistle but didn't hear it back. He wasn't stupid, but he was only ten. Maybe, if he couldn't see over all the heads, he'd try to bolt across the Avenue to get a better view. "Buddy!" The pitch of the engine's howl jumped an octave, screaming from the far end of town and the dark shapes of mountains like the cry of something damned let suddenly free.

I dodged through the crowd of kids pushing up against each other and craning for a better view of White Lightning, ready to yell and cheer as it streaked Ojala Avenue. "Buddy, damn it! Buddy, answer me!" And then it was all scream and pounding engine. I wedged myself between two boys at the front of the pack and saw the white shape just as it rounded the curve at the light, its front end nearly suspended as if clawing the air for speed. A yell went up from the crowd. I felt a tug on the back pocket of my jeans and there was Buddy. In all the noise I could only read the words as he desperately mouthed them. "I can't see! I can't see!" and so I pushed him in front of me and held on like a vise as the Ford, in a wild rush of light and metal and gasoline fumes, hurtled past the screaming crowd and back into the night. For several seconds after Tommy passed, no one moved or spoke. Then, as if in unspoken agreement, the crowd shifted and broke. "Happy New Year!" someone cried, and then everybody remembered. Lips fumbled for lips. Corks popped. Somebody fired several shots into the air.

"Wow!" Buddy cried, breaking free. "Did you see that? Did you see that, Bron? Wasn't that *cool?*"

My heart hammered like a tiny fist banging on my ribs. I looked down at Buddy. He was one of them in miniature, one of the guys, right down to the Levi's that hung precariously on the points of his skinny hipbones and dragged the dirt at his heels. What had happened to him had happened so fast that I hadn't even noticed.

I was sorry now that I'd kept my promise to wake him up for Tommy's run. Someday, in imitation of his heroes, he'd wrap some flashy piece of metal and himself around a tree. He'd try that hard to be cool, I knew how it was, and it would be my fault. Something in the pounding, driving, screaming rush of a gasoline engine could get to you, could pull you with it over the edge of some personal line you drew against risk, even against death. You stopped thinking at some point. You left behind the rational, reasonable parts of yourself and just went with it.

"Go on," I said, pushing him before me. "Get on home. This was a stupid thing. He could have killed himself, or somebody else coming the other way." But Buddy knew, as we all did, that the police had cordoned off the Avenue for Tommy because they knew he'd do it every time, every New Year's Eve, no matter how long they locked him up in between. It was his identity, what set him off from everybody else and gave him the stature he didn't otherwise have. Sure he was crazy, sure he was a dropout, but did you see *that!*

We crossed the vacant lot and cut through the back streets toward home. Overhead were the tiny pinpricks of stars and not a trace of moon. The night wind shuffled eucalyptus branches against each other so that they seemed to talk in dry whispers, conspirators floating around us like dark shaggy giants.

"Bron," Buddy said after a while. "Are you scared?"

"No."

He slipped his small hand into mine. "Me neither. It's just hard to see in the dark sometimes."

"Yeah," I said. "I know how it is."

11

THE RAIN STARTED UP in my dreams. Isolated drops, tapping my window like pebbles. And then I was awake, clearheaded, as if a part of me had been fending off sleep. I looked out the window and there was Lanie ready to throw another pebble. I held up my hand to let her know I'd be down. Climbing into the clothes I'd dropped in a heap hours before, I slipped past the curtains where Buddy and my parents lay in sleep.

Lanie stood in the shadow of the porch huddled in her Navy pea coat, collar pulled up around her ears. "You okay?" I asked.

She shook her head. I followed her across the dining room, where she looked out the window onto the Avenue, then drew back. "He's such a bastard," she said in a fierce whisper, more to herself than to me. *"Bastard!"* She pulled a chair out from under Number 6 and dropped into it, forehead cradled in the palms of her hands. I sat across from her and waited, because that was how it always went. She would talk when she was ready, and I would listen.

At first I'd been as impassioned as she, ready to tear Jimbo to pieces for this or that awful thing he'd said or done. Now I found myself wondering how many times we'd play this out, her pretending she would finally end it with him, me pretending I believed her. What good did it do? She went back to him every time, no matter what I said, no matter what she promised. I'd begun to wonder if I wasn't just the latest in a long line of friends who'd given up on her. Maybe I wasn't so special after all. Maybe I'd just happened along at the right time, when there was no one else.

I murmured the usual things while she cried softly into her hands. "You don't deserve this, Lanie . . . he isn't worth your little finger . . . there are dozens of nice guys who would . . ."

"Promise you won't hate me, Bron," she said at last. I wasn't sure I'd heard her right. Hate Lanie? Who could ever hate Lanie?

"Don't be silly," I said.

She dropped the collar of her pea coat and my breath caught. "Pretty bad, huh?" She reached across the table, grabbing both my wrists. I stared at her face, unable to form words. After a fight, a boxer might look like this. An accident victim might stumble from a wrecked car looking like this. But not a beauty queen, not someone I knew. The right side of her face from the corner of her eye to the soft curve of her chin was a single spreading bruise, grayish purple in the semidark of the dining room and garish in the occasional headlight that streaked the window and lit her up, monstrous, pathetic, lipstick smeared like war paint down her chin. Blood, black and thick, leaked slowly from her left nostril. She dabbed at it with a wad of toilet paper.

"God, Lanie . . ."

"*Say* it!" she insisted, as if she were angry with me. "Say you don't hate me."

"I don't hate you, dummy. Why do you say that?" I'd begun to cry, sick and scared and out of my depth. "I'm not the one who hates you." Our hands clutched like the hands of shipwrecked sailors grab across the upended prow of a lifeboat. Everything I'd ever said before seemed senseless now, as if she'd gone into some dark place I could not find her in or help her out of.

"I never want to see him again," she said. "I never want to see his face." Tears welled up in her dark eyes, and I could tell she was seeing his rage all over again, his fists as they came at her.

"I know . . ." I murmured. "I know."

She'd begun to shake. Her hands were cold and damp. "Can you get me something to drink? A shot of something," she said. "Whiskey."

I went into the kitchen and felt behind the cans for my father's bottle. My hands shook. *Old Crow*, the label said, *The Original Sour Mash Bourbon Whiskey*. I poured two water glasses half-full, leaving the bottle on the counter in plain sight for my father when he came into the kitchen in the morning, or for my mother should she see it first. I was full of something black and turbulent, something that felt like rage, but that couldn't be rage because I'd never felt rage. Killers felt rage, madmen. Rage was not a female trait. Girls got mad. Not angry even, just mad. And then they got over it. But this was something else. This spun off in all directions at once, shooting back impotent and ultimately directionless, leaving me shaking in its wake.

Lanie swallowed the whiskey with a little aftershudder. "I gotta get out of here," she said.

"I'll take you home."

"I mean out of Ojala. For good. Away from everything." She sounded bitter and years older than she was. "From everybody."

Two cars, one on the bumper of the other, sped through the dark streets. I watched their headlights zip through Lanie's dark eyes. "Let's go," I said. "Let's go for a drive." I reached for my keys in the pocket of my Levi's. They lay on my palm, solid and practical. We could get away, like Lanie said, from "everything" with those keys, at least for a while.

Outside, the air was cold with a metallic edge you could taste. We pushed Silver out onto the Avenue so we wouldn't wake my parents, but they were dead sleepers and we probably needn't have worried. By midnight there was nothing left of them but hands that did what hands had learned to do, the scrubbing and cleaning to ready the place for the next day's lunch. They knew little of my whereabouts or what I might be doing. They hardly had the energy to supervise Buddy, who spent more and more time next door with the Alvarez family. As if testing stagnant water, I'd begun doing little things I knew would anger them or make them sad, caking crimson on my lips like a warning flag, wearing tight cardigans buttoned up the back so that my Living Bra poked out in sharp relief.

"Be home before twelve-thirty," my mother would call as I left, plates of pot roast stacked on her arm, *au jus* sloshing, but I hadn't been in before three in months. Sometimes my father would call me back and I would turn, half expecting a lecture, some warning or piece of useless but well-meant advice, but he wouldn't really see me either.

Instead he'd pull one of his old tricks: "How far would you have gotten," he'd ask, "if I hadn't called you back?" There'd be a film of sweat across his forehead, grease on his chef's whites, maybe a bandage on his thumb where he'd sliced the beef too thin. "Give your old dad a kiss," he'd say, and I was free, a small price to pay, I thought, for freedom.

But it was an empty freedom, too easily won, too wide. I would embark into it like an unattended ship slipping anchor, sails luffing, nothing in mind but to catch a passing breeze and hold it long enough to feel steady in the water. For Lanie it was worse. She'd sailed into the first harbor that seemed safe and stayed there, unable to change direction. She thought she deserved Jimbo, as she must have deserved her parents and that meager sad excuse for a life in the trailer park.

We coasted to the corner and I started Silver, her engine catching on the first try. I knew her better than I knew the inner workings of my own body. When her fuel pump needed replacing, Chick supervised but I did the work, digging down into Silver's greasy insides like a surgeon. Her pistons beat with the rhythm of my heart, or the other way around.

Sometimes I'd catch Frieda looking at me as if I'd gone crazy, but my gratitude was so genuine and my payments so prompt that I could always work her around. "Just remember, we're talking metal and rubber and glass here, girl," she'd say. "Not flesh and blood, not feelings. . . ."

We wound slowly through the back streets of town, past the small shabby houses near Lanie's trailer park. There were cars parked all along the sides of the street, more cars than houses, some of them immobilized with flattened tires and covered with coats of fine red dust. Mexican laborers lived in these houses, many of whom were the backbone of the community, if backbone meant sweat, freeing the city of its garbage, hauling avocados and oranges by the ton from the trees of wealthy ranchers. At school, you saw the kids who lived in houses like these clumped together at the rear of things, of basketball games if they attended, or dances, appearing and disappearing midway through the evening like a bright and chattering band of birds. They never seemed unhappy to me, though I thought they must be. How could they be happy out there on the edge? Yet they exhibited a brash confidence, at least among themselves, speaking a fast tangled language and ignoring most of what went on around them. The girls with their olive skin and shy dark eyes were strikingly beautiful, more beautiful, I thought, than the blond who won Homecoming Queen or any of her court, who, with their similar features, might easily have been her sisters.

We threaded our way out of town. "I think there's something wrong with Jimbo," Lanie said after a time. She held her hands to the heater, rubbing them together to pull the life back in.

I kept my mouth shut. It was never good to agree with Lanie when she began to pick away at Jimbo, probing like an archaeologist through layers of time and sediment, painstakingly, as if a single faulty move might collapse a whole theory. If you tried to help, she'd turn on a dime and defend him. This was because, as she said, "nobody else would." It was as if she'd been given a job for life, one she wasn't allowed to lay down or set aside or even do halfheartedly.

"No . . . I mean something really wrong. Like a sickness or something, something he can't help. Did I tell you that he said he'd probably kill somebody someday? Would a normal person think something like that?" She rummaged through her purse for a pack of her mother's Marlboros. She slipped two out of the pack and lit them, coughing on the exhale. I always got a kick out of the way she pushed out her bottom lip on the exhale. Soon the car was filled with smoke, but it was too cold to roll down the windows. "The thing is, it happens so fast. One minute we're fine, he's got his arm around me and I'm feeling, oh, I don't know, *whole*. I know this sounds crazy after what he did, but that's how I feel when I know he loves me. And he does love me, Bron. . . ."

My fingers tightened on the wheel and I watched the dark road unwind itself and roll beneath the hood. Inside, I felt hollow and sick. There were times when I believed I had the words to make her change the way she saw things; now I knew that whatever drove her back to him time and time again went beyond any words I ever had. Still, I couldn't let her think I agreed. I was the last of her friends to put up a fight. Giving up, I'd be consigning her to the cave I'd dreamed her into once, a cave too deep to climb out of all alone.

We drove past orchards of orange trees, dark round Alice-in-Wonderland shapes, and up into the hills. There were few houses in the hills, and these were scattered and set back from the road. The people who lived here were generally well-to-do, my mother's term for "the richies," but they were not really rich, nor influential like the Callahans. They were artists and musicians as well as some fairly well-known writers, an author of a mystery series and one very old poet who had once won some prestigious prize nobody remembered the name of. The houses were all very private affairs, hidden behind overgrown bushes and untrimmed trees, and had an air of serenity about them as if they were generating a quiet and solemn creativity. This is where I would live someday, I'd decided, when I was a famous writer or pianist. That was the day I realized how far I'd come from New Jersey and how fast. That I could be so fickle came as a surprise.

Lanie was my opposite in many ways. She was sweet and unselfish and, most of all, loyal. But dogs were loyal, too, blindly loyal. You had to know when to cut loose and save yourself, but Lanie never seemed to know just when, and so she never did.

"I think you're right about one thing," I said, shifting Silver down into second for the long climb to the summit of Topa Ridge. "You need to get away from him, some-how. . . . "

"I could go live with my aunt Ella in Arkansas."

"Arkansas?" Crossing the country, we'd bumped into Arkansas, another adventure. All I remembered of it was a skinny boy with one leg and the startling fact that despite his age, thirteen, fourteen, he'd wet his pants.

"Yeah. I could get a hog-callin' certificate. Beats cutting hair for a living."

"Oh, Lanie, can't you just stay away from him? Jesus . . ." I coasted Silver toward the edge of the lookout and cut her engine. Lanie and I opened the doors at the same time and got out. The cold mountain air made us shiver and pull our jackets close.

Lanie dropped her cigarette and squashed it with her heel. "I told you, I'm not going back with him." She shin-nied up onto the hood, leaning back against the windshield. I did the same. We stared together at the black canvas of the sky. "I didn't think he'd ever go this far, Bron. I don't even know how it started. We were talking about, I don't know, about the police, something about which ones were the good guys and which ones weren't and all of a sudden, bam! I didn't even know what happened. There was just this empty gray space, I guess I went out, and then I bounced back for the next one. He was yelling and crying, something about my screwing around with Tony, you know, Chief Alcott's son? I was too dizzy to think. I could taste blood and I thought, What if he doesn't stop? What if he kills me?"

"Oh, Lanie . . ." I heard an engine and my heart froze, but it was a sedan, a late-model Ford. A grown-up, not Jimbo. Picking up speed at the turn, the car continued to climb, the engine fading into silence.

"And you know what, Bron? You know what scared me even more than Jimbo coming at me was that I didn't care. I didn't really care right then if he killed me or not." The tears had begun again, slipstreaming down from the corners of her eyes, but it wasn't as if she were feeling sorry for herself or knew the tears might bring some relief or help her heal. She hardly noticed them. She looked like a statue to me then, as if she'd hardened into something as unchangeable in the short run as stone. She would go back to him. That, too, was set in stone. I knew it, she knew it, but neither of us knew why. We were going through the motions of change, but nothing would change.

I wanted then to turn to her, to take her in my arms like a child and rock her silently against all the dark shapes in the night. I wanted somehow to let her know that no matter what she did I would always love her. That seemed important right then, even critical. But except for a quick, shy embrace after a contest she'd won or a publication of mine in the lit magazine, we'd never hugged or held each other close. Instead, paralyzed by all the things we didn't yet know, by our youth, our homophobic fears, by the accidents of our separate fates that brought us together for this time, we stared out into the night or down into the lights of town scattered at the bottom of the bowl of mountains like captured fireflies.

12

*T*HE SMELL OF GREASE and gasoline saturated the air, our clothes, the coffee in my paper cup. Buddy and I stood behind the yellow sawhorses at the edge of the strip, Buddy so excited I had to shake breath into him. He couldn't even talk, a rare event for Buddy. His hair was slicked back on the sides with something that stayed wet-looking, and he had pulled so faithfully at a lock over his forehead that it had begun to curl down in the cool and proper way, like Kookie's on *77 Sunset Strip*. On the back of Buddy's navy bomber jacket was the black silhouette of a cowboy on a bucking bronco. *Vaqueros*, it said across the silhouette in the looping letters of a lariat, the logo of Ojala Elementary. He looked like a ten-year-old going on eighteen.

"If I ever catch you with a cigarette, you're dead," I said.

"Huh?"

"Nothing."

(99)

Before us stretched the gleaming asphalt black snake of a runway, dancing mirage of glassy black water at the far end. Stretched out over the water was a green-and-white Castrol banner, drooping a little, like a damp diaper.

When we'd first arrived, only a few cars were clustered in the pit. I'd expected them to look different, to have numbers or names painted on their sides, racing stripes, something to set them off. But most were like the cars that cruised Ojala Avenue or raced on Carne Road. Now more and more engines began to accelerate, each with its own individual sound familiar only to its owner, who might hear a tiny miss or a ping that would tell him something, nobody knew what exactly. But again and again he would wind his particular combination of cams and lifters to a fever pitch, almost, in a peculiar way, like a conductor with his ear tuned exactly to the soaring melody of violins against cellos, so intent and serious was a driver's face as he pushed the pedal to the floor.

The racers—at least the older, more experienced ones— were obviously stars and seemed very aware of their star status. They'd go about their business with solemn faces, studiously ignoring the crowd. Then I saw J.C. and knew suddenly why I had come. Not that he'd give me the time of day, I didn't expect that. It was enough just to look at him. In all the bustle and noise, he was the only one who seemed at all relaxed, wandering with his hands in his pockets from car to car, peering in, dropping a word of advice or encouragement. Everybody knew he'd win his heats; he always did. He could relax, even lose once in a while without any loss of status. His advice was like money in the bank.

"Hey, J.C.!" Chick called, and J.C. turned, frowning. But when he saw Chick, he smiled and ambled over. He wore a red satin jacket, like the one James Dean had in

Rebel, zipped halfway down to reveal the dazzling white T-shirt underneath. I felt like running. One look at my face and he'd see what I was thinking.

"What's happenin'?" Chick and J.C. jostled each other, what all the guys did in lieu of a handshake, before they could settle into saying anything. Then there was the usual preamble: "Nothin', what's happenin' with you?" "Nothin' much. . . ."

There were fine creases around J.C.'s green eyes that deepened when he laughed but that made him look a little worried otherwise, as if he'd once flinched away from something painful and never regained his balance. But it was said that he hadn't been much of a father and husband, not really. That he'd carried on with his life as it always had been, racing cars, hanging around with the kids, and that Susan had given up in disgust. But, of course, she was "such a bitch" that whatever he'd done got justified in the end. He loved Jeffrey, his son, he said, more than his own life, even—if you could believe it—more than his Deuce.

"So . . ." Chick said after a while. "You gonna put her through her paces or what?"

"Oh, yeah," J.C. said with feigned humility. "She's running like it's her last race and, you never know, it just might be. Hey," he said then, turning to me. Blood rushed into my face. "You ought to let me race that car of yours sometime. John built her for the track, you know. She's fast as a greased pig." His eyes seemed to be laughing at something he'd remembered from before, or maybe at me.

"She doesn't let nobody touch that car," Angela said. I could have sawed off the tip of her tongue, even though she was right. No one would ever race Silver, not as long as I had her.

Then, right then, staring back into J.C.'s laughing eyes,

I thought, Why not me? I'd race her. There were women racers, a few anyway. Older women, battle-hardened tough-looking women with bleached-out hair and bad skin, but they could do it, they could drive, some of them as well as men. One had tattooed knuckles, like Robert Mitchum in *Night of the Hunter*, L-O-V-E on one hand, H-A-T-E on the other. I thought, If those women could do it, why not me? How hard could it be to jump the line as the flag dropped? The rest was only holding on for the few seconds, half a minute at the most, that it took to reach the finish line.

"If anybody races Sil—my car, it'll be me," I said.

J.C. grinned, appraising me like I'd said something strange or brilliant. "Well, well, look what we've got here, Chick. A little spitfire. Teach *you* a lesson or two, huh?" He punched Chick lightly on the arm. Chick looked away, embarrassed. Angela's death grip had always kept him from racing, even though he'd spent a fortune beefing up his engine. It was a little like having all the equipment, he'd leer, grabbing his crotch, and not "getting any." He got all he needed from her, Angela said. She and Chick could talk about "doing it." They'd been engaged for two years and she had their lives planned, right down to the number of children. They were the same as married. But Chick didn't have the option of splattering himself across the asphalt or the river rock wall at the end of Carne Road. That wasn't written into her plans. He was "pussywhipped," J.C. said, but he said it with a slow, sassy grin at Angela. They'd dated years before for a short while, so there was history in that look only they knew about.

"Watch the fifth heat," J.C. said. "I'm going to wipe the smile off that Okie's face." He nodded toward a brand-new Chevy with a factory aqua-and-white paint job. "He's bumped the carburation a little, bored her out, but she's still a dog, count on it." He touched his index finger to his forehead in the popular salute and ambled off. Helpless, I followed him with my eyes.

"I can't believe it," Lanie said.

"What?"

"The way you look at him. I thought you were smarter than that." She'd been quiet most of the morning, and grumpy. I knew that she'd come along only for something to do. She came because she thought Jimbo might be there, or because she knew he wouldn't. I didn't ask. I just wanted her to get over him. Like a grisly nightmare or a bad case of acne. Just like that. Why did she have to make such a big deal about it? It didn't seem that hard.

A charge ran through the crowd as a crackling loud-speaker voice announced the first race. No one we knew, but my heart began to pound just the same. Buddy shrugged free of me. I knew it was time I stopped trying to catch his hand, at least when people were around, time to let him grow up and find out how to be a man.

I wondered just how much Buddy knew about Dad, about his accident. It was hard to tell. He seemed so much the typical bratty-sweet ten-year-old that it was easy to let him go his way and hope for the best. I was sure he didn't understand what had happened that night. I didn't, and I was fairly sure even my mother didn't. None of us had a language for it. The right words, *attempted suicide*, held a dark-edged horror that we flinched from. Somebody had to be responsible for an attempted suicide, unlike an accident that just "happened"; somebody had to do the attempting. And the failing. Somebody had to mean it. Though I hated myself for it, I wondered sometimes if I might have loved him more had he succeeded.

Still, I ached sometimes to close the gap between my

father and me. I wanted to be able to soothe away all the doubts he had about himself, the way I'd done so easily at Buddy's age with a simple kiss and another promise that, yes, he was the best daddy in all the world, but I hadn't ever really understood how real and how deep those doubts were, how deep the chasm he stumbled into again and again without warning, or why it was he stumbled in. "It's just one of his moods," my mother would say, the way she'd dismiss a "blue day" of her own, just before a period. We rode the roller coaster of those moods, up one day, down the next. Until his "accident." Then we rode it with one hand on the brake.

When I looked back to that night, like watching a horror film through my fingers, I could never find Buddy. Who brought him in from the car? Did he sleep through it all? I hoped so. He was a good kid. And even if he weren't such a good kid, like all kids he deserved his innocence.

The flag dropped and the cars zipped past, a '53 Ford with gray primer spots and an older black one, '49, '50. The '53 won by two seconds and both cars idled back to the pit, accelerating in snarling bursts like prowling lions in heat.

The crowd stirred and loosened, broke up and wandered away from the sawhorses toward the soft-drink stand or the outhouses. "Wow," Buddy said, softly, to himself. "Wow."

Chick ruffled Buddy's hair. "Not much to it, huh, kid?"

Buddy looked up with round eyes. Was Chick crazy? "J.C.'s even faster than that, huh, Chick." It wasn't a question.

"J.C.'s the fastest, smoothest man around, that's for sure," Chick said straight over Buddy's head, at me.

We watched three more heats, heart-catching blasts of

metal and smoke and gasoline always over in the blink of an eye, then broke for soft drinks and greasy hot dogs smeared with sticky sweet relish and mustard. Buddy ate two, wolfing them down as if he'd used up all his energy racing each car that zipped by. The next heat would be J.C.'s first, the one against the "Okie."

Sipping my Coke, I watched J.C. slip out of the satin jacket and toss it casually into the backseat of the Deuce. From hanging out the driver's window, his left arm was tan up to the line of his shirt sleeve. He walked to the front of the Deuce and, almost lazily, popped the hood, propping it up with one arm while he peered down at something inside. His arms were strong and muscular, not a boy's arms. His white T-shirt tapered neatly (had he actually ironed it?) into the soft faded blue waistband of his Levi's. Dropping the hood halfway, he caught it, then eased it down and let it click into place. Nothing about the way he moved was staged. Still, it seemed as if he calculated everything in advance, if not for crowd appeal, then for efficiency. Then he'd walk on through, letting nothing get in the way. Where had such confidence come from? I wondered. Were some people born with it while others, like my father, had to scrap their whole lives for just a tiny piece? How fair was that?

J.C. slipped into the driver's seat and started the engine. Then he just sat for a while listening to it idle. He didn't jam the accelerator to the floor as all the others did. He might be heading out for a Sunday drive in the country for all you could tell. Mesmerized, I watched him peel the foil from a piece of Wrigley's peppermint, bend it double, and pop it into his mouth. Dropping the gearshift into low, he coasted toward the starting line, the deep thrum of the

Deuce's engine enough of an announcement for others to turn and watch. Buddy, who'd never once taken his eyes off J.C., ran off toward the barricades.

The Deuce and the Chevy approached the line from two different directions. The Okie pulled up first, revving his engine in three sharp bursts. J.C. let the Deuce's engine build and build, bit by bit, until it was singing for its freedom. Over the loudspeaker came the names of the racers. A cheer went up for J.C. His arm lay out the open window, just as if he were cruising the Avenue; then he slowly rolled the window up. Why the small tight frown? Had he heard something in the Deuce's engine that we hadn't?

The flagman stood between the cars, not a stone's throw away, and hoisted the green flag. Both engines began to shriek as J.C. and the Okie held them back, balancing gas against clutch, so that they were perfectly still yet ready as rockets. The crowd was still, too, holding a collective breath, almost humming with excitement. The flag dropped and the Deuce came off the line as if taking flight straight into the air, but the Chevy began to fishtail, sending clouds of black smoke into the crowd, fighting for traction. Finally the wide back tires caught, but by then J.C.'s Deuce, like a small black bird, had sailed across the finish line.

"Attaboy, J.C.!" yelled Chick. On his shoulders, Buddy bounced with excitement.

"God, he can turn a girl on, can't he?" Angela sighed, just loud enough for me to hear. I stared at her profile as she gazed at the Deuce making its way back to the pits. She wasn't a beautiful girl, but it was the first time I'd even thought that. She had strong Latin features, a generous nose and dark dancing eyes, a wide mouth with pillow-soft lips. I tried to see her as she appeared to Chick, and before that to J.C., in bed—a bed with, of course, satin sheets, a tangle of smooth dusky limbs and black hair, spent from the kind of ecstasy I'd imagined from reading my romance novels. Angela was as far from me, from my life's experience, as one species is from another. Yet I couldn't bring myself to talk to her about any of it, any of what I needed to know if I were ever to get myself someone who already knew what to do. Ten minutes in bed with me and the guy would die of boredom.

"You like him, don't you?" Angela teased. We'd both watched J.C. slither under the Deuce to check something before his next race.

"I don't even know him," I said, looking away. "And, besides, he's too old."

"Too old for what?" Lanie joined in. I felt like a cornered mouse.

My face grew warm. I'd always blushed too easily, and the more I blushed, the angrier I got with myself, though there wasn't a thing I could do about it. "Watch yourself, Bron," Angela said. "He likes being first, J.C.... I mean first with everything. No one breaks in an engine like he does, or so he says, and it's the same with girls." I found myself staring at Angela's eyelashes. They were curled and coated with thick black mascara like a matching set of tarantulas. You had to do individual coats over a period of about an hour to get them to look like that.

"I don't need breaking in," I said almost under my breath, glad that Buddy had gone off to the outhouses with Chick.

"Yeah, right," Angela said dryly.

"What's that supposed to mean?"

"What do you think? You trying to tell me you're not a virgin?"

"Knock it off, Ange," Lanie said, back in my corner.

"I don't remember trying to tell you anything about it," I said, but I was losing ground.

"You can always tell, you know," she said, popping her gum several times in succession.

"Right," I said, imitating as best I could Angela's dry sarcasm.

"You *can*," she said. "Ask anybody. It's all in the walk. You can always tell."

J.C. slid out from beneath the Deuce and stood up, brushing the dust from his pants. "Hey," he said, nodding his chin at me. "Come here a minute." I froze. He couldn't mean me. He hadn't said my name after all, which probably meant he didn't even know what it was.

"Hay is for horses," I said.

"Oh, Jesus," Angela muttered.

"You wanna race?" he said.

The floor of my stomach dropped and I felt myself grow cold. "Me?"

"You said you wanted to race, right? So, let's do it."

"I don't know how, exactly . . ." I said. "I was just, you know, thinking about it."

"Well, think about it behind the wheel," he said, opening the Deuce's door and stepping aside like a doorman. J.C. went around to the passenger side. "Start her up," he said, sliding in. I turned the key and the engine caught, smoother than Silver and with a deeper, slower beat like far-off drums. "That way." J.C. pointed to an empty expanse of field and runway at the far end. I popped the clutch and the Deuce died on the spot. "Shit," I muttered.

"Ahhh, ahh," J.C. admonished. "Not ladylike. Start her up again. And this time take it slow on the clutch. Let her out like fishing line. Ever fish? Or like a long, slow shit. I mean kiss. . . ." I didn't dare look at him. My face stung like I'd eaten one of those tiny yellow chili peppers, the kind a *gringa* didn't dare eat.

I drove to the far end of the field, the Deuce idling under me like a well-trained horse, my left knee shaking so badly I was sure J.C. could see it. On this end were a half-dozen airplanes, so small they looked like insects. Happy insects with propeller smiles. There were tin shacks, oil drums, a stack of old tires. "Okay, turn her around and pull up on that runway," he said. I did exactly what he said, as if there were no other choice. "Okay, stop right here. No, don't turn her off. Let her idle." And then to me or to the car, I didn't know which, "That a girl."

Off in the distance, I could barely make out the green-and-white letters on the Castrol banner. People, like bits of colored fluff, drifted through clouds of brownish dust. "Now I'm going to count down from ten," J.C. said. "Are you listening?"

I nodded.

"Then, when I say go, you pop the clutch and jam the gas, okay?" I nodded again. My teeth chattered so hard I was afraid to open my mouth. Nothing inside me was still. Everything danced with sparks of sick nervous jitter. "Now rev her up just a little." The Deuce climbed to a high whine. That's it. Now," he said over the sound of the engine. "Let the clutch out just till you feel it start to catch. That a girl. Now hold her, just like that! Ten, nine, eight . . ." My hands had turned to water and threatened to slip from the wheel. "Seven, six, five, four, three . . ." The arch of my left foot cramped. "Two, one, GO!"

The Deuce leaped forward. I clung to the wheel like chewing gum as she sped down the runway, sixty-five, seventy, eighty, eighty-five. Was I driving? I felt a hand touch my knee and turned, surprised to see that J.C. was still there. *"Okay!"* he yelled. "Let off." The horizon settled into place and I noticed for the first time that the sky was the perfect blue that skies are supposed to be. Seventy-sixty-fifty miles an hour. A single cloud shaped like a hot dog floated at two o'clock. Fifty miles an hour was like standing still. "Let's go back and try that again," J.C. said. "That wasn't bad."

Back at the pits, Buddy ran over and jumped up on the running board. "Hey, kid," J.C. said. "Your sis is going to race. What do you think about that?"

Buddy looked at me for confirmation. "I guess so," I said. The Ladies' Heat was the last of the day, plenty of time to chicken out if I needed to. Right then I felt fine, hollow and loose like Angela on her satin sheets.

"Okay, little lady," J.C. said, sliding over and bumping me with his hip. "Out you go. I've got a race to run."

I didn't see another heat. Instead, my mind went over and over J.C.'s instructions and tried to feel again that point of balance just before acceleration, seconds before the flag came down. I walked past a couple of the women I knew would be racing. The one with the tattooed knuckles smoked like a man, an unfiltered cigarette pinched between her thumb and index finger. Her voice was raspy and deep, but she had a great laugh that came bubbling up from some deep place inside and crinkles in fans around her eyes.

She was talking to a blond with skin so pale you could almost see through it to the veins and bones that made her up. The two women leaned hip to hip against a green '56 Ford with chrome spinner hubcaps and *Delaney* scrolled across the door in gold script. I watched the easy way they looked at the men, laughing or nodding like they understood each other perfectly, though the men never would. You weren't supposed to like this kind of woman. They were often loud or told dirty jokes. They hung around the bars like men. In fact, they *were* just like men, which wasn't right at all. But I found it hard to keep my eyes off them. They had a raw kind of energy you couldn't argue with, that wouldn't back down.

Buddy couldn't wait for my heat. He'd stopped asking Chick a million questions. He didn't even have eyes for J.C. Instead he kept thinking of things that might go wrong during my race, even with a car as perfect as the Deuce. Buddy was learning fast, but there wasn't a whole lot he really knew about engines. "What about the lifters?" he'd ask, his eyes wide.

"What about the lifters?" I'd tease.

"Well, did J.C. check them?"

"Sure, that's what he was doing under the car a while ago. Didn't you see him?"

"Oh, Bron," Buddy said with ten-year-old disgust. "The lifters aren't down there."

"Oh, no? Well, where are they then, smartie?"

"They're under the hood. You know, in the engine."

"Yeah? Like where in the engine? Connected to the carburetor?"

"Aw, Bron . . ."

"Don't worry, Bud," I said. "If anything breaks down, it's going to be me, not the Deuce."

Buddy was scared now. "Maybe you shouldn't do it, Bron," he said. "If Dad found out . . ."

"What? What if Dad found out? And how would he find out, huh?" I pinched his nose.

"I mean maybe something will happen. . . . Maybe you

could get hurt." He scuffed his desert boot back and forth over something I couldn't see. Was he going to cry? Buddy never cried.

"Hey," I said. "Have a little faith. J.C. says I can do it. He says I've got the feel for it." I wasn't going to tell Buddy how our eyes connected when J.C. said that, or how my heart skipped as if he'd touched me.

"I wish I could do it," Buddy said. "I wish I could race."

"Someday I'll let you race Silver," I said. "Someday" was safe enough.

"You'd let me race Silver," Buddy said, gazing up at me as if I'd grown wings, turned to pure light.

"Sure I would, silly. Now quit worrying about stuff." But I could feel the nervousness settle back into my stomach and slosh there in a puddle like the inch of dirty water left over in a dishpan.

What could happen? What was the worst thing that could happen? Buddy ran off to find Chick and I stood there as if glued suddenly to the skin of the earth. Why was I doing this? Why climb into a metal bomb and hurl myself through space at a hundred miles an hour? Suddenly the whole thing seemed crazy. Not only crazy, but really dumb. What was I trying to prove? What had happened to the PHS honor student? the girl who got the attendance award three years in a row? who always did her homework, no matter what? She seemed like somebody else to me now, a nice girl, a worker bee, someone who believed what she was told, who wandered through life with wide eyes glazed over with an empty innocence (like a Disney heroine), a girl who trusted everyone. A good pet, more or less. But how far had that gotten me? What my father had attempted that Thanksgiving night in Plainfield had driven one point home: You were a fool to believe too much in anything or

(112)

in anybody. You had to count on yourself; you had to be tough.

But I wasn't tough. Inside, I was soft, easily swayed. There seemed no reason not to do whatever came up, whatever sounded like fun. What was there to stop you? Once I'd believed in God. Not passionately or even very thoughtfully. He'd been a kind of Superparent I took for granted, the way I'd once taken everything, with a child's innocent greed. Now I was grown-up and rational. I needed hard evidence. Praying was like talking on the telephone with no one on the other end. God was for children and people afraid to face life on their own.

None of this happened overnight, though it seemed that way. In truth it had taken years. My father's accident was simply the benchmark, as I saw it now, of my growing up. Of my getting smart.

But I wasn't smart either, not really. Smart people didn't listen so closely to what everybody else said before they made up their minds. Smart people knew things about the way the world worked, about the right way to act, to dress, to talk, to walk, to feel. . . .

Suddenly the outlines of everything around me, cars, people, the words on plastic banners hanging limp in the still air, became sharply clear, as if I'd put on a pair of glasses I'd needed all my life but never knew I needed. I wanted to cry out for Buddy. Where was Buddy? Somewhere in the crowd. But I knew I'd have scared him. What I needed right then, more than air or food or life, was for someone to tell me who I was.

The heats ticked off, one after another. The crowd thinned, nobody particularly interested in watching what the women would do, which was fine with me. Lanie and I drank watered-down Cokes. We blew smoke into the hot still air. "Maybe they'll cancel it," I said. "Maybe none of the women want to race."

"Maybe they're on the rag," Lanie said. "Maybe they decided to take up knitting instead." But when J.C. came walking over, I knew it was time.

"You're racing Sticks," he said. "Delaney's old lady. She's good, maybe the best one out here. Well, the best woman anyway. And the Ford's faster than it looks. . . . Hey, you changed your mind?" He lifted my chin and shot me that half grin of his.

"Did I say I'd changed my mind?" He tried to read me, then shrugged as if it didn't matter much to him one way or the other.

I followed him to the pit, where Sticks was arguing vehemently with her husband, a guy with a gut and an old man's gray undervest smeared with grease and wet with perspiration. It was hard to follow what they were saying, a kind of engine talk too advanced for me.

"Sticks, Harv . . ." J.C. said. "Meet the competition."

Sticks turned her pale gray eyes and yellow eyelashes on me. Her face took on the uninterested look of a cat.

"This is Bron," J.C. said. So he knew my name after all. "It's her first race, but don't you go easy on her."

Sticks wiped her hand on her sleeve and stuck it at me to shake. Her mouth twitched in amusement. But her eyes were stagnant, like water standing too long in a dishpan. "I don't go easy on my own children," she drawled. "Race is a race."

"Nice meeting you," I said, but Sticks and Harv had turned away, picking up the argument where they'd left off, as if I hadn't happened in between.

"How come you're letting me do this?" I asked J.C. as we got into the Deuce, me on the driver's side as if, this time, I knew what I was doing. "I wouldn't let anybody race my car. I *wouldn't*. . . ."

"Why not?" He laid his left arm across the back of the seat, fingers not two inches from my shoulder.

I shrugged. "I don't know. It's like, she's mine. Like if something happened to her . . . I know, it's silly. . . ."

"Naw, it's not silly," he said. "It's your first car. Like first love. You never get over it, not really. Kind of like that, right?"

"Like Angela?" The words slipped out before fully forming in my mind.

"Angela?" J.C. hooted. "Jeez! Where did you hear that? Angela and me . . . ." He paused, deciding just how much to tell me. "Naw, Angela's not my first love." He laughed again, a short staccato bark. "And I sure as hell wasn't hers!"

"So why then?" I traced a line around the steering wheel with the tip of a damp finger. All I could think about was how it would feel to kiss him.

"Why what?"

"Why did you decide to let me race the Deuce?" I gathered my courage and looked him in the eye.

"I don't know," he mused. Then that half grin again, what Chick called J.C.'s shit-eating grin. "Maybe so's you'd owe me one."

"Unh-uh," I said. "Nobody's gonna get their hands on Silver, not even you."

"I don't want your car, little girl." With his finger, he traced the line of my jaw, then my lower lip. "Start her up," he said.

"Huh?"

"Time to go."

I drove, heart stuck in my throat. I couldn't swallow it,

couldn't spit it out. Somewhere in the crowd Buddy was watching. I'd keep him in my mind, just Buddy, nobody else. I'd pull it off, somehow, for Buddy.

Idling up to the start line, I saw out of the corner of my eye the green Ford pulling even with me. I didn't dare look over. "This is where I get off," J.C. said. He slid out and came around to my side, leaning his crossed arms on the window ledge. "Remember, now. Not too much gas or you'll fishtail all over the runway." That's just what I was going to do, I knew it. He knew it. The whole crowd knew it. For months, years maybe, the talk in Ojala would be about how that dumb kid from Jersey blew the race at Santa Maria. And of course J.C. wouldn't give me the time of day ever again.

"You okay?" J.C. said.

"My teeth," I said.

"Huh?"

"I can't hold my teeth still," I croaked. My mouth was dry as toilet paper. "I'm okay, except for that."

J.C. left and came back with a Pep Boys matchbook, Manny, Moe, and Jack with their blown-up heads and stunted little bodies. "Here," he said. "Stick that between your teeth." I bit down on the matchbook till my back teeth ached.

Sticks give the Ford several quick kicks of gas. I looked at J.C. for my orders. "Just rev her up a little," he said. "None of that greasy kid stuff. Just feed her enough to make her beg for more." He said this in a slow and lazy way, as if there was all the time in the world and just he and I in the middle of it.

I pushed the accelerator with my big toe. "Now think nothing but flag," he said. "The flag comes up, you hold 'er, just like you did out there. That flag comes down, you're

(116)

out of here. Easy as that." He slapped the roof and walked away.

Alone, I began to freeze over inside. But with the cold came an unexpected calm. I looked across the track at Sticks and was surprised to find her looking back at me in that same detached way as before, yet studying me like I might be something good to eat, or at least to wear down before the kill.

The flag went up. I let the clutch ride partway up, inched the accelerator down, finding the exact place as if I'd always known it, the place where the whole world stood perfectly, absolutely still. The place where the power was. Only the green flag fluttered, caught for a moment on an errant breeze. And down it came.

The Ford and the Deuce jumped off the line as if shot from the double barrels of a shotgun, then seemed for some reason to catch in stop action. The green hood of the Ford rose and rose, Sticks's thin hair lifted lightly from her neck, her arms floated forward as if urging a horse from the gate, the gold letters of *Delaney* danced in the air. The Deuce stayed with her, winding through first gear. I glanced down at the tachometer, jammed the clutch, popped her into second, and yelled through my clenched teeth as she leaped forward again, gathering speed and strength. Second was her best gear, J.C. had said. But the Ford was a half-car length ahead, Sticks leaning into the steering wheel, the bones of her bare shoulders nearly poking through her skin.

The Deuce was nearly to her limit in second, her nose even with the *n* in *Delaney*, then the *a*, the *D*, and finally the side mirror. I glanced quickly over at Sticks, who seemed to be smiling, a pencil-thin stretched-out smile. Up into third, feeling the Deuce jump again, the Ford standing still now, *Delaney* slipping out of sight, the Deuce pulling up, pulling even. Sticks turned her head and that was when I saw the fear clear as a child's prayer in the gray of her washed-out eyes. I remembered the beefy arms and hands of Delaney, a man who J.C. said "didn't like to lose."

And then the Ford was gone, whipped back as if pulled by a giant hand, and I realized it was all over, the race was over. I let off the gas, touched the brake, and began to shake, hanging on to the Deuce's steering wheel as if it were a ring thrown out to save my life. All the way back to the pits, my stomach heaved and fluttered.

Buddy came clear of the crowd like he'd been tossed. He leaped on the running board and we idled back together, the Deuce, Buddy, and me, Buddy chattering nonstop. "I think you won, Bron . . . well, maybe it was a tie, but that's good, too. Chick said it was a tie. He was yelling like crazy, you shoulda heard him!" My eyes pulled people away from each other, threw them aside. So *what* about Chick? So what about *anybody*? Where was J.C.?

I cut the engine, Buddy jumped down, and I stepped out, legs bent and stiff. A hand clamped the back of my neck. I turned and the hand dropped but I could feel it still and felt it for the rest of that day, like heat, like a brand. "Good job, girl," J.C. said.

"You tied old Sticks!" Chick said. His neck was bruised with a half-dozen hickeys Angela had sucked there the night before. Angela hung back, subdued for once. "Congratulations," she muttered. "We didn't know you could drive like that. You been practicing?"

"Hell, no," Chick answered for me. "She's a natural, ain't she, J.C.?"

J.C.'s grin was unreadable. A half-dozen heartbeats later he said, "She did all right." I let that be okay. By the deliberate way he moved, the look in his eye, those maddening grins, he always said so much more than he said. You could know him, I told myself, if you could just read him.

That night I lay on my mattress gazing up, not at James Dean with his funny little smirk, not at Elvis, spread-eagled and floating, an angel in studs and black leather, but up through my window at the moon. It seemed close enough for somebody to walk on, a crazy thought. J.C. could be looking at the moon, too. Right at this moment. Why not? And he didn't have a girlfriend, Angela said, at least not a steady one.

When he took the keys from my hand, I'd been hoping for a ride back to Ojala. I'd pictured us seriously discussing the race, going over every little detail: how it all went by in slow motion (was it that way for him?), whether I got all I could out of second gear. And we'd talk about other things, too, exactly what I didn't know. But I didn't see him after that. In the last heat of the day, Sticks raced her friend with the tattoos, beating her, but J.C. was nowhere to be seen, the Deuce gone, too, like the mirage at the far end of the strip, there one minute, gone the next, a trick of heat and light.

13

VALENTINE's DAY, and both dining rooms were full. My mother and I had long before switched jobs, each better suited to what the other had been doing. As hostess, with her sweet good nature, she would take names as new customers entered, seating them with glasses of wine on the porch. ("Make sure you charge them," my father would call after her. "That beer and wine license wasn't free!") This night, for the promise of a table "in two shakes of a lamb's tail," people huddled in the cold February air sipping jug wine. "Isn't it romantic?" my mother would chortle, and they would smile through frozen cheeks.

My mission, or so I saw it, was to feed them fast and get them out the door. The more tables I turned ("Like tricks," I told Frieda, who was not amused), the more money I would make. I had lots of money now, could throw as much as anyone into the hat for beer. Dyed-to-match skirt-and-sweater outfits in Cerise, Buttercup, Azure, and

Peony hung in my closet like trophies. Each had matching angora socks that I'd roll carefully down over a hair ring, the way everybody did. I had two pairs of white bucks, too, so that one pair would always be sparkling clean. What I used to do for Silver, I now did for my white bucks.

My hair was still an abomination. No matter how long I left the curlers in, lacquered the whole creation with Aqua Net, wished it into bounce and shine, it lay stagnant and dull as a case of bad breath. Nothing short of surgery, the kind they gave FBI informants, could be done about my chipmunk cheeks either, or my pug nose. I looked thirteen. I supposed I always would.

I didn't care much about the way I looked when I was a waitress. Nobody from school ever came in, though I swore to my father that I'd walk right off the floor if they did. For work, I'd just yank my hair back in a ponytail. I didn't even bother with lipstick unless my mother nagged me.

It was a romantic night to be somebody's valentine at the Welsh Kitchen, or it could have been if you weren't the waitress. Hanukkah candles twinkled in their little cut-glass jars. Each table had a single red rosebud. My mother had suggested we have something appropriate on our menu, but when my father suggested braised lambs' hearts, she decided not to push it.

I scurried from table to table being efficient and occasionally, if the mood hit me, charming. Why my mother in all her clumsy forgetfulness always made better tips than I did I never understood. I was faster than anybody, faster than Frieda. I'd watch Frieda linger at a table after the check went down, chatting and smiling, and I'd say to myself, Wasted time. Set up Number 8. There'd be a sure buck-fifty there.

(121)

Dropping the salads at Number 3, I heard a commotion at the door, less a commotion, really, than a kind of serious buzz. I turned and saw my father, hands on his hips, talking to a tall thin woman and three young men. "What's going on?" asked the lady at Number 3.

"I don't know," I said. "Maybe they don't like waiting." They didn't look like the waiting type.

Then I heard my father say, "You'll have to check that, son," and saw the gun in the holster slung on the hip of one of the boys. The boy was as tall and thin as his mother, with the same long face and sharp nose. Her bushy eyebrows, gathered over concerned gray eyes, were salt-and-pepper, his a thick dark brown. He frowned, too, not in anger, but as if he was puzzled.

"I can't do that, sir," he said.

My father looked stumped for a minute, then said with unaccustomed firmness, "Then you'll have to leave."

The boy turned to his mother, said something to her I couldn't hear. Then he turned and went out the door. My father, like a majordomo, led the mother and her other two sons to the table they'd reserved. No one looked up as they passed, though every ear had been tuned in, every eye had glanced at least once toward the door. This was the drama of the old West, or what was left of it, something not to be missed.

I wondered why the boy decided to leave rather than check his gun as my father had suggested. (I pictured my father with the gun belt snagged between his thumb and index finger like a dead cat or a string of fish, carrying it into the kitchen where it would hang alongside his spare aprons until ransomed.) When I had a minute, I stuck my head out the door and there was the boy standing at military parade rest, feet apart, hands clasped at the small of his back. He was staring straight ahead at some spot in the distance.

Frieda waited on the boy's family, but I couldn't help looking at them whenever I passed their table. They were different from anyone else in the dining room, different from anybody I'd ever met. How exactly I didn't know, except for the obvious things: the way they sat, straight and still, leaning toward each other to speak in modulated tones punctuated with smiles of gentle amusement. And their eyes gleamed with something I recognized much later as intelligence. Intelligence and wit with just a trace of natural arrogance.

I kept wondering about the boy standing outside on the porch like a palace guard. What was he trying to prove? Why was hanging on to that gun so important? Whatever his reason, it was worth being hungry over. Grabbing a bottle of Coke, I said to my father, "I'm going to give this to that kid on the porch, okay?"

"Oh, not you, too!" he cried. "There go the profits." It's what he said every time my mother poured a glass of wine or popped another Brussels sprout into her mouth. It's what he cried when a glass shattered or a dish cracked or he ran out of bulk flour and had to buy from Bailey's Market instead of the wholesale place.

The boy was standing in the same position, except that now he had his hat on, one of those very tall cowboy hats that he'd taken off before coming into the restaurant. It looked as odd with his tailored gray suit as the polished leather holster and the ivory-handled gun. He turned as I approached, the Coke in my outstretched hand the way you'd offer a bone to a dog. Would he bite? "I thought you might be thirsty," I said. "I could bring you a sandwich or something, too, if you want. . . ."

"No, thank you," he said. His tone was polite but firm.
"The Coke, then?"

"No, thank you." The corner of his mouth came up as if he might just smile, but then he swiveled his head back into position as if an order had come down from somewhere in a voice that only he could hear.

"Suit yourself," I said.

When his family finished their meal and paid the bill, I watched through the window as they walked to their car, an old Ford station wagon, hunter green with pine paneling on the sides. They were laughing together about something. You could tell that by the way their bodies moved, like tall willows dancing on the bank of a river. The boy who had stood on the porch held the door for his mother and she gathered her long dress to step in. Because he was tall, the boy had to bend a little and anyone might have thought he was bowing. Then he went around to the other side to drive them away. I knew where they lived without being told, out in the hills with the artists and the eccentrics my mother thought were so wonderful.

"Well, that was an odd duck," my father said afterward. He sipped his Old Crow out of a water glass now, right out there for everybody to see, like there was nothing wrong with it, as if he were just anyone, as if the window to our collective past had been sprayed and wiped clean with a swish of Windex. Not a trace of apology in his eyes now, no plea for understanding, just a grim and unhappy defiance.

"That child with the gun?" my mother said. "Wasn't he the sweetest thing? He was cute, wasn't he, Bron?"

I shrugged, dumping dishes carelessly into a bus tray.

"You liked him, didn't you? I think she liked him, Tom."

"I didn't say that. I didn't say I liked him. He was weird."

"Class," Frieda said. "Breeding. The Hardings are patrons of the arts, or were, at least, when they had money. Every music event, the classical ones anyway, she's got a hand in somewhere. Her father was some famous conductor. You could do worse, Bron."

I rolled my eyes.

The next morning, a Saturday, I was upstairs in the asylum listening to my favorite song, "In the Still of the Night," on my phonograph, playing it over and over and thinking about J.C., when my mother came rushing up the stairs. "That boy is here," she said.

"What boy?"

"The one with the gun."

"So?"

"He asked for you."

"So?"

"Bron," she said in her most sadly disappointed voice. Whatever had become of my manners? I rolled off my mattress with a sigh and followed her down the stairs. What did the boy want with me?

"Oh, dear!" my mother cried, realizing that in a haze of absentmindedness she had left the boy standing outside staring at the door. He had a strange little smile on his face when I opened it. He was embarrassed, too. That a boy could blush as easily as I, as any girl, put me at ease.

"Hi," I said. "Did you want that Coke after all?"

"No...well, yeah, sure. I just came by to say thanks...."

"You said thanks," I said.

"I brought you this," he said, pulling from behind his

back a slim book with a dark blue cover. "It's . . . poems, Robinson Jeffers." He shrugged. "I just thought, you were so nice and all last night. I mean, if you don't like poetry, it's okay. You don't have to. Not everybody does. . . ."

"I like poetry," I said.

He stuck his hands into his back pockets as if, having given me the book, he didn't know what else to do with them. His Wranglers were worn nearly to threads and on his feet were a pair of dusty rough-out boots. The silver gun and polished leather holster hung below his belt, dipping over his right hip. "Who's your favorite poet?" he asked.

I thought for a moment. I did like poetry, sort of. But I hadn't spent a whole lot of time with it. "I dunno. Robert Frost, I guess."

" 'Two roads diverged in a yellow wood . . . ' " he recited. "Do you know that one? It's great. Oh, by the way, my name is William, Will Harding." He stuck out his hand.

"Bron," I said. "Short for Bronwyn. It's Welsh," I added as if in apology. As long as I could remember, I'd had to explain my name. I felt silly shaking hands, but I could see he didn't. His hand was cool, his palm rough with calluses.

"That's beautiful," he said, and ducked his head. "That's a beautiful name." We both looked away at something across the street.

"Well," he said. "I just thought, well, would you like to ride horses sometime?"

Will Harding towered over me like Ichabod Crane, all angles and knobs. He was what my mother would call "a nice boy," definitely not my type, with dark serious eyes and a long narrow nose. But horses, that was something else. "Sure," I said.

"Tomorrow?"

"Yeah, sure."

"I'll come get you about two, okay? I've got to muck out the stables in the morning."

"Muck what?"

"Clean the stables," he said. "Two okay?"

"You don't have to pick me up," I said. "I have a car."

"Oh, no," he said. "I'll pick you up." Then, like an apology, "It's a little hard to find and there's a gate and anyway I'd just like to come and get you. Is that okay?" He was blushing again.

At two on the dot the next afternoon he was at the door, wearing what I thought might be the same jeans and a faded blue-and-gray plaid shirt with pearl buttons. I figured he probably slept with the gun or slung it over the bedpost, the way they did after a long day at the O.K. Corral. "Do you always wear that?" I asked.

At first he didn't know what I was referring to. "Oh, this," he said, slapping the holster. "Yeah, I guess I do."

"How come?" We climbed into a Jeep, a World War II model, olive drab green without a top. The windshield folded flat against the hood.

"Critters," he said. He looked at me to see what I'd make of that. Then he laughed.

We drove through town, down Ojala Avenue toward the foothills and Topa Ridge, where Lanie and I had gone on New Year's morning. Passing the Frostee, I turned my head away, hoping no one, not even Lanie, would see me riding in that Jeep. I knew what the Frostee crowd would say about someone like Will Harding. There were a few old codgers who hung around the pool hall in rough-out boots and hand-tooled leather belts with rodeo buckles, and Lanie's father always wore a white Stetson when he and his ladies drove through town, but playing cowboy wasn't a cool thing to do. You wouldn't be caught dead in a pair of boots unless it was Halloween.

But Will wasn't pretending; nothing about him was pretense. That was one of the things that I knew without knowing how I knew it and, later, how I knew that he would never have done what they said he did. His mother knew it, too, had always known how perfect the match was in this son between character and action.

It was as perfect a day as any I'd known in Ojala, cool and sunny, the air so clear you could see beyond the first set of ridges in the Topa Topas to a whole new vista beyond, where wisps of cloud floated as if too contented to move on. The January rains, more than in recent years but nothing to brag about in my book, had greened the foothills. Pampas grass, like ostriches with their tails in the air, waved us past. We turned at Carne Road and began to climb, jogging left before reaching the summit, then climbing again. I turned once and watched Ojala falling behind, shrinking, as if I were seeing it through the fat end of a telescope.

"Have you always lived out here?" I asked. The wind in our faces made conversation difficult, and it was just as well. Neither of us seemed to know what to say.

We stopped at a wooden gate with DOUBLE J RANCH burned into the top rail. Will leaped out, unlocked the gate, and pushed it open. He moved with a grown man's ease and an unself-conscious grace. Only when he looked at me did his composure crumble. "We moved here when I was ten, after my dad died," he said. We drove through and he hopped out again to close the gate.

The Double J was a breathtaking expanse of land with soft yellow grasses and hills humped like giant gray-brown cats asleep in the sun. The narrow dirt road we followed wound through dozens of oaks, their rough twisted limbs dipping at times to a foot or so above our heads. Occasionally the Jeep would hit a rut in the road and we'd be sent nearly flying off the seat. We'd laugh then, easier than we had been with each other.

At last we reached a scattering of buildings, a weathered gray barn and two white frame houses, one smaller and set behind the other. "I told Mom not to expect us for lunch," he said. "I thought, well . . . what I thought was that you'd probably want to get to know her a little first." He turned the key and the Jeep's engine died in pieces, like a stubborn soldier. "So it's just tea."

Lunch? Tea? All I had in mind was a horseback ride. The image of his mother with her impeccable posture and 1920s vintage silk came back to me and I was sure I never wanted to meet her, much less "dine" with her. "That's okay," I said. "Let's not bother her. Where are the horses? Back here?" I headed off toward the barn.

"Oh, she wants to meet you," he said. "She thinks your father's terrific!"

"I'll bet," I muttered.

I was so caught up in the anticipated terror of meeting Mrs. Harding that nothing of the living room registered at first. Then I fell in love, just like that, like falling. It was one of those rooms that looks tossed together on the spur of the moment by some ingenious highly paid designer, a heap of pillows here, a vase of tulips there, knickknacks that weren't knickknacks at all but collections of wonderful, clever things never gathered before in one place, in that exact place on that tiny round table with its spindly giraffe legs bathing in the sun. The couch was a pillowy bower of faded, overblown roses in several shades of rose and peach and made for sinking into. Against french doors at the far end of the room sat a huge and gleaming grand piano with its lid raised. Except for an ancient, nearly threadbare oriental rug beneath the couch and coffee table (piled with books about exotic birds and ships and places I'd never heard of), the dark, almost black, foot-wide floorboards were bare, worn where they were walked the most and gleaming with a finish that must have been rubbed in by a thousand hands.

She came through the doorway with her arm extended, giving me a nod and a no-nonsense handshake. "It's very nice to meet you, Bronwyn," she said. "We all enjoyed your father's little restaurant so much."

I mumbled thank you, pleased-to-meet-you. She was intimidating, nearly as tall as Will and as thin as someone starved in a closet. But the skin on her face was sun-browned and leathery and she didn't look a bit frail. Once she pinned you with her clear gray eyes, you couldn't shake her loose. You quivered there like prey. "Will tells me you're from the East."

"Yes, ma'am."

"Check the tea, will you, darling?" she said, and Will left the room.

"Where in the East?" she said. Now, I thought, was when the mother gets to ferret out all the details of the girl's poor but humble background, the way it happened in the movies, out of earshot of the duped and foolish son.

"New Jersey. Plainfield." I'd considered saying Four Hills, the ritzy suburb we kids had always raided on Halloween, but there was something about her that wouldn't accept anything but absolute truth, even if you were going to be put to death for having told it.

"Ah!" she said, pouncing. "I have an acquaintance in Plainfield, a rare-book collector."

"Yeah, it's not exactly—"

"Fine public schools, he tells me. Some of the finest in the country. Did your parents have a restaurant in Plainfield?"

"No, ma'am. My father was . . . my father worked in restaurants."

"And he always wanted to have one of his own, is that right?" She seemed delighted with herself, or with my father. Will came in carrying a silver tray, setting it down without spilling a drop of the tea. "Thank you, darling," she said. "He'd make a good waiter, wouldn't he?" Will grinned at me. "But of course he has other obligations, which I'm sure he'll tell you all about." She poured the steaming tea into one of the tiny fluted cups. "Do you take cream?" The cookies were the kind you couldn't eat in mixed company, crumbly and covered with powdered sugar.

We sipped our tea. The pendulum of the grandfather clock clicked back and forth, back and forth in the maroon velvet of its coffin. Somewhere a horse whinnied. "That's a beautiful piano," I said, just to say something.

Mrs. Harding gazed over at the piano as if she were actually seeing it, not just recognizing that it was there. "Yes," she said. Then she looked at me. "Do you play?"

"Uh . . ." I thought of Miss Nicholl with her double Steinways, her sharp little pointer, her relentless drills. "Sort of," I said.

"Oh, then, you must play something for us!"

I always wondered at times like these why I'd begged for the lessons. I knew it wasn't only that my best friend, Paula, got to play while I waited, listening, outside on Miss Nicholl's brick steps. Paula's family had lots of money. Our money went for food and necessities, not ballet and piano lessons. But it wasn't jealousy. And it wasn't just whim. It was the music itself that pulled me to it, and I felt then as if, playing the notes myself, in some strange way I might be returning to something already known. But this was impossible to explain. I had only the weapons of childhood, a blind and single-minded relentlessness that my mother with her pleas to reason could not match. "Perhaps just a few lessons . . ." she said, her voice trailing off.

With a kind of dogged passion, I worked my way through the Thompson series to Mozart, from sonatinas to fugues. Miss Nicholl was persistent to the point of belligerence, personally offended if I didn't practice (which had to be done on a neighbor's piano). Her little pointer would ping against my knuckles. "Count! Count!" she would cry. "This is a march, not a ballad!" She believed in my talent. Or maybe her persistence was a gift she lavished on all her students. But the day I saw my mother's prized Hummel porcelain bluebird perched on Miss Nicholl's mantel, I lost my taste for lessons and quit soon after. The lessons, I learned, had been free. Perhaps from the beginning when, breathless, she'd placed my ten fingers on the ivory keys, the lessons had been free. I was Miss Nicholl's charity case. Months later, unable to help myself, a fugitive from what I'd learned to love, I went back and the lessons resumed.

"Mother . . ." Will warned. They seemed to have this way of understanding each other, a kind of code.

"Nonsense," she said. "Bron?"

I shrugged. "Sure," I said. I set my teacup on the silver tray and crossed the floor with a kind of light-headed, crazy sense that had gotten me through dozens of recitals: The music would play itself—all I had to do was allow it to seep down through me like water through a filter.

The keys were cool beneath my fingers, unfamiliar and familiar at the same time. I took a deep breath. I began to

(132)

play. And Mrs. Harding, Will, even Ojala dropped away, lost to notes imprinted long before on my heart. My last recital. First Congregational. Ascetic saints caught in a moment of pained glory, staring down. We would move in three weeks. Afterward Miss Nicholl had cried. I played, she said, as Mozart should be played, her highest compliment. I had never thanked her for the lessons. But I had played for her, and maybe she knew that.

This time, though, as the piece ended, I felt for a moment disoriented, not knowing or really caring whether or not I'd played well. Something else mattered, something meant for me alone, that had nothing whatsoever to do with pleasing or winning favor, but it was a lonely feeling for me then and I shied from it. How could you know how you were doing at anything unless someone let you know, told you how good you were or talented or smart or pretty? Someone had to tell you.

I watched my fingers drop from the keys and came slowly back into the room, wanting suddenly to please Mrs. Harding more than anyone I'd ever played for. Pleasing her, I'd have won something in that living room or taken back some piece of myself that stayed behind at the door, still wiping its feet.

When I turned, Mrs. Harding was perched on the edge of a couch cushion as if struck by lightning in a Victorian rose garden. Her wiry fingers were clenched in a ball on her knees. Her face was impassive, the gray eyes overcast. Then she blinked. Her eyes cleared. "That was well played," she said at last, the way one might drop a nickel into a collection plate.

"Well played? Mother! You get your wish and that's the best you can do?"

(133)

Mrs. Harding turned to Will with a charm-school smile, a small stretch of the lips with nothing at all in the eyes. "My wish?"

"You bet! '*Someday somebody's going to play that piano the way it was meant to be played!*' Come on, now, admit it. Didn't you say that?

"We all took lessons, Bron," Will explained, turning now from his mother, who'd begun with unnecessary clatter to clear away the tea service. "All three of us. And we stank. Phew! I was the worst, and I was supposed to set the example. Finally . . . " He began to chuckle, remembering. Even then I'd begun to warm to the spark of mischief in his brown eyes. "Finally old George Hazard—Father had saved his life in the war and so he owed us one—finally he told Mother he couldn't give us lessons any longer, that he was moving somewhere—where was it, Mother?—but we knew we'd worn him out with our clumsy fingers and our tin ears. For all I know, he never left Ojala."

"That's ridiculous, Will. Your memory, as usual, is highly selective." She hoisted the silver tray before Will could take it from her. "It was a pleasure to meet you, Bronwyn. Will has so little time to entertain, you see. . . ." Whatever else she might have said evaporated as she headed for the kitchen.

For a moment, Will looked puzzled or maybe annoyed. Then he shrugged off whatever had crossed his mind. "Ready to ride?" he said.

The mountains were just mountains to me then, so much rock. On either side of the trail were things I called "cactus" and "bushes," all thrown into a heap like unsorted laundry. But the saddle creaked comfortably under me and I rocked easily to the heavy rhythm of Millicent, a mare of indeterminate origin who'd been in the family as long as

Tim, Will's youngest brother. Nearly blind in her left eye, she was to be allowed to lead with her right for as long as she stayed on the trail. If she wandered off, I was to nudge her back with my heel and the reins that were clumped together in my damp hands. Millicent, Will assured me, couldn't buck if she were bitten on the butt. Still, I wasn't taking any chances. I gripped her with my knees until they gave out and bounced uselessly against her fat sides.

Will rode like all the Saturday matinee cowboys of my childhood, with a loose ease, the reins looped through the fingers of his right hand, left hand riding his thigh. He loped ahead and from time to time would circle back and slap Millicent on her rump to get her going. The air was clear and cool and laced with something pungent that Will said was anise. After a while, when a musky dankness sifted past, he said "Fox" but I saw nothing. I had no eyes for the unfamiliar. I was thirsty. My back and legs were stiff. I was relieved when Jack, Will's pinto, turned off the trail and Millicent followed. "There's a creek back here," Will said. We ducked under the branches of some willowy kind of tree, Millicent in a semi-lope now as she smelled the water.

We dismounted and let the horses dip their long necks into the stream. Will stretched himself full out with his Stetson on his stomach. I sat Indian-style, a few feet away. "You're now in my second favorite place on the face of the earth," he said. The wind-ruffled surface of the creek was shot through with sunlight as if it were filled with gold coins. Behind us, the leaves of the trees that were not willows after all rattled, then were silent.

"What's your first favorite place?" It seemed the thing to ask, though I'd started to feel a little uneasy as if, in sharing a favorite place, he was assuming things he shouldn't. Like we'd spend more time together. I didn't want him to get the wrong idea.

"The wrong idea." That was my mother's line. "If you let him kiss you on the first date" (or touch your breasts, or put his tongue in your mouth—which she would never come right out and say), "he'll get the wrong idea." Well, as far as I could figure, boys always had the wrong idea. If you looked at them sideways, they got the wrong idea. So maybe it wasn't wrong, after all. Maybe they just couldn't help themselves. Like dogs. I'd fought off my share of boys in backseats of cars and felt pretty much like a veteran of the make-out wars. It was always fun for a while, in the kissing and petting-above-the-waist stage. Then they always got a little crazy and forgot you were there—the you they brought to the drive-in—and would have settled for a sheep or something if they'd been able to get their hands on one.

"We'll go to my first favorite place next time," he said. "It's a longer ride."

Thinking about all that make-out stuff while sitting on a rock with a boy I hadn't once thought of kissing made me blush, so I was glad Will had his eyes closed. His eyelashes were long, the kind girls were supposed to have, the kind I'd have given a kidney for, and the skin along the sides of his face was rough, acne-scarred, as if a wildfire had raced across it years before. He opened his eyes and caught me staring. "I'm sorry about Mom," he said. "She's kind of pushy sometimes." He sat up, dangling his long arms over his bent knees.

"I didn't mind playing the piano," I said. "Really. It was just that . . ." How to explain what it was like to see her frozen in place? Had it been my imagination? Did she have some kind of illness? sudden fits that turned her into stone? "Did I do something wrong? I mean, most people like Mozart. . . ."

Will laughed shortly and shook his head. "Yeah . . . well, she likes Mozart all right. He's one of her favorites. I watched her face while you played. She didn't expect what she got." Will tossed a pebble, then another into the creek, with a loose overhand pitch. "Davy's girlfriend plays. Not like you. She plays these little things, you know—minuets and stuff. Show tunes. That's what Mother was expecting. She didn't know what to make of you. Didn't know what to say. Damned unusual for my mother, believe me!"

I was thinking that if I ever saw the woman again, it would be too soon.

"You surprised me, too," he said.

"Why?" I knew why. I just wanted to make him say it.

He shrugged. "I'm not sure. . . ."

"You didn't think a dumb waitress would even know who Mozart was, right?"

Several emotions chased across his face, confusion, surprise, maybe hurt. "No . . ." he said. "That wasn't it. I guess I just didn't think of you as the Mozart type. . . ."

"Which is what?"

Will hesitated, looking up at the sky as if the answer were up there somewhere, written in a jet trail. "Snooty, I guess. Highbrow. I don't know. Like I said, I've got a tin ear. . . ."

"Snooty? Mozart is *snooty*?" I had to laugh. "That's the dumbest thing in the world! I thought you were surprised because, you know, here was this . . ."

"Waitress," he said quietly, bringing my eyes back to his.

(137)

"Yeah, waitress. Your basic low-class waitress and . . . *Mozart*!" At a loss for words, I threw up my hands.

"Now, *that's* the dumbest thing in the world," Will said. "Low-class! Where do you get that stuff?"

"Oh, come on," I said. "Don't pretend you don't know what I'm talking about. Where do you go to school, anyway? Villanova? Thatcher?"

"Yeah . . ." It was always so easy to tell. You could spot a "richie" at fifty yards, my father said. You could smell them. Will shrugged his wide shoulders. It occurred to me how often people of our age shrugged off explanations, how often we were probably misunderstood.

"Which?" Thatcher was one of the most prestigious private boarding schools in the country. Presidents' sons went there. A Saudi prince was placed on the waiting list at birth. Villanova had a quieter reputation, but tuition there could support the average family for a year.

"Thatcher," he said. "I'm a day student."

"Well, see? Your typical low-class education."

For a while he didn't say anything and neither did I. I didn't know why I was so heated up. What did I care about Will Harding, anyway? Or his mother.

"You've got the wrong idea, Bron," he said after a while. "We're not rich. I'm a scholarship kid. I got in only because my father was this war hero . . . ! And the ranch? We're caretakers, we don't *own* it. We don't even own the horses. And the piano lessons? Free! Gratis! So I guess, according to you, we're low-class, right? Funny, I never thought about us that way!"

I thought back to the night I saw Mrs. Harding in her black vintage silk. So maybe the dress was just old, not haute couture, just something she'd had in the closet for decades. The way she wore the dress, though, *that* was genuine, too, the real thing. "It isn't just money," I said. "It's, I don't know . . . class, breeding, blood lines! It's the way people talk, and walk, and eat! Yeah, it's even the way they eat." I remembered Lanie's description of the Callahans at dinner.

"Oh, Bronwyn," he said, shaking his head. "You're a strange one."

"What? Tell me you're not from some good family, people who came over on the *Mayflower*, Boston bankers. . . ."

"Virginia," he said. "We may be bad, but we're not Yankees."

"Aha! Blue blood," I said.

"You're such a snob!" he said, his eyes wide and full of amusement.

"Me? *I'm* a snob?"

"Well, you don't have to be rich to be a snob," he said.

"Ho!" I cried.

"Ho?"

"Just ho! Never mind. . . ." I brushed away whatever he might say next, and he laughed. His laughter bubbled up, as if from some reservoir deep inside. But I wouldn't give him the satisfaction of joining in, even though I wanted to.

Millicent and Jack, side to fat side, bumped companionably against each other. They'd had enough water but didn't seem anxious to go anywhere. Clouds had begun boiling up from behind the far ridges and a breeze lifted, clattering the leaves, lifting the horses' tails and manes. "Smells like rain," Will said. "Smell that?" I couldn't.

"Maybe we'd better get back, then," I said, realizing as I'd said it that I didn't really want to leave all that much. Will wasn't what I'd expected him (or maybe what I'd expected a cowboy) to be. He wasn't simple or even very predictable. He said none of the things teenagers said, the

(139)

"half things" I'd grown used to, broken-off sentences, short-cut phrases meant to convey much more than they ever did, *What's the haps? You cool?* filling spaces with words because space was somehow frightening. I didn't know yet what Will might be afraid of, but it wasn't space. For what seemed long periods of time he'd stare at the jagged mountaintops or watch a hawk tracing circles in the sky, saying nothing at all. Then he'd come up with something that really made you think, looking you squarely in the eye, expecting what? I didn't know, and it made me very uncomfortable.

I wasn't comfortable in Will's country either, in this Ojala that I couldn't have imagined from down below. But I was caught up anyway, intrigued in spite of myself. The land was dry and unfamiliar but beautiful like an old woman could be beautiful. What you got at first was just impression, folds and wrinkles, a brown sameness. But, looking closely, you began to differentiate, to see beyond the surface.

Now, as the clouds climbed, their shadows preceding them down the folded ridges, I could see that the mountains were not simply the gray-brown of house cats but a multitude of colors, russets and sage with patches of white and blackish green, a color I had no name for. And they were massive, even from where we stood on the bank of the creek. What we'd climbed, first in the Jeep, then on horseback, were foothills—what we'd have called mountains in the East but what, here, were just preludes to the real stuff.

Will gave me a foot up into the saddle. Millicent shuffled as if she'd just as soon shrug me off. "She knows the way home," Will said. "You can just go along for the ride." He swung his leg over Jack, and Jack turned toward the trail, easy as that.

Millicent was friskier going back. I bumped along on

the saddle, trying to grip with my knees, but I didn't seem to be the natural I was with cars, at least according to Chick. Chick. Angela. J.C. Lanie and Jimbo. How far away they all seemed now, as if there were two completely separate Ojalas, one fast and loose, the other slower and wider, harder to fathom.

Ahead, Jack began a slow gallop and Millicent, to my dismay, began to jog after him, bumping me higher into the air. "Wait!" I yelled, but Will didn't hear. I grabbed the saddle horn, though I knew I wasn't supposed to, and hung on for all I was worth. "Damn you, Millicent!" I yelled. "Shithead!" But she wasn't impressed. All she had on her mind, it seemed, was to keep up with Jack, to get to the barn for dinner. The ground rushed by under our feet, Millicent's hooves kicking dust into my face. "Whoa!" I yelled, pulling back on the reins, yanking hard on her mane, but nothing slowed her down. Will and Jack danced ahead in smooth and perfect unison as if on a carousel. You could almost hear the music.

Then finally I saw the barn ahead, but so did Millicent. Lowering her head, she began to gallop harder, streaking past Will and Jack, me clinging on like a coat of paint. She came to an abrupt stop at the barn door, nearly bucking me over her head. I slid from the saddle on my stomach, leaving a damp streak behind, shaking with fatigue. I felt like punching Millicent's fat face but didn't have the strength for it. She rolled an eye my way as if to say, "What's your problem?"

Will came loping up, a little too casually, I thought. "Hey, you really got her moving!" Buddy's face always had that particular look on it when he'd pulled off a good trick, but his eyes always gave him away. Will had known exactly what Millicent would do; probably he'd pulled that trick dozens of times on greenhorns like me. Then he'd go home and laugh about it with his mother.

I bent to hide my hot and sweaty face. I slapped the dust of my jeans. I blinked back angry tears. "Very funny," I said. I nearly said, "So funny I forgot to laugh," but only children said things like that. "I could have broken my neck."

Will swung off Jack. He'd stopped smiling, but his eyes still invited me to laugh. "And it's a nice neck, too," he said. We faced each other, a foot or two apart, miles apart, while the horses waited, noses to the barn door. If another eighteen-year-old boy had said I had a nice neck, I'd have known what he really meant all right and why he was saying it. Teenage boys I knew said more or less the same things, mostly things they thought they could get away with or impress you with, cool things. But with Will I didn't know what to say back. A smartass comeback didn't seem appropriate somehow.

On the way back down the bumpy road to Ojala, as my teeth clattered, Will chatted easily about life on the ranch. It sounded like a lot of work. He had to keep after both brothers, even David, who was only eighteen months his junior. He made it sound like a game but I didn't see how it could be. It sounded like a whole lot of responsibility. Even as he drove, his eyes scanned the meadow as if he were watching for cattle rustlers or a mountain lion to jump one of the horses. Then suddenly, before I knew what was happening, he whipped out his gun and shot straight out the side of the Jeep, two shots. Blam, and then blam again. He didn't stop the Jeep, he didn't even slow down. He just drew the gun and shot. "Snake," he said. "Sorry, didn't mean to scare you."

We didn't talk much after that. I'd sneak a glance at

him and could feel when he did the same. He seemed easy in the silence. There were things I wanted to know about him, but I didn't want to ask the questions. It was easier to let him be strange. Anyway, he wasn't what I wanted for a boyfriend, so why bother?

"You can ride Jack next time, if you want," Will said as we came to a stop in front of the Welsh Kitchen. "He looks mean, but he's just dumb. He'll do exactly what you want him to do."

Next time. Did I want there to be a next time? I thought about it for a minute and finally I said, "Could we skip the tea next time?"

14

*L*ANIE HELD OUT against Jimbo for six weeks, but she was like a hooked fish. One minute fighting like hell for her freedom, the next she'd be flirting with the net. Jimbo always knew right where to find her. He'd cruise by as we sat at the Frostee sipping our milk shakes, leaning his elbow and his spiky bald head out the window, grinning like a moron with his prized gold tooth. *A matter of time, just a matter of time. . . .*

Lanie had been with me the day Silver made her debut at the Frostee, and with none of the fanfare she deserved. Everybody acted like we'd been there all along. Now we were regulars, Silver and Buddy and me, sometimes Lanie, and easy to find if you wanted to find us. Jimbo wanted Lanie back, but he wasn't pushing it. He'd drive through and give her the once-over, like a picky shopper, his eyes slippery, greasy as Frostee's four-for-a-buck tacos. He'd look Silver over with the same mouth-smacking leer he practiced on Lanie and on any other girl who'd stand still for it. "Wanna race that thing?" he'd tease, even though he knew his pickup was a dog. After the Drags he'd called me a dyke, Lanie said. Only dykes raced cars, he told her. But she knew he was impressed because of J.C. J.C. had been his idol since junior high. Once he even punched somebody's lights out because they dared question J.C.'s authority on the matter of camshafts. He worshiped J.C., and J.C. had let me, Bronwyn Lewis, a girl, race his car.

Usually I ignored Jimbo. I'd be too busy studying the words on the wrapper of my cheeseburger or picking the polish off my fingernails to give him the time of day. But sometimes I'd think how sweet it would be to lose him in the dust out on Carne Road. Maybe Lanie would see how foolish he was, choking in Silver's exhaust. By then she'd adopted Silver, too. In some funny way that cars have, Silver was our armor, our fort in a wilderness where boys ran like renegade cowboys and made all the rules. But I never seriously considered racing Jimbo. An airport runway surrounded by miles of empty land was one thing; Carne Road was another. I doubted that Jimbo, showoff that he was, wanted to flirt with that rock wall any more than I did. And besides, I knew I could lose my car if Frieda was good for her threat. I thought she probably was.

This time, Lanie let me know in advance that she was going back with Jimbo. I suppose I should have been grateful for that. Usually I found out like everybody else, when they showed up together in his pickup looking like newlyweds back from a honeymoon in some cheesy place like Vegas. Probably they'd just gone to the orange orchards, where everybody went to get it on.

We were parked at Topa Ridge when she told me. It was dusk and we'd been watching the lights twinkle on in the valley, one by one, then in little clumps. It was a peaceful thing to do. You could let your mind drift like a paper boat, away from things that got you down. I'd swiped a pack of my dad's Camels. Lanie had a pint of Jack Daniel's tucked in her purse. We lit up. The Camels made you dizzy with the first hit. "Jimbo wants me back," she said.

"So what's new," I said, the expected thing. No use pretending I was anything but disgusted. I took a deep drag of the Camel and nearly choked. Anybody who'd go back for another punch in the face was stupider than she had any right to be. How long would it be before Jimbo broke her nose or an arm, or even killed her? Lanie knew, everybody knew, about the woman in Ventura who'd been killed by her jealous husband not long before. It was the kind of thing the *Sun* really played up. Above a grainy photograph showing three solemn-looking policemen and a mummy wrapped in sheets lying on a stretcher were the bold black words HE LOVED ME. "According to friends and family, those would have been the words of a young Ventura wife and mother, had she been able to utter them."

We stared out our respective sides of the windshield as if waiting for a movie to start, neither of us knowing what to say, what was worth saying. Mountain peaks in jagged silhouette seemed to rise into the sky as the last of the daylight faded, and finally they, too, were gone. Then the sky was a black dropcloth with a single slit for the quarter moon.

Lanie laid her head back, closed her eyes. She would do what she would do and that was that. I fidgeted with whatever would turn or push. The odometer on its second time around was stuck at 34,948 (a lucky number, my mother would have said). Into the dead quiet, I wanted to cry or yell or throw something. Things I would never have said to anyone I cared about batted the walls of my brain.

(146)

"So what's new?" I croaked again. But I didn't really want to talk. I wanted to slap her.

My heart dropped the way I dropped my clothes at night, all in a heap. I took a deep breath and looked at Lanie, just as she turned her head and opened her eyes. They were dark as the night sky and full of pain, but it was as if she were feeling mine, my pain, and none of her own. It was the way my mother sometimes looked at me, expecting me to have followed her into a place beyond logic and reason where I was expected just to understand. For some reason a look like that only made me madder.

What was it about Lanie that made you want to hurt her? Did Jimbo have so much ugliness inside, so much anger, that he needed to destroy what was best in his world? Did that somehow right things for him? make them even? And what did that say about me, who could feel what a Jimbo could feel, if only for a second?

"Look, you've come this far," I reasoned, calmer now. Still, I had glimpsed for a moment a self that shouldn't be, and my insides shook with that vision. How could such an ugly inner self fly with Mozart? And yet it had, again and again, and those two parts seemed to me irreconcilable.

Lanie took a sip of the Jack Daniel's, winced, and passed the bottle to me. It had a good solid burn going down.

I ran through the litany with Lanie of all the things we both knew, and that we knew would make no difference. "You've made it through the hard part. You said you didn't even miss being with him. You said it just the other day!"

"I know...." She sounded sorrowful, the way a ship sounds way off in the distance having left you behind on the dock, waving your sad little hand.

"But you do," I said flatly. "You do miss him...."

"I guess."

(147)

"But what is there to miss? I mean, come *on*. You guys fight as much as you make out. At *least*! So what is it you miss?" The thought of Lanie kissing Jimbo was enough to make me puke.

"I dunno. I guess the . . ." She frowned, shook her head once, and almost smiled, would have smiled if I weren't watching, ready to bite her head off. "It's the excitement, I guess. When I'm around him, everything has this, like this *edge* to it, you know? Like you never know what's going to happen next. . . ."

"And that's *good?*"

"I know it sounds crazy, Bron. I didn't say it made any sense. . . ." But it did. It made the crazy kind of sense that drag racing made when you were out there sitting on the line.

She twisted the butt of her cigarette into the ashtray. Once I'd cleaned Silver's ashtray with toothpicks and Q-Tips. Now Lanie and I played a game to see who could jam in the last lipstick-tipped butt and not spill the whole mess. The backseat was another heap, clothes and books, Frostee wrappers, all tossed together.

"Jeez!" I blew a plume of smoke at the ceiling where it dispersed like fog. Silver was beginning to smell like the pool hall. "I *guess* it doesn't make any sense."

"I mean it's fun running around with the girls and all," she said, meaning mostly me, and that it really wasn't so much fun, not when you could have a boyfriend. "But isn't this what us girls do, you know, *in between?* We're all just looking for the same thing, for that one special guy, right?"

I shrugged. Was that really what it was all about? Was it all that simple? Were *we* all that simple? I took another slug of the whiskey and passed it to Lanie.

"Maybe we could, you know, double-date," Lanie said

after a while, as if this were something so normal it could have occurred to anyone.

"Yeah, right," I said. "You and Jimbo, me and Buddy. Or how about me and Pitts Heimer?" Pitts had earned his nickname by digging at his zits so zealously they bled.

"How about you and that guy, you know, what's-his-name with the Jeep?"

"Will? Will Harding? He's not a date. I told you that. We rode horses together, that's all. One time."

"Well, I'm not saying you gotta marry the guy. Just see if he wants to double sometime. You said he was real nice. Maybe some of him will rub off on Jimbo."

"Jimbo needs a complete overhaul," I said. "Not just a tune-up."

"Oh, Bron . . ."

"Oh, *Lanie.*"

THEY WERE BACK together the next day, cruising the Avenue, Lanie bunched up against Jimbo like they'd been glued, the fuzzy dice she'd given him hanging from his rearview mirror. I waved as I drove past, at her, only at her. He knew that. He knew how much I hated him, how much I hated that stupid pickup truck. Silver could leave it standing still, I *knew* she could. Instead of tears, I let the anger build. We could beat him, Silver, I said. We *could*. If I cried, I knew some of those tears would be for myself, self-pitying tears, the kind I wouldn't cry over my own father, the kind I hated, and so I wouldn't cry. It was back to Buddy, and Chick and Angela, and of course Silver, the steadiest of them all.

15

HOLD ON A MINUTE," Frieda called as I headed for the door. It was a Friday night in early April and the front door was open to let the spring air, as my mother put it, "dance through." A few regulars were seated at "their" tables having the usual, Meat Loaf Parmigiano for Leo the Lecher, who would grab whatever body part he could reach before you dropped his salad down; Greta Garbo with her *"une petite soupe à l'oignon"* and water in a wineglass. Greta's real name was Edith and she had never been a movie star, but with her floppy hat and scarf and dark sunglasses, she could pass for Garbo all right.

Frieda had that "pay attention" look in her eye. Her curls were gathered in loops on top of her head like Lucille Ball's and wrapped with the leopard-print scarf. Welsh leopards, she'd probably say if anybody asked.

"Out here," she said, leading me onto the porch. "You've got some time." Already I didn't like the sound of that. Had she read my mind? Did she know where I was headed?

(150)

Silver had been singing to me in a whole new way since my race in J.C.'s Deuce, as if she were jealous or itching to show what she could do. She was light and fast, made for racing. Owning a car like Silver was like having the atom bomb and no place to drop it, all that power just waiting. It made you look for an excuse to use it, to try it out just once. But Frieda would never understand that kind of urge. I leaned against the porch post, ready to bolt.

She lit up with a practiced, unhurried motion, shaking the match several times before sticking it carefully under the cellophane of her cigarette pack. I envied her her long copper fingernails. I'd stopped biting mine. Mostly. But the cuticles were ragged and sore-looking. I kept my hands out of sight as much as I could, curling them in my lap or sticking them deep into the pockets of my jeans. I almost understood how a Pitts Heimer felt, but Pitts was somebody you didn't want to think about for long.

"Where ya headed?" I knew she wasn't really interested. Anybody headed down Ojala Avenue in a car on a Friday night was up to No Good. Or if they weren't, they'd find it waiting for them.

"I dunno." I shrugged. "Somewhere. . . ."

"Cruising." She flattened the word. So she didn't really know. I relaxed a notch. She just had to do this second-mother thing from time to time and I had to put up with it. Probably she just missed the old routine with Johnny.

"Cruising," I said.

Then came the question she had in mind all along. "What do you plan on doing with your life, Bron?" She curled the coppery fingernails of her free hand together and frowned down at them, as if she saw a flaw there, a hairline crack, trouble.

Her question threw me. I hadn't thought much about the

future since coming to Ojala, I guess because nobody else did. Kids in Ojala more or less fell into things, as far as I could tell. Or something would just "happen," like a girl would get pregnant and have to get married. There were few abortions in those days, at least that we knew of. You could cross the border into Mexico if you wanted one bad enough, or were desperate. Tijuana was a half-day's drive straight down the coast, but at least one girl we knew about died in a botched attempt. Her tragic story circulated from time to time like Asian flu. It didn't keep anybody from "doing it," though, any more than the flu kept people from breathing.

Then there were the kids who went to college or opted for the military. But nobody talked much about what would happen later, when we grew up, when we had to get serious.

"I dunno," I said, sounding even to my own ears a little like a moron. "Go to college, get a job. . . ."

"You're sixteen. Time to do a little thinking about it, no? Unless you want to end up pushing pancakes in some two-bit coffee shop." She peered into the window to make sure she wasn't needed. "Not that I'm not happy here, you know that. And this ain't no two-bit place. Your folks are the finest people. . . ." Then she stabbed her finger at me. "You're not a whole lot of help, you know."

"What do you mean?" I knew as well as she did that I worked only for the tips, that when it came to doing the cleaning and the upkeep I was always on my way out the door.

"Things aren't exactly hunky-dory right now, Bron. Business has been dropping off, haven't you noticed? We haven't done thirty dinners any night in the last three weeks. They're worried. Your folks work their fingers to the bone, and they're worried. This place is all they have."

Whenever my father lost weight, his neck would get

so thin you'd wonder how it could hold his head on. But his fingers had *always* been bony. I thought of telling that to Frieda, to kind of lighten things up, but I didn't think she'd appreciate it. "I know," I said.

It wasn't as if I didn't worry about them. Did she think I was some kind of monster? But I couldn't spend my life in the place like they did, scrubbing and waxing floors, cleaning ovens, defrosting refrigerators, scraping grease off the kitchen wall—and they didn't expect me to.

"Well? It's your place, too," she said. "It goes down, you all go down with it."

"Like the *Titanic*," I said.

She poked her tongue into her cheek, narrowed her eyes, and studied me for signs of disrespect. "You think this doesn't have anything to do with you, right?"

There was so much she didn't know. "It has something to do with me," I said.

"Something." Dragon smoke blew out her nose.

"Look, if it'd been up to me ..." I rammed my fists deeper into my pockets. "And it *wasn't*." I shuffled from one foot to the other. Why were we having this conversation anyway? "If I'd had anything to say about it, which I *didn't*, we wouldn't even be here. There wouldn't be any damned sinking restaurant to worry about!"

Frieda smirked, brushed a dropped ash off her knee. "Didn't ask to be born, right?"

"Huh?"

"What John used to say. '*I didn't ask to be born.*'" She whined out the words, screwing up her face like a toddler in the throes of a tantrum. "Of course John was all of about eight years old when he came up with that one. That's a child's way out of being responsible, Bron. I expected better from you."

Now I was heating up. Who did she think she was anyway, and what did she know about me? about our family?

"None of this is going to last, Frieda. Dad's a loser, don't you know that? He's never kept a job more than a year in his life. Things get too bad and, zip, he's outa here!" I sliced a finger across my wrist. Frieda's eyes widened just enough to let me know she got it.

She ground her cigarette into an ashtray she'd brought from inside, then ground it some more. Whatever she was thinking went a long way down. "You're one pissed-off young lady, aren't you?" she said quietly, looking up.

"Better pissed off than pissed on," I said, but her expression didn't change.

"Everybody makes mistakes, Bron. You, me, everybody. Some are the kind you can't take back, but all of them, *all* of them, are forgivable." When I didn't answer she said, "Think about it, kid. Just think about it."

So I did what Frieda said. I thought about it. I knew she meant for me to think another way, to see what happened from another vantage point, maybe even from my father's. But what did she know? Did her father try to off himself? Was she kidnapped by her own parents and taken clear across the country to some dusty little burg? Did she, at the impressionable age of sixteen, that very *impressionable* age of sixteen, have to start her whole life all over again? Sure, I thought about it. And the more I thought, the angrier I got.

And besides, there were other things I had to think about and think about fast, like how far I was willing to go to beat Jimbo out on Carne Road.

It had been stupid to let him get to me, I knew that, but stupidity was a kind of virtue in the crowd I ran with.

(154)

I was missing Lanie and angry with Jimbo for taking her away, for treating her like trash, for even thinking his pickup could ever beat a car like Silver.

And I was full of myself. These days whenever I cruised into the Frostee, heads turned. I wasn't just the girl from Jersey now, I was the girl who raced J.C.'s Deuce and tied Sticks Delaney.

But the glory began fading when Jimbo started in on me. Racing the Deuce was one thing, he said, picking his teeth, staring bullets through his mean little eyes, *any*body could win in that car. But *my* car, my pretty little pussy of a car? Now, *that* was something else.

Lanie said to just ignore him, and at first I did. But in truth I wanted that race as much as Jimbo did. I'd played it start to finish over and over in my mind a dozen times, each time easing off long before the wall came looming up because Silver was so far ahead. Jimbo wouldn't win. He couldn't win. But we had to show him that, Silver and I would show him that.

A bigger-than-usual crowd had gathered at the Frostee by the time I got away from Frieda, all the regular bunch plus some kids from out of town who'd come trailing a rumor like they sometimes did. I got a glimpse of Lanie as I passed and could tell she was angry, fit for bear, as she sometimes said. Her fists were on her hips, her mouth in a straight no-bullshit line. Oh, hell, I thought, another lecture. I parked and Lanie stomped over, hopping in. "Don't say it," I said.

"Don't you try and shut me up, Bron. You're not the only one who knows what's best for people." Lanie settled her behind in for a stay, crossing her arms over her chest. She had the cutest outfit on, tight white capris and a blouse with a wide collar and sailor stripes. Her earrings were tiny silver anchors. In that outfit, I'd've looked like a first grader, but she could get away with anything.

"I didn't say I did. I don't know what's best for anybody." But I did sometimes. I sure as hell knew Lanie was better off without Jimbo.

"Look," she said, trying a new tack. "Jimbo doesn't want to race all that much. He just can't back down. You know how it is with guys."

"But I could, right? It's okay for me to back down and look stupid, right?"

"It's not the same thing and you know it."

"No, I don't know it, Lanie. That's the thing. You're always cutting guys some slack, as if they can't help who they are or what they do. But us girls? We're supposed to take stuff, give in, apologize when we get our faces smash—" She looked away, so that I was staring at the back of her head. "I'm sorry," I said.

"No you're not," Lanie said, looking back, her dark eyes glittering. "You're not sorry. Jimbo's right, you just think you're better than me, better than anybody around here." She waved her hand to take in the crowd of cars and kids milling around like ants on a coffee break.

My heart fell. "You really believe that?"

She looked down at her hands, nails bitten to the quick like mine, then up again but not at me. Jimbo had a crowd around him now like he always wanted. He was leaning against the door of his truck, arms crossed, fists tucked under his biceps to make them poke out. "Look," she said. "What I really wanted to say, what I was going to say before you tried to shut me up, is that I'm worried, that's all. You know how dumb it is to race out there. You said so yourself."

"You don't have to worry about Jimbo," I said. My

throat was a sharp ache that wouldn't swallow down. "He'll drop out, wait and see. Something will happen to his engine, so it won't be his fault."

"I'm worried about the both of you," she said. "Please, Bron. Please don't do it. I'm asking you as a friend."

We said all the things with our eyes that words are never equal to. "Ask Jimbo," I said.

"Shit," she said. "You're every bit as stubborn as he is. So kill yourselves, I don't care!" She jumped out and slammed the door behind her, stomping off, an elbow-pumping ninety-seven pounds of fury.

Chick came over and slid in. "I'll cruise out there with you," he said.

"Angela coming?"

"Naw. She's at her sister's. They're doing all this wedding shower stuff. Jeez! What a production." He ran his hand over his hair, just like Kookie. "Sure you want to go through with this here race?"

"It's no big deal," I said, wanting to believe it.

"Right," Chick agreed. "No big deal."

I wanted to ask if he'd seen J.C., but I couldn't. I couldn't speak J.C.'s name without giving myself away.

"So, what do you say, then? Let's get on out there. Get this show on the road." He stuck his head out the window and howled, one long howl followed by little barking yips.

Silver started like she'd been waiting for me to turn the key and settled into her familiar cheerful hum. Chick waved a victory sign as we drove past the crowd and out onto the Avenue. My hands began to sweat. In the rearview mirror I saw other cars pulling out and lining up behind us. Then we were a procession of headlights cruising, bumper on bumper and up to No Good.

Out toward Carne, past Ojala Lanes and the last of the

streetlights, the Avenue became just another dark road. A three-quarter moon cast the rounded shapes of orange trees across Silver's hood and I thought about Chick and Angela getting married. Chick was nineteen, Angela not yet eighteen. If things went as she planned, they'd have a couple of kids before she could legally drink. As far as I could see, that wasn't anything worth celebrating. But what did I know? I didn't even have a boyfriend.

I slowed down and turned onto Carne. "Take the right side," Chick said. "It's safer." The orchards on both sides narrowed to a V at the far end where the wall was, but you couldn't see it from where we were. Cars pulled around us on either side, some racing to the far end, drivers hooting from their windows, waving beer cans. A few cars pulled along the sides of the road and parked. Someone would stand sentry at each end, watching for the police.

Jimbo charged up, gunning his engine, toasting us with his beer. "May the best man win!" he yelled. Lanie threw him a disgusted look and got out. Chick hopped out, too. "I'll start you," he said.

Jimbo gunned and gunned his engine, a loose ratty sound like a bad cough, but I kept Silver at a notch over idle, smooth and steady, whetting her appetite. She sometimes stuck just a little in second. I'd have to double-clutch her, but by second gear I knew I'd have the edge on Jimbo. The way he was goosing the pickup, he'd probably flood out and die on the line.

I wasn't afraid. I was almost too calm, jaw loose, limbs loose and easy.

Jimbo chugged the last of his beer and tossed the bottle into the orchard. "You ready, girl?" He leered. I could see he'd had a few.

(158)

I nodded once. We both looked out at Chick. In the headlights, his face looked spooky, pale as buttermilk. His eyes were wide, frightening, maybe frightened. And then, like a cheerleader, he smiled and both arms lifted. Silver's hood rose up and she began to sing, moonlight sliding over her hood like a white cape. I held her, balanced, ready to fly.

Jimbo's pickup vibrated beside us. Chick's arms stayed in the air it seemed forever and then, in a snap, he brought them down. We zipped past, Jimbo leaning forward like a jockey. I double-clutched Silver into second and she sailed ahead in a singing scream, Jimbo dropping behind. Too easy, I said to Silver, no race, and I let off the gas enough to let Jimbo catch up. Our headlights pierced the thick darkness as if we were racing through a tunnel. Dropping into third, I punched the gas again. Jimbo looked over, his mouth dropping as he fell behind a second time.

And then the wall came out of the darkness. It didn't loom. It just appeared, a four-foot wall of river rock shadowed in headlights at the far end. I let Jimbo come on again and then again, let him drop behind each time like soiled Kleenex. Silver sang and laughed. Jimbo hurled himself forward. The wall grew. I hesitated, and the pickup pulled ahead. I stomped Silver's pedal to the floor and we began to gain again, but the wall was bigger now than I'd imagined it all those times I'd run this race in my mind. Silver's nose caught the pickup's front fender, then she was even again. We tore toward the wall like horses in the stretch, neck and neck, no sound but the drumming wail of pistons pounding like wild hooves.

Then Silver slid ahead, clearly ahead. She'd won. Everybody could see that, could see Jimbo fall behind. I eased off and turned my head just enough to see his face, grim and set in the moonlight. And I knew, just as if I'd known him all our lives, that he would never go down.

The pickup came on again, pulling, heaving itself at us. I watched as it passed in a pounding burst, Jimbo wound like knotted rope around the wheel, and I watched as he braked and tried to stop, the old blue pickup in the slowest, most graceful move of its life, back end sliding, sliding. The pickup hit the wall like a plane plowing into a runway with an aftersound like a gunshot, a sharp crack, metal and glass against stone. It rocked twice and settled. Dust rose in clouds around it.

I braked, leaped from Silver, and began running with the others. Steam rose from under the hood of the pickup. Its windshield on the driver's side was a web of radiating lines, Jimbo's forehead slumped against it, a single stream of blood in a dark red line down the center of his nose. Jimbo's eyes were closed, his lips hung slack. One hand lay over the wheel, fingers in a half curl, the other hung to the floor.

"Somebody get an ambulance!"

"Don't touch him! Don't touch him!"

"Is he dead? Is he dead?" There were kids all over the hood, on both running boards, peering in and staring as Chick arrived. A girl about twelve, a dark skinny girl with a single braid down her back, began to cry as if she'd been shot, both hands over her mouth.

"Feel his pulse," somebody said. All around and quiet, the night was a silent accusation.

Chick reached in for Jimbo's hand. "Shit," he said. "I can't feel nothin'. Damn it! God *damn* it! Get somebody. Call an ambulance!" He looked from face to frozen face, pushed the shoulder of a boy who came to life and ran for his car. The others backed slowly away, as if Chick were their accuser and it had somehow been their fault. For the longest time I watched Chick holding Jimbo's head against his chest, his dark eyes full of fear. Blood seeped through his fingers and down onto his jeans. You'd have thought he was Jimbo's brother, when in fact he'd never had a good thing to say about him. Death could do that.

At last the thin wail of a siren rode toward us over the tops of trees. I thought about Lanie at the other end of the Avenue. Would she be on her way? Should I drive back and get her? I didn't want to be here, didn't want to think. I stood apart from all the others with my arms wrapped around my ribs, cold, anonymous as the kids from out of town.

The ambulance cut its siren and slid in behind the pickup. Two men got out. One hurried toward the pickup. He was overweight and already sweating. He reached through the window of the pickup and placed his fingers on Jimbo's neck. The practiced mask of his face told us nothing, but I knew. He nodded to his partner and together they wheeled a stretcher toward the pickup. They hurried but not a whole lot, which was because Jimbo was dead. Jimbo was dead. *Lanie, Jimbo is dead.*

They eased open the pickup door and took Jimbo from Chick. There was too much blood. I thought about Lanie's face the way it looked on New Year's Eve. This had been quicker. A single sharp crack. The men tightened belts across Jimbo's chest and thighs. *Lanie, Jimbo is dead.*

And then he moaned. It was Jimbo all right, no mistaking that voice. Even in pain it had a wheedling, disgruntled sound. "He's alive!" somebody cried, as if Jesus had stepped whole from the grave. Three girls began to cry, hugging each other for comfort.

(161)

I walked back to Silver. Her door lay open. Inside, the tiny map light on the dash glowed. She looked cozy but she was just a car now, a pretty little blue car, no longer mine.

IT HADN'T BEEN hard as I thought to leave Silver at Frieda's, to drop her keys under the seat and walk away. In the time it took to drive from Carne Road to Frieda's house, I'd frozen Silver out. I thought, If I could do that with people, with my father, I could do it, *couldn't I?* with a car. Metal and glass and rubber. No heart.

If Jimbo had died, I'd have just kept on going, down the single two-lane road that brought us here, out the ring of mountains to the sea and then into that, walking and gulping and choking and floating. And stupid. So stupid the thoughts I sometimes had. Where was there to go, really?

But Jimbo wasn't dead. He was even for a little while a hero, driving through the Frostee the very next day in his battered blue pickup, a bright white patch on his forehead where they'd shaved off what little hair there was. He drove up beside Chick's Olds, his head poked out the pickup window like a gander on the attack.

"What'd I tell ya?" he said. I tried to blend into the tuck and roll of Chick's backseat.

"Hey! What'd I say? You remember? She's a *pussy*, I said. Didn't I, Chick? Aw, don't feel bad, little girl. You ran a pretty good race. You just didn't have what it takes to go all the way. Right, Chick? Hey, you know what? Me and Lanie's gonna get hitched! Now, what do you think about that?"

My head shot up to see if he was lying. Angela said, "You're kidding! When?"

"Goin' ta Vegas," he said. "This weekend. Party time! Yow!" He gunned his pickup and squealed out.

"Dumb bastard," Chick said.

"You think he means it?" Angela turned to me.

"He's all talk," I said. But what did I know? Lanie wasn't speaking to me.

"They're gonna do it sooner or later." Angela sighed. "But I didn't want them to beat us to it. *Chickie!*" she pleaded.

"We could do a double," he suggested. "Go to Vegas with them."

"You got shit for brains or what?" Angela said, smacking his arm. "My shower's not till next month!"

I bummed a Kool from Angela. She stuck one between her pillow lips and we both lit up.

"I thought Lanie'd lost it in the hospital," Chick said. "We couldn't calm her down to tell her Jimbo wasn't dead. That's what she'd heard from whoever was hanging around." My heart thunked. What kind of friend was I? "This nurse had to shoot Lanie with something to shut her up and she went out, bam, like *that*." Chick slapped the dash with the flat of his hand. "Hey, she loves the guy, you gotta give him that."

"I'd give him my dirty underwear," Angela said.

"Oh, no you don't." Chick grinned, pinching a nipple. She slapped his hand away, bored, like she was swatting a fly.

All that week, I was good, just to prove to myself that I could be. I did all my homework, painstakingly, the way I'd done it when I was that other person, the honor student, long ago in New Jersey. It felt good somehow, like climbing onto the worn soft seat of a bicycle and turning the pedals again. I'd forgotten the feeling of a job well done, the neat satisfaction in that. But I still dropped my work off after

(163)

school and fled from Mr. Demski's room as if I'd been hit on the spot with a case of the runs.

In the restaurant I worked beyond my shift, doing all the side work I'd slipped away from so many times before. Now I married catsups like it was my particular calling, setting them mouth to mouth, screwing on soaked clean caps, and wiping the bottles afterward with a damp rag. I became the darling of customers, all except the regulars, who knew better than to trust so sudden a convert. I'd pour hot coffee into nearly full cups, replace slopped saucers, change clean ashtrays for dirty, all the time smiling in imitation of Frieda and all the world's good waitresses.

It was in all the papers the next day, the three that we knew about, the *Star-Free Press*, *The Sentinel*, the *Sun*. As usual, the *Sun* had the best splash, Jimbo's pickup smashed against the wall, Jimbo being wheeled away on the stretcher, the crowd gaping and young. *Youth Escapes Race with Death*. My name wasn't mentioned. Maybe the editors thought that would stretch the limits of credibility, a girl drag racer.

But Frieda knew. She knew when she heard my car pull in or before that, nodding off in her darkened living room, when her police band radio said '46 blue Ford. Then, when she knew that I was safe, she switched off the radio and went to bed. I'd tell my parents or I wouldn't, it was up to me.

I'd walked away from her house, loose-limbed, like I'd just grown legs. I never walked anywhere anymore, not two blocks to the market for whatever we'd run short of, a dozen eggs, a head of lettuce. Climbing the stairs, carefully to avoid the two that squeaked, I heard the rumble of my father's deep snore. I was tired, so tired suddenly that I could hardly make the last steps and stood there, breathless, as if I'd run the race on Carne on foot.

(164)

The attic was flooded with moonlight. In silhouette against the sheets, my mother spooned against my father's back made a single snoring being with two heads. I peeked in on Buddy the way I always did. Some part of me believed he wouldn't be there, that he'd slip through the cracks and disappear. He was small, it could happen. He slept on his back, arms and legs flung out like a sky diver, gulping life through his open mouth.

I'd have to explain all this to him, this thing I did, this dumb-ass thing I did. I shucked my clothes and climbed into bed, but I couldn't sleep. The world was too bright, too full of jangle and sharp edges. My heroes floated above me like guardian angels. Elvis was having a good laugh at my expense, but James, he knew.

16

SOMETIMES FROM my attic perch I'd watch my father walk to the pharmacy for the morning paper. Chin on my arms, I'd watch him trudge the three blocks, then the three blocks back, the *Sun* tucked under his arm. He'd be in his chef's clothes, whiter-than-white, his white apron tied in a bow over his stomach, and those worn-out combat boots with the turned-up toes, now slopped with gravy and tomato sauce, the clear gray snot of fish guts.

Sometimes he'd wave and smile at someone passing on the Avenue, but mostly he'd be deep in thought, glazed over, and if someone honked, he'd jump. Then he'd wave, but it would be too late. You could have picked him right out of a crowd, not simply because of what he wore, but because of his hair. He had a great mane of it, silvery white, brushed back from his high forehead in a single cresting wave. It was his crowning glory, my mother said.

I couldn't watch my father go for the paper the morning after my race with Jimbo. Instead I hung around the kitchen watching my mother roll out the piecrusts. She was fast as anything, as efficient as my father with his soup stock and his sauces, but about half the time when you talked to her now, she didn't answer. Like her mother, she'd gone to live somewhere else, somewhere she liked better. I held my coffee in the bowl of my hands, letting the warmth seep in where it could, and waited for my father to return.

As he came through the door several things happened to his face, one after the other, like in flip cards you got in boxes of Cracker Jack. At first he seemed perplexed, as if he'd been told a joke and didn't get the punch line. He always understood jokes. His eyebrows were raised and there was a sort of smile or smirk on his face. Then his mouth fell open as if he were about to speak. He even laughed, once, a short bark.

I chewed the skin at the tip of my thumb. His face settled, dropped. And everything else fell with it: chin and shoulders, spine. "What is this?" he said, unfolding his copy of the *Sun*. There was Jimbo's pickup, the rock wall, the stretcher, all the life gone out and stiff the way it is in news photos. In another shot, a thin pale girl in a white turtleneck stood off to the side, both hands raised to her mouth, eyes wide in horror so complete that it looked staged. But it wasn't. If I hadn't seen myself there in black-and-white, I'd have thought maybe it didn't happen, that this was the kind of thing that happened to other kids, to the bad kids.

My mother slid the paper from my hands. "Good Lord," she said. "What's this? Bron? Is this you?" She looked at me as if I were changing on the spot before her eyes, growing horns and a tail.

I shrugged. I did that a lot, words being harder, especially the ones that made sense.

My father poured himself a cup of coffee, stirring swirls of cream in. He couldn't go for the Old Crow, not now, but I could tell he was thinking about it.

"This just isn't right," my mother said, reading through the text for a second time as if she might find something there to exonerate me, turn me back into someone she could relate to.

"It was just a race . . ." I said.

My father's coffee cup stopped on its way to his mouth. "A race," he said. He put the cup on the saucer and the saucer on his worktable. "A boy was nearly killed and you say it was just a race." He removed his glasses. They'd been wired together a half-dozen times, but he wouldn't give them up. One earpiece hung limp like a broken arm. "What's happened to you? Don't you realize what you've done?"

"Well, it wasn't *all* her fault . . ." my mother said. "It wasn't her idea, was it, Bron? It wasn't your idea, was it?"

I didn't answer.

"It doesn't matter whose idea it was, Helen. There's a human life involved here. A boy's life, and she says it's *just* a race!" My father's fingers combed his hair, leaving furrows like a tractor through a wheat field or runners in the snow. He didn't know what to do next, what fathers did with naughty children. There was no precedent to draw on.

And then there was his own guilt that overshadowed everything, always, and robbed him of his power.

"You could have been killed," my mother said. "This . . ." She tapped the photo of Jimbo on the stretcher with the back of her hand. "This could have been you. Is this the way you spend your time? Racing cars? If we had known . . ."

"No car," my father said. "That's it. Put the car up for sale. Put it in the paper. No car. That's what got you into trouble in the first place, that damned car."

"I gave it back," I said. "It's at Frieda's."

"Well," my father said, deflating. "Well. That's exactly what you should have done."

"She's sorry," my mother said. "See, Tom? She's sorry, aren't you, Bron?"

"I'd like to hear her say it," my father said.

"I'm sorry," I said.

"Well," my father said. "Well. Let's not hear another word about it, then!" He waved his hand at the paper, laid out now on his worktable like a blueprint. "Give your old man a hug." I placed my arms around him. "That's a good girl." He swatted me on the rear as I left the room. "Bron?" he said when I'd reached the door. I turned. "Come back here a minute." I walked back into the kitchen. "How far would you have gotten if I hadn't called you back?"

I worked the dinner shift with Frieda. It was busy for a change. Frieda didn't say much but I figured she was saving it. She got Johnny's car back, but she'd want more than that, she'd want her satisfaction for being right all along. I didn't mind. She'd been straight with me from the beginning, and I figured I owed her.

Ten after nine, I cashed out the last customer and joined Frieda at a table for two. She had her cup of Sanka and a clean ashtray ready to fill. Frieda always started over like that, as if she didn't want to share a dump with strangers. I pulled a pile of quarters, dimes, and crumpled bills from my pocket and there were Silver's keys, her ignition key and the little key that unlocked her gas cap. I looked at Frieda, tried to figure how she'd gotten them into my pocket without my knowing. She didn't smile, didn't look angry. I couldn't read her expression exactly, but I knew I was supposed to, that there was more to know there than her words would say. She stacked and rolled her quarters. In the kitchen my father's pots banged against the sink. "I believe in second chances," she said. "Don't you?"

IT WAS OVER, and yet it wasn't. Not inside me. Not in that place that doesn't let you off the hook, no matter what anybody else says. If I were a Catholic, I thought, I could confess. If I were a kid again, I could be spanked. Who was I kidding? I'd never been spanked. It wasn't as if I'd never done anything wrong. I'd scribbled on walls, thrown tantrums. I was a normal kid. But we were a reasonable family. That was how my mother described us, to us, as well as to others. We reasoned things out. They trusted me to behave myself, and if I didn't, they trusted me to reason things out and learn from my mistakes. When Frieda told them she'd like me to have Silver back, they agreed at once. "She'll work things out herself," they said.

I'd nearly caused another human being's death. No matter that it was only Jimbo. He was human, more or less. No matter how much I tried to shift the blame or even share it, it shadowed me. I ate it for breakfast, found it in books, in the mirror. At night it cornered me.

In desperation, I returned to the little church, not to pray but to play. I knew someone there now, the custodian, an ancient Mexican man who would stand just inside the door, a dark and silent presence, and listen until I was through.

At first it was mechanical, a shot in the dark. I'd watch my fingers do Mozart as if they belonged to someone else. And then my ears began to hear the notes, and finally my heart. Where were you? the music seemed to say. Where were you all this time?

17

*I*T WAS TRUE. Lanie and Jimbo were getting married. There'd be a shower, spur-of-the-moment at Angela's, and then they'd go to Vegas right after. Stay at the Flamingo, where Bugsy Siegel and Virginia Hill had been lovers. They'd drink pink champagne. Lanie was barely sixteen. I got a shower invitation in the mail, a tiny white card with pastel umbrellas floating through green drops of rain.

If a shower was meant to anticipate oncoming storms, this one was right on target.

I thought a dozen times about calling Lanie, picked up the receiver and put it down again, or dialed and pushed the button down. People could avoid each other forever if they knew each other well enough, even in a town the size of Ojala. Still, I thought maybe I'd run into her by accident. But I knew she wouldn't talk to me. I even thought for a while she was getting married just to spite me, to get back at me for nearly killing Jimbo. But then I knew it was because she'd almost lost him. She had this one way now, this ultimate way in which to say no matter what happened they would always be together. It was the no-matter-what that chilled me.

I couldn't go. I wouldn't go. How could I sit around the punch bowl pretending?

But I couldn't not go either. She'd want me to be there. She'd want my blessing, though there wasn't a chance in hell that she'd get it.

And then it came to me. I'd go as a spy. Just one of the girls. I'd shop for a gift, something festive and hopeful like a toaster. You couldn't kill a good toaster. I'd dress for the shower like all the others, in heels and hose, maybe even white gloves. My dress would be fairylike, gossamer. I'd float in it like the swan who'd always before been the ugly duckling, Cinderella's stepsister, the bridesmaid who was never a bride.

I'd have to buy the dress. Nothing I owned came close.

I couldn't believe what happened to girls at showers, how their mouths cleaned right up, how they became on-the-spot matrons, exclaiming wildly over matching towel sets and toilet brushes, exchanging cleaning hints passed down by their mothers. *Clorox will keep that ring out. . . . Toothpaste works great on silver!*

A half-dozen girls were sitting in a semicircle when I got to Angela's. One ancient woman sat by herself on the couch sucking on her bottom lip. The room was dimly lit as if for a wake, and crammed with overstuffed brown velvet furniture. On the wall over the couch, a grizzly bear of a couch, was a gold crucifix: tiny points of thorns, Jesus' thin bare feet *en pointe*, one over the other. Yellow and white crepe paper streamers crossed the room in several directions. There were yellow balloons in a cluster hanging at eye level from a ceiling fixture.

I said hi. Several girls said hi, too casually, and went back to their enthralling conversations. I sat next to the old lady, on the edge of the couch, my knees together and to one side like I'd seen the models do, hands clasped in my lap to anchor my crinolines. I was in love with my dress. It was muted mauve, princess style, with lace and tiny maroon rosebuds at the neck and on the edge of the sleeves. Slipping it on over the nylon slip the saleslady provided made me shivery and shy. I bought it on the spot because of that, because of the way it felt going on.

The old lady gave me a malevolent look and went back to her gumming.

Then, as if she'd been popped straight out of a child's musical windup toy, Lanie burst in. "Hi, you guys!" she gushed, and the girls jumped right up and surrounded her. In their pastel dresses, they looked like flowers dancing on thin white stems. Lanie wore a tailored suit, cream-colored, with a cream lace camisole. Gardenias with deep green wet-looking leaves nested on her shoulder. I'd have bet my last dime that she bought them herself.

"Hi, Bron," she said, giving me a little four-finger wave as she headed for the kitchen. "Angela!" I heard her cry. "This is so wonderful! I'm so excited." The girls in pastel smiled at each other with the smug satisfaction of having done wonderful things. Gifts waited in a pile on the floor. There were tiny pastel mints in a dish on the coffee table. There were mixed nuts. I ate three cashews, then pulled my hands back and anchored them again in my lap as if they were naughty children with minds of their own.

Angela served fruit punch in tiny paper cups. Everything had umbrellas on it. Then she said we'd play a game. She went around the circle ripping sheets off a game pad and handing them to us along with tiny pencils, the kind with no eraser. "It's a scramble game," she explained.

I looked at the list of scrambled words and unscrambled three on the spot. They were all words having to do with love and marriage: *nrig, rmray, gnaegtmene.* We all set ourselves to the game as if something important might be revealed in the right combination of words, the key to a successful married life, foolproof ways to hold a man forever. I finished the list and was about to call out when I looked around at the others. They were bent over the words with their little pencils, working away, their faces screwed up in grim concentration. "This is hard," Lanie said with a little laugh. "But I'm not supposed to win anyway, am I?"

The winner got a box of stationery. "Oooo, neat . . ." she said.

"Time to open presents," Angela announced. She knew the order of these things, having had three older sisters and a half-dozen cousins for whom showers had to be given. Lanie slipped to the floor, tucking her silky legs and size five pumps under her. "Oh, you guys . . ." she gushed. "I don't know where to start."

"Here," Angela said, handing me a paper plate with a slit in the middle. "Pull the ribbons through. Like a bouquet."

Cindy, who'd plumped down next to me on the couch, said, "Here, I love to do this," and snatched the plate from my hand.

"Don't break the ribbon! Don't break any ribbons!" Saundra cried. You'd have a child for every ribbon you broke, that was the rule.

"Oh, God, no!" Lanie blushed. "No kids for us. Not till after Jimbo gets a steady job. No way!" She carefully slid a yellow ribbon from the large box on her lap. "Oh!"

she cried, lifting out an electric blanket. It was beige and came in its own plastic storage bag. "This is just great! It gets so cold around here sometimes." Did they even have a bed? Where were they going to live? with the Callahans? And what did Jimbo's parents think about all this anyway? Surely they weren't happy about it. Surely Mrs. Callahan had been invited and chose not to come. Neither mother was present, a real faux pas. I don't suppose Lanie's mother could have gotten out the trailer door, and it was just as well.

Cindy drew the yellow ribbon through a slit in the paper plate, leaving the bow to bob on the top like an Easter hat. The next gift was from the Callahans. I knew it would be good, no matter what they thought about Jimbo and Lanie's decision. They were that kind of people. Lanie's face lit up as she lifted a silver tray from the box and laid it on her lap. "Oooo . . . oooo," everybody said at once. But Lanie just kept gazing at it as if it had been delivered to the wrong address and might get snatched away. Her reflection in it wobbled, as if she were peering through rain.

My gift was next, the toaster. "Thanks, Bron!" Lanie said as if there'd been no bad blood between us. My heart melted. I loved her so much. Cindy pulled my pink ribbon through the plate and I felt like one of the gang.

The cake was a great success. It was in the shape of a volcano with yellow and white flowers dripping down from a center cone like lava. Angela's mother had made it. Everybody exclaimed at once that she would make all their cakes from now on, for every occasion. I sneaked a second slice and thought about a third. There were only so many ways you could keep your true feelings down: Drinking was one, eating another.

"Smokers outside!" Angela declared, and headed for the backyard. Lanie followed.

"Too bad there's not a wedding." Cindy sighed. "Spring weddings are so . . . I don't know . . . springy! Don't you think?"

"Definitely," I said. "Definitely springy." I went out the back door.

"Bron . . ." Angela said. Their faces had the cagey look that faces get when the subject under discussion walks into the conversation. Angela looked from Lanie to me and back to Lanie. "Gotta brew some coffee," she said in mock horror. "I almost forgot."

It was a soft night in a miniature orchard, all the trees covered with blossoms like tiny white stars. Their fragrance was thick and sweet and made you unaccountably sad. "I'm such a jerk, Lanie."

Lanie blew some smoke into the sky, her lower lip out the way only she did it. The sky was stuck somewhere between banker's gray and navy blue, with wisps of cloud hanging low beneath a scattershot of stars.

"I didn't want Jimbo to get hurt. That wasn't what I wanted." What I wanted was to show him up. She knew that. But was she supposed to understand it?

"I know," she said. A shriek of laughter from inside. A fat gray cat brushed my leg and moved off into the night.

"Are you happy?" I said. "I mean, dumb question, but is this what you really want?"

"To marry Jimbo? You bet." In that tailored suit, she could have passed for nineteen or twenty easy. Her makeup was so perfect. She had this way of looking and acting older than she was, but it was just that, an act.

"What about Arkansas?"

"Huh? Oh, that ..." She chuckled a little uneasily. "Don't tell anybody, okay? but Jimbo's gonna get a job in Texas, with his uncle, on the rigs. As soon as he hears, we're leaving."

My heart dropped. I'd been working on getting used to a certain kind of loss, but not a permanent one. Texas. Oil rigs. Lanie in a checkered apron living in a trailer, one kid on her hip, another on the way. "You're dropping out? You're not finishing school?"

She passed me her cigarette, brushing at a bit of ash that clung to her lapel. "Oh, I'll finish . . . sometime." Then, in response to what she saw in my eyes: "Oh, come on, Bron. You know me and school. There isn't one test I didn't cheat on. You know that. You're the one who lets me. I'm not exactly an Einstein." She laughed and I could see that it didn't really matter to her how smart she was. Long before, she'd settled for someone else's low appraisal of her intelligence. That's what schools were for, to pound you early into some predetermined slot and keep you there, no matter what you might show later. And yet Lanie was the one who figured out who owed how much for the bag of tacos and Cokes. She did it in her head, fast, and was rarely a penny off. She was the only girl we knew who could read a map or figure out how to piece together a dress pattern.

"And what happens when he gets mad again? What happens then?" I sucked smoke deep into my lungs and blew it out in three perfectly round rings that wavered for a minute in the still air and, in a blink, disappeared. I tasted Lanie's lipstick on the filter. Looking out into the dark yard, I found myself wishing we were little girls, that we'd been little girls together and that we never grew up. This was a yard to run and squeal in, racing around the blossomed

(178)

maypoles of trees, carefree and silly. I passed back her cigarette.

"That's not going to happen," Lanie said. "He promised. He actually put his hand on his mother's Bible when he said it." I nearly choked. Jimbo with his hand on the Bible was like a pervert with his hand up a woman's dress.

"So, can we spend some time together? Before you go? We could shop for stuff you need, or something. . . ." I shrugged.

"Of course, silly," she said. She turned and put her arms around me then, not in the way that ladies do after church, their rears stuck out behind like gawky flamingos. She hugged me very deliberately, chest to chest and belly to belly. She was wearing Shalimar, her hair tickled my ear, and she was very light and fragile, like a jumble of hangers wired together. I hugged her back for all I was worth. Then, with her hands on my shoulders, she leaned back and said, "You be careful, hear?"

I nodded, tears on the rims of my eyelids. "You, too."

18

*T*HAT NICE BOY came by again," my mother said, whipping up a bowl of egg whites. Beside her on the worktable were six filled and six unfilled piecrusts. Every day but Tuesday she made at least a dozen pies, rolling and crimping and braiding, one after another. Her hands had a life of their own now. She only had to check in on them once in a while to make sure they were doing what they were supposed to. The rest of the time her face wore a dreamy faraway expression. You had to say things twice to get her attention.

Mitra cut lemons in half and squeezed the juice by hand, humming something tuneless and eerie. She was smiling, but just to herself, as if the memory of something ephemeral and sweet had crossed her mind.

"Which one?" I said. Like my only dilemma in life was to choose between all the nice boys who came by to "court," as my grandmother would have said.

"You know perfectly well what nice boy. The one

with the gun," my mother said without a trace of irony. "William."

"Aghhh," Mitra said. "Cwillam! Yah. . . ." She rolled and fluttered her eyes, wriggled her skinny backside. Even in my blackest moods, she could make me laugh.

So maybe Will's family didn't read the local papers. Maybe they read only the *L.A. Times* or *The Christian Science Monitor*. "What did he want?"

My mother dusted sugar into the meringue and tasted it with her finger. "What do you mean, what did he want? He wanted to talk to you. I told him you'd call."

"Gee, thanks," I said sarcastically. But sarcasm went right over my mother's head, like a dirty joke or the news that her daughter was a drag racer.

"You're welcome," she said, dumping little heaps of meringue onto the translucent yellow filling of three pies.

I drove out of town without thinking much about where I was going, tracing the familiar road toward Topa Ridge. Everything was blooming, shooting yellow out of the dry soil or climbing over rock in a profusion of flame-colored petals. You had to wonder how. The last rain had been months before, and yet there was all this that shouldn't be but somehow was. The air was dry and warm, blowing tangles in my hair.

I'd see how *he* liked it, somebody showing up on *his* front porch in the middle of the day. If I'd really known where I was going, I'd've brought some poems, Ogden Nash, a book of limericks. To keep things light.

It wasn't exactly as if I hadn't thought about Will. I had. More than I cared to, more than I'd intended. Something about him stuck, but I had no idea what it was. All I knew was that around him things got more real, had keener outlines, mattered in a way they normally didn't.

Probably that wasn't good. Probably that demanded something of me that I wasn't used to giving. It wasn't just fun with him.

I stopped the car at the gate, hopped out, and lifted the latch. A stiff breeze blew here, as if this were a different country, and I pushed the gate hard against it. In the distance two horses raced across the field, tails whipping high. Oak leaves in tiny curled fists fell in a dry rain. I drove through and pushed the gate back where it was.

I'd tell him I happened to be in the neighborhood. He'd get a kick out of that.

But what about his mother? "No thank you, Mrs. Harding. I no longer take tea. Bladder problems, you know. . . ."

But there was no one home and so I needn't have worried. Then I saw the open barn. I parked and walked over. Inside, the barn was dark and cool. It smelled musty and ripe, a composite of wet straw and leather and animal hair. "Hello, Millicent," I said, but it was clear she had forgotten me. In the distance was the rhythmic slide and alternating silence of a shovel on concrete. "Will?"

A face wider than Will's but with the same serious cast poked up over the top of a stall. "Oh!" I said, surprised. "Is Will around?"

"Hey! Bron!" Will came out from the adjoining section, slapping the dirt off his hands. When he was excited everything moved at once, eyebrows, elbows. His Adam's apple rode an elevator up and down his throat. There were these ways in which he reminded me of Buddy, but other times he seemed very old and wise and to know more than a boy his age should know.

"Hey, Dave, come on out here and meet Bron."

David Harding strode out, leaning his shovel against

the wall. He had a scowl on his face that looked permanent. He wiped his hand on his shirt and offered his hand. "Nice to meet you," he said, which I found pretty hard to believe.

"Same here," I said. Dave turned and went back to his shoveling.

"You're a real mess," I said to Will. There was a swipe of dirt across his nose and forehead where he'd brushed something away. Horseflies buzzed over our heads in formation. "My mother said you came by."

"Yeah ..." Will slapped his hat against his thighs to shake the wet straw off. "So. You came to help me muck? Or shall we get Mother to make us some tea?"

"You're not serious."

"Naw ... she's not even here. She's been gone for a week. It's her twentieth college reunion."

"Let me guess. Vassar."

"Smith," he said. "Close. Come on inside while I wash up."

I followed him into the house. "Let me see the soles of your shoes."

"Huh?"

"The soles. Let me see them."

I turned my right foot over. "I wiped them on the mat," I said.

"You can hike in those," he said.

"Oh, yeah, well ..."

"I promised I'd take you to Hurricane Deck, my first favorite place."

"You didn't say I'd have to walk there."

He stopped with his hand on the door handle. His height always took me by surprise, as if he added inches on the days I didn't see him. His brown eyes sparkled. "Got something against walking?"

"Nope. I like to walk. I do it all the time. Maybe you didn't notice."

We stepped into the living room I'd fallen so hard for. The Steinway gleamed as if it had just been polished. "Go ahead and play if you want," he said. "I won't be long."

But I didn't want to play, didn't want to open all that up again. I'd done the one piece just to show off. It didn't mean anything. All that was over now. While he washed up, I studied the family photographs framed and hung along one wall. Will looked enough like his father to break a mother's heart.

We climbed a trail that rose in quick increments from the flat of the ranch land. It was narrow and littered with bits of broken rock. Will kicked some aside as we passed. I listened to the bump, bump, bump of it on its way down. Will's long legs took the climb in stride, but I was out of shape, if I'd ever been in, and I had to hurry along to keep up. Soon I was breathing hard but shallowly so as not to give myself away. "Redtails," Will said. We stopped to watch a pair of hawks float, air caught in a hollow of wing. Then one dropped, so fast my eyes couldn't follow. Then up it came with a snake wriggling in its beak. "A good omen," Will said.

"Oh, no," I muttered. "Not you, too."

"What?"

"Nothing." But he waited. "Just this thing my mother does. Like that. Omens and stuff."

"Well, the Chumash believed in this one. They knew what they were talking about."

We stopped to drink from a spring that trickled down over rock and moss. The water was cold and tasted like dirt, but good dirt. I splashed some on the back of my neck. It was hard to settle into the quiet. Except for the trickle of the water and once the quick scurry of something in the bushes, there was no sound. I didn't know silence. It made me uncomfortable. It made me fidget and search for things to fill it up with. "You come up here often?"

"Uh-huh."

And then we were climbing again, straight into the sun. The plants we passed were spiny and brittle, the kind that could survive on a dead planet. I wondered how high we were and how far we had to go. I wanted to give up and turn back. Pieces of sharp rock bit at my soles through the rubber of my tennies. I'd begun to sweat and my calves ached. Will clomped ahead like a packhorse, holster slap-slapping his thigh.

And then we were on level ground, or almost level, level with the clouds if there'd been any. I stopped and caught my breath. Not only because I'd lost it climbing but because of what we'd come to, what seemed to me the top of the world, a world so wide and deep I had to take it in like a thousand-piece jigsaw puzzle, a little at a time. They say a newly sighted person has to learn to see, that it doesn't come all at once, like you'd think, but in pieces the way I saw the world from Hurricane Deck that day, just shapes and colors. It was furry at first, green and gray, ridges and folds slapped over top of each other, spilling in every direction straight down. It cut you to size. And yet it was so beautiful you didn't know how to breathe it all in, how to be in it.

Will sat near the edge on a jutted-out rock, watching me. It made me uncomfortable, him watching me, but I didn't know what to do about it. What was he thinking when he looked at me that way?

I searched for something familiar in the distance, some-thing to anchor on. Ojala was a tiny cluster of tiny buildings in the gray distance, a fist in the pocket, an error in judgment. Who had staked the first claim to such a place, and why? Whoever it was must have seen the ring of mountains around him as protection. He must have felt secure there, and so he stayed. It was different for me. I'd had no choice. The mountains were barriers holding me back from a real life somewhere else, keeping out all the good things, whatever they might be. Somewhere in that settlement was my parents' restaurant, a made-over house, an embarrassment with tentacles firmly attached to my heart.

I was restless, jumpy, hollow inside like I might be hungry, but it wasn't that, it wasn't food I wanted. I couldn't just sit there like Will did, but finally I sat, hands in my pockets so that I couldn't chew on my fingers. He could go so long without words. "I suppose you saw the papers," I said to get it over with.

A puff of warm dry air blew a part into his dark hair and he squinted against the sun. His hands were in his pockets, too, but they seemed easy there, not ready to jump out and head for his mouth. He seemed easy all over. "Yup."

"Well?" I gave him what Lanie called my snotty stare. "What did you think?"

What started as a smile turned into a frown, as if he didn't know what he was going to say at first, which card to play. "I thought, now that's a strange thing to do. . . ."

"For a girl."

"No . . . for *any*body. But then it isn't something I'd do, so it's a little hard for me to understand."

"What did your mother say?"

"She was gone. I didn't save the paper. She'd have found it hard to understand, too, I guess."

"I guess." I scratched a circle in the dirt with a stick. Then I made a sun out of it, with spokes all around, a grade school sun.

He slid off the rock and plunked down next to me. He smelled like the barn, but it was a smell I was already accustomed to. He took my hand and turned it over, like an astrologer, except that the palms of his hands were like leather. Then he smiled and laid my hand back down. I wanted to say, What's that for? But what would he have said?

"So why did you do it? Why did you race that guy?"

"Jimbo? Oh, Jimbo . . ." I said, as if that explained. But I didn't want to think about Jimbo and Lanie. When they got back from Vegas, Jimbo tied cans to the bumper of the pickup and kept them on for a week. Lanie looked different to me, but I couldn't put a finger on why. I guess she just looked like a wife. "What do you do when you come up here?" I said.

"Think," he said. "Sort things out. . . ."

"Does it work?"

"What do you mean?"

"Do you get things sorted out?"

I watched his eyes trying to read mine. On his long nose were tiny beads of sweat. His face was close. His eyes went from my eyes to my lips. Something inside me jumped. "More or less," he said, and then he looked out into the gray distance, as if that were where he found all his answers.

He began to talk about his father, easily and as if we'd already started this conversation somewhere else. I knew without his saying that he'd inherited the burden of the eldest son, that he'd have to set the examples. Between Will and his mother there was an almost easy give-and-take, but there were expectations, too. "Your mother said you had obligations," I said.

"Oh," he said with a little shrug. "I suppose she meant West Point. My father went there, and his father."

"And now you."

"And now me," he said with a little grin.

"Do you want to go?"

He didn't answer fast, and so I wondered. "I never thought much about whether or not I wanted to go," he said. "It's always been just one of those things in the future. If I don't like it, I guess I'll come back home." I didn't think it would be that easy. "So what are you going to do when you graduate? Race stock cars?"

"Very funny."

"No, really. Are you going away to college? Are you going back East?"

"Not without a scholarship," I said. "Probably I'll just stay around here. Go to the CC." That's where the kids with no direction went, the ones who wanted high school to last forever.

"There's a music academy in Santa Barbara," he said. "A good one. You should go there, Bron."

"Sure," I said. Sure. We could barter my mother's pies for tuition. There were sounds everywhere that I hadn't heard before. Little clicks and skitters, the wind through dry brush. A fat lizard darted past my hand and stopped to look back over its shoulder, absolutely still as if listening to the tune of its own heart.

"I'll be leaving in a couple of months," Will said.

"In the summer?"

"Yup. Summer school. I can get a head start." He released a deep breath and said, "But, until then, can I see you?"

"You're seeing me," I said, my heart starting to tick like the wings of a moth trapped in a tin can. He didn't smile. He even looked a little sad. Then our faces were moving at the same time in that little dance that faces do before a kiss, one going one way, one going the other, as if a plan's been made beforehand. His lips seemed to know just what lips were supposed to do, which surprised me for a second. Mine sure did, but then I'd done a lot of kissing. I guessed that maybe he had, too. Our tongues touched. Everything was warm, our hands, the air, his arms as they came around. After what seemed a long time we pulled back, slowly, as if underwater, out of breath. Will threw his head back and began to laugh.

"What's so funny?" I said. Did I kiss like a virgin after all? Could he tell just like that? But then he'd already seen the way I walked and so he must have known.

"Nothing's funny," he said. And then he said, muffled through my fingers that he held against his lips, "I'm just happy." How could a boy's eyes be old and sort of sad and still be dancing?

"Wanna come to my prom?" I said, just as easily as if I'd practiced. But until that very minute I hadn't thought about asking Will. Lanie'd been pushing me to ask somebody. She wanted to double, she said. She'd find somebody for me if I didn't. "I mean, if you want to," I said to Will, who was more than willing, I could tell. "But you can't bring that gun."

As if in answer, Will slid the gun from the holster and, with an arm straight as a fence, aimed it high at something in the distance. The silver of the barrel dazzled in the sunlight and held your eyes, as if you were a rabbit caught for a moment in the headlights of a car. And then he pulled the trigger. Crack, crack, crack went the sound of it, skipping half a dozen times across the tops of mountains. He holstered the gun with his eyes still fixed on the distance, as if he could see the bullets going on and on.

"What was that for?" I said when all the little unseen things that lived in the world around us started up again. "Why did you do that?"

He came back from wherever he was, slowly, even reluctantly. Then he smiled and was himself again.

"Why do you shoot at things?" My heart was still hammering.

"I don't shoot at things," he said quietly. His face had closed down, like a bank after hours.

I got up and dusted off my seat. "Then what's the gun for, Will? Indian raids? I was just beginning to like this place, too." I turned away and he caught my shoulder.

"Hey," he said. "Bron. I'm—*damn!*" He looked at the sky. His Adam's apple bobbed. He looked down and met my eyes. There was stubbornness there I hadn't seen before or maybe a little resentment. "I don't know why I did that. Showing off, I don't know. . . . I'm sorry. I won't do it again. I didn't mean to scare you."

"You didn't scare me," I said automatically. Of course I'd been scared. I'd felt like scurrying off into the bushes like something hunted. "I'm just not used to guns."

"I'll teach you to shoot," he said.

"Why?"

"You don't want to know how?"

"Sure, I guess. . . ."

Going down the trail wasn't much easier than going up. You had to watch your feet or you'd stumble on the scattered rock, and all around that incredible view. It made you want to fly or just fall forward into it and to hell with where you landed.

Will set a line of Coors cans along a fence out behind the barn where the pasture land began. "You drink all these?" I asked. David banged out of the barn and into the house without a glance in our direction.

"Nope. I don't like beer, do you? Timmy gets a nickel for every one he can scrounge for me. I owe him about ten bucks. Hey, Tim," he called, and a kid about Buddy's age came out of the barn. "Come meet Bron."

Tim was a miniature Will, right down to the boots. The same dark hair and long nose. The only difference was the glasses, thick lenses behind which a child's brown eyes were wide and owlish. All the Hardings seemed cut from the same mold. I thought that was probably the way it was in all the old aristocratic families. Tim came at me with his hand stuck out. "Pleased to meet'cha," he said. And then he was just a little boy again, jumping all over Will, begging to shoot.

"What's Dave up to?" Will asked him.

"I dunno. . . ."

"You're supposed to be helping him with the fence, right?"

"Well, sorta. . . ."

"Sorta." Will gave Tim the kind of don't-bullshit-me look I used on Buddy and Frieda used on me.

"Aw, c'mon, Will. You said you'd teach me." The glasses were heavy. There were streaks of dirt on the sides of his nose from where he'd had to push the glasses into place.

"And I will. Only today you're learning fences. Get!" Will gave his brother a kick in the jeans, more a push than

(191)

a kick, with the side of his boot, and Tim took off, scuffing dirt clouds ahead of him.

There wasn't much to the lessons once you got to them, but the safety part went on for a while. Will was very serious during this part. He sounded like his father must have sounded or as if he were reading from a book. The gun was heavier than I expected. The grip was warm from Will's hand. Will stood behind me, his right arm extended along mine, his breath tickling the edge of my ear. I sighted down the barrel, matching the little pointed thing at the end to the *OO*'s in one of the Coors cans. "You don't just pull the trigger," Will said. "You squeeze it, okay? That way the barrel won't jump. Okay, ready?"

I squeezed the trigger, the barrel jumped. The can stayed where it was. There was an acrid metallic smell to the air, not exactly unpleasant. Like some of the plants we'd passed on the way up the mountain, the anise and sage that Will had pointed out. They took some getting used to, but once you knew what they were, it was like you'd always known them.

I sighted again just under the *OO*'s, squeezed the trigger, and the can disappeared. Then I was hooked. I shot cans until my arm dropped under the weight of the gun. "Dale" Will called me, for Dale Evans, but he made me set up my own cans and load the gun myself.

We kissed again when I'd gotten behind the wheel and started Silver up. I guess we kissed because his face was just there in the window, like the moon. I tried to remember who else kissed so easy, who matched me so well, but then I couldn't think, just taste.

We bumped off down the dirt road, Silver and I. Wind swirled leaves across Silver's hood and my mind swirled with them. Will hadn't said yes to the prom, but I knew he'd come. I knew he'd do things to make me happy, it was as simple as that. We all knew things about boys and this was one of them: Either they were put on the earth to make you miserable or they tumbled along at your side like easy water. There wasn't much in between. Will was easy water. Or so I thought until I got to know him better. He didn't run on the surface and there were things about him I might never know, but he didn't play the games that kept a girl guessing either, hopping from one foot to another like a firewalker.

And then I was sorry I'd let him kiss me, though it really wasn't like that, like letting him. I'd wanted that first kiss just as much as he did, the second one, too. But some people made a whole lot out of a kiss and I figured Will would be one of them. Like my mother said, he was a nice boy. For me, what was a kiss? Sure, his were good. In fact, I couldn't stop thinking about it, the way his lips were softer than they looked and so *there*. I never did want to pull away, not really.

But now what did he think? That I was his girl? And isn't that what everybody would think once they saw us at the prom? By the time I was headed down Ojala Avenue, back to the arcades, the dusty shops, the Frostee, I was miserable and as split from the world I'd just left as if I'd never gone in the first place, as if the afternoon had been nothing more than a daydream.

I thought about calling Will, telling him the prom had been canceled, that the gym had flooded out, that I had to work, that I'd been grounded for drag racing. I'd have done that with somebody else but not with Will. With him, it would have to be the truth. They'll call you a shitkicker, I'd have to say. You'd embarrass me. You don't fit. And how could I ever say that?

(193)

Besides, Lanie was thrilled when I said I had a date. We were a team again, the way we were before she became a wife. I wouldn't even have to buy a dress. She had a closet full of them (one of Saundra's closets) from all her contests. She'd do my hair, we'd have a ball.

"But Will isn't . . ." I said. But there was too much he wasn't, in this world anyway, and too much that he was in the other one.

"Isn't what? Is he tall?"

"Yeah . . ."

"Well, what else matters?" she said. I guessed that husbands could be any old height. Or maybe she'd have married Jimbo that much sooner had he been six inches taller. "You can wear heels!"

She got me in the mood, like I was Cinderella now and she the fairy godmother. I tried on a baby blue chiffon first. It was a gorgeous Grace Kelly thing, one-shouldered, with a chiffon trail floating off the back. I slipped it over my head and stared at my blue reflection in the floor-length mirror. With my flat chest and bony shoulders I looked like a Greek goddess after a sex change. Lanie gathered up my hair and held it on top of my head, waggled her own head back and forth, frowning. "Nope," she said. "Not your type." What she didn't know was that there wasn't a type for me. I just wasn't prom material. She was wasting her time.

Then she pulled out a pink net strapless thing sprinkled with silver. I giggled my way into it, but when it was in place, it fit like somebody'd sewed it on. "From my first contest," Lanie mused. "Miss Junior State Fair."

"You were what? About twelve, right?"

"Fourteen," Lanie said.

"Which explains," I said, hitching the top an inch or two where there was supposed to be at least a *little* swelling.

"It's perfect!" Lanie cried, and dived into the closet again for shoes. She handed me a pair of silver sandals that I knew would fit. Cinderella's prince would have had some trouble choosing between us on the basis of shoe size. With the shoes on, I pirouetted a couple of times through the room. "It's the Sandra Dee look," Lanie said. "We'll do your hair like hers, those baby curls. We could even make it blond if you want."

"Shouldn't I stuff something in here?" I said, pulling the bodice out so that Lanie could see what was painfully obvious: no boobs. "Some socks or something?"

Lanie stood back and gave me a serious once-over. "Here, try it," she said, handing me a box of Kleenex. I stuffed a wad in each side. Then the dress looked just the way it was supposed to. I stood sideways to admire my new figure.

"I've got a rabbit fur jacket in here somewhere," Lanie said. "You've gotta wear something over that or you'll freeze."

"Yeah," I said. "I'll freeze my tits off." Then we were howling so hard we had to roll on the bed. It was easy to forget for that little while that Lanie was anybody's wife.

19

F YOU WERE a normal American girl you began looking forward to your Junior Prom about six years
early. That way you'd have all your expectations in
place and ready to be shot down.

I figured even with the floppy pageboy and the chronic
need to finish my homework, I was a fairly normal American
girl. I had certain expectations for my Junior Prom for how
that magical night would unfold. None of them were exactly
spelled out. In fact, they weren't really spelled out at all.
But I knew it was supposed to be the most romantic event
of my life, at least so far.

Thanks to Lanie I had the dress and the right shoes.
That was number one. Probably even more important than
the right date was how you looked going in. But now that
I had that taken care of, I spent all my time worrying about
the way Will would come across. It was never good to
bring an outsider, someone from another school, and Will
was stranger than most. For all I knew, he'd wear the gun

the way he did the night his family came to the Welsh Kitchen. Our principal would step out of the crowd like Wyatt Earp and have Will arrested on the spot. Me, too, for being an accessory. But worse than that would be the embarrassment. I'd spent half my waking hours trying to avoid embarrassment and here I was walking head-on into it.

And all because of a kiss that worked.

Three times I saw J.C. in the week before the prom and thought, What if I'd asked him? It wasn't out of the question. And he'd graduated from Ojala. He was a bigger-than-life alumnus. Each time our cars passed I'd wave, casually as if we'd once closed a mutually profitable business deal, and he'd wave back. The last time, he winked. I was sure of it. I should have *asked* him, I hissed to myself. I should have asked *him*!

Worse than anything, Lanie and Jimbo and Will and I would all have to go in the Jeep. Four couldn't fit in Jimbo's pickup, and when I'd offered Silver, Lanie said no, that you didn't go in the girl's car. It just wasn't done. Besides, she said, the Jeep would be fun. We'd be sitting right out there in our formals for everybody to see. Hers was white chiffon and clung like Saran wrap. I could just see us cruising the Avenue, her doing that little beauty-queen wave.

My mother was full of all the excitement I was supposed to have. She'd been a little let down that she and Daddy wouldn't be buying my first formal dress. "I thought you'd say we couldn't afford it," I said self-righteously. The truth was that I loved borrowing Lanie's clothes. You never knew when a little of her glamour might rub off.

"Well," Mother harrumphed. "Some things you just have to afford." She fluffed the ruffles on the pink formal hanging from a nail in the rafters while we waited for

Lanie. The boys would pick us up together at the restaurant. "Better your folks than mine," Lanie said, and I guessed she was right. I suggested the Frostee. After all, we spent more time there than we did at home. But Lanie wouldn't hear of it. Afterward we'd drop in at the Callahans' for an after-prom party, a grown-up thing, since the Callahans would be hosting it.

"I always thought we'd shop together for your first formal dress," Mother said a little wistfully. "The way mothers and daughters are supposed to. The way you do the first bra, and later the wedding dress. . . ."

"I sent for my first bra from the Sears catalog, remember?"

My mother frowned. "Oh, well. . . ." She looked so tired and sad that I put my arm around her and patted her shoulder, like I was the mom and she the daughter. "If I ever get married, we'll pick out the wedding dress together, okay?"

"If?" my mother said. "*If?*"

"You up there, Bron?" Lanie appeared, hair in rollers, the white dress in a plastic bag. Already made up, her eyes looked dark and mysterious, like a lady spy's, her lips perfectly etched on and brushed with shiny fuchsia. "Hi, Mrs. Lewis! I brought all my makeup, half a ton of it. I know we don't need it all, but what the hey!"

"Well, I'll let you girls carry on," my mother said, sadly but a little hopefully, too, like the kid left out of the hopscotch game. "Call down when you're ready. Your dad wants to see you all dressed up. And of course we'll take pictures." My father had an ancient Brownie that worked about half the time. Usually he cut your feet off or else the top of your head. In the three shoeboxes full of photographs we'd carted across the country, only about half had heads and feet both.

Lanie rolled my hair in about five minutes, pulling the pins from between her teeth and anchoring the whole thing down with a net. Then she set up her portable dryer. I pulled the plastic hood over my head and sat there like an alien on life support until my hair was dry.

"Your mom's just the sweetest thing," Lanie said, tugging the rollers out. My hair sprung out in giant loops. Already I could see it was a disaster in the making, that I should have gone for the bleach after all. Bleach gave your hair some body, at least it did that.

"Uh-huh . . ." I said.

Lanie started in on my makeup. I watched her face while she did it for signs of hopelessness but she just looked like an artist on a mission, serious and purposeful, humming to herself the way she always did when she was fixing hair. At last she stepped back, aimed the Aqua Net, and sprayed me stiff. "Okay," she said, passing me the hand mirror. "Look."

My smile gave me away. I was pretty, magazine pretty. Just what I wanted. My hair had a cotton-candy look to it, fluffed out all over and sprayed in place like a motorcycle helmet. A tornado couldn't have taken the shape out of it. Lanie lifted the pink net dress over my head and when it was in place, I stuffed the Kleenex in. "You'll knock 'im dead," Lanie said.

"Who?"

"Who else? Your date. Will." She slipped into her dress, gave her makeup the once-over, pinching a speck of mascara from one smooth cheek.

We tottered around like ladies at a Sunday afternoon

tea, waiting for Jimbo and Will. If we sat down, we'd muss ourselves. Lanie was so exotic-looking, so grown-up. Beside her, I looked about fourteen.

I didn't have to go to the prom. Nobody could make me go if I decided not to. In fact, maybe I'd just back out while there was time. Faint or something. Break my ankle. Just then I heard the Jeep. It had a miss in the engine every third stroke. I knew the engine as well as I knew Will, better. "Well, he's here," I said, and we teetered down the stairs on our spindly heels.

I'd hoped nobody would be in the dining room but it was about half-full. Heads turned as we came out and Lanie turned on her smile. "Oh," said one woman. "Aren't they gorgeous?" *They*, she said, *they*. So I smiled, too. Stretched my mouth all out the way that Lanie did. I felt like doing pirouettes. I was gorgeous.

Then my father popped out of the kitchen, Mom just behind. In my father's eyes was such a combination of things. He looked almost shy. But then he rose to the occasion. Taking one of Lanie's hands and one of mine, he danced us through the room, stopping at tables to introduce us. "My daughter, Bronwyn Lewis," he said. "And . . . and my other daughter, Lanie Lewis." It didn't seem to matter that he knew only two of the customers by name. He charmed them all.

Meanwhile Will had slipped in. He watched the show from the door, wearing his goofy little grin and a dark suit like an undertaker, but no gun. He kept that grin on the whole time my father waltzed me around, and I pretended I was Lanie, the "adopted" daughter, not the real one.

Then Jimbo arrived, gunning the pickup several times. I heard a bottle drop to the road as he got out. Carrying the corsage Lanie had bought, he looked like an eighth grader on his first date. I had to pinch myself to remember he was a husband.

My father took pictures, hunched over like he had a portrait camera on a tripod instead of our little square Brownie. "One . . . two . . . three!" he said. "Say whissskey!" and the camera wobbled and clicked. Then the boys presented their corsage boxes. Lanie's slipped right onto her wrist, but mine was meant to pin on. Will came at me with the orchids and the hatpin, looking uncertain but determined. He didn't know that if he stabbed me in the boob, I'd never feel it. But Lanie stepped in and saved him, pinning the white orchids to my waist. My father took another picture, the four of us lined up with the sheep posters, the apple-cheeked British children playing tag.

"What a character your father is!" Will laughed, opening the car door the way he'd done it for his mother, with that little sweep back of the professional chauffeur. As elegantly as she did everything else, Lanie stepped into the backseat, Jimbo behind. Gathering my ruffles and sparkly net, I climbed into the front seat. "Yeah, right," I muttered. It wasn't the first time I'd heard my father described as a character.

Will stopped, his hand on the door as if he'd forgotten something. But it was the tone of my voice that stopped him. "He was drunk," I explained. "He's like that all the time."

Will pushed the door and it snapped. We studied each other's faces, his hands on the edge of the door. I thought, What does he know about me? I thought, He's doing that little balance sheet people do when they're just getting to know somebody. He's thinking, *There are things I don't know*. He's thinking, *Not a good family*. He's thinking the way his mother does, the way "proper" people think.

(201)

"You look really different," Will said after a while.

"Gee, thanks," I said. "You look nice, too."

"No, I mean—*damn*, that didn't come out right. I mean, you look beautiful and all that, but really *different*. You know?"

"Let's get this show on the road!" Jimbo bellowed.

"It's okay," I said to Will, who looked like he was going to stand there until he got it right. I pushed the netting down so that I could see out the window. "I'm just getting used to it myself." Will came around and hopped in to start up the Jeep.

As if Will were from another country, Jimbo shouted instructions from the backseat: Turn here. Slow down! Now turn around and go back. . . . Will didn't seem to mind. I could tell he was enjoying himself though I didn't know why exactly, except that it was a beautiful night, warm with a breeze like the touch of a soft hand. We drove slowly down Ojala Avenue, Lanie waving to everybody, Jimbo yelling, "Where's the party? Getting any? Yowza!" from the back. Will reached over and took my hand and suddenly things felt right, like they were supposed to on prom night.

Everybody was out and cruising. Jimbo popped a cap in the back. He must have stowed a six-pack in the Jeep before coming into the restaurant. In a certain kind of way Jimbo was always thinking.

"You'd better keep that down," Will said quietly, but I knew Jimbo heard him.

Then I saw J.C.'s Deuce and the silhouette of two heads, one a girl's, and my heart fell. They passed us, Jimbo yelling, "J.C., my man! Getting any?" J.C. lifting his chin in greeting as he passed. I craned my head to see who the girl was, somebody I knew? Somebody had asked him to the prom!

It had been that easy. He'd *wanted* to go. He'd have probably even gone with me.

"There's J.C.," I said over my shoulder to Lanie, like a Braille interpreter. She couldn't have missed J.C., nobody could, especially with Jimbo yelling out. I said, as if it didn't matter, "Who's he with?"

"That's Saundra," Lanie said. "Didn't you know they were going out?"

"Yeah," Jimbo said. "Me and him's gonna be brothers-in-law! Yowza!"

"Oh, Jimmy," Lanie said. "This is their second date. And she's leaving anyway in a couple of weeks." Saundra was doing a European Tour. It was something you did in the best families before you went off to college.

J.C. and Saundra. J.C. and *Saundra*.

Saundra was a woman, rounded like a woman, slow-talking and wise. Just the way she moved around a room was a source of fascination. It was as if she had no bones or will. She'd drape herself in a chair or lie on a bed like a sultan's woman, all rosy and open. She wore loose-fitting clothes, clothes no one else in Ojala would think to wear or even know about, things imported from Morocco and Pakistan. They were always drooping off one of her shoulders and she'd pretend she didn't know that, just letting them droop there. She had the biggest boobs of anybody. They even swung a little when she moved, like ripe pears.

"I didn't know they were going out," I said in the same voice I'd have used to comment on the weather. What did I care? But Lanie knew. I hadn't told her much, but she knew just the same.

"Oh, they're not *really* going out," she said. "They just

thought it would be fun to hang around with us kids. They're friends, that's all."

"That's what *she* thinks," Jimbo said. "That's the way she gets herself in trouble." Rumor had it that Saundra had had an abortion, not in Mexico but in some private clinic up north. I thought if the story was true, it could account for the sadness in her eyes. Or else they weren't sad at all but only kind of lazy. I didn't know Saundra all that well.

The gym had been transformed. Snow Dreams was the winning theme, even though we were halfway into April. Kids had spent a week getting the room ready, and I had to admit they'd done a good job. With the lights dim, the whole room sparkled like an ice cave. Lanie and I floated in on Jimbo's and Will's arms and claimed a table under a frosted cluster of white balloons.

The band was just setting up. They wore white jackets and black slacks and bow ties. I thought they'd be corny, forties stuff like my folks used to dance to, but the Dusters could play just about anything, all our favorite songs. The top of my head, even with all the hair puffed up, came only to the ridge of Will's right shoulder. I spent a lot of time with my head tilted back, and after about three numbers, it was kind of stuck back permanently.

Will was a smooth dancer, I figured cotillion, which was also what the better families did. You learned the waltz and even the minuet before you could walk practically. He could jitterbug, too. Not like some of the cooler guys, throwing their dates over a hip and then up in the air like Russian acrobats, but we looked pretty good, I figured. Kids I knew would give Will the once-over and he didn't seem at all uncomfortable with that. But I felt like grinding my heel into a couple of insteps.

Call-me-Cynthia Spellman was there, dolled up like a

teenager in pale blue net and silver ballet shoes. So was Wide-Body Betty. Her dress was hospital green satin and the shoes dyed-to-match. Her feet looked like they'd been pumped up and then pushed in. It was the chaperones' job to pry apart the couples that got locked too hard onto each other during the slow numbers, though Cynthia and Betty didn't quite know what to do about married couples like Lanie and Jimbo. They glided around the room glued to each other, their moves perfected over the years since junior high. Will had manners. He danced just close enough to let me know he wanted to be there, just the right distance. Call-me-Cynthia gazed at me soulfully, as if I'd caught the biggest fish. Now and then Will's lips would graze my ear (though getting through all that hair wasn't easy) and I'd look up to see his eyes kind of dreamy.

J.C. and Saundra arrived like visiting royalty. Wide-Body Betty even hustled a couple of nervous sophomores out of a prominent table and waved the royalty in. Couples mostly danced with each other at proms, nobody switched around much, which was fine with me. I'd have rather wrestled Jimbo to the floor than dance with him. But that meant J.C. was off limits, too, and why did I think he'd even notice I was there?

"Time to powder noses," Lanie said when the band took a break. We headed off with dozens of other girls for the girls' room and wedged our way in. Girls shrieked and laughed, hugging each other like they'd been recently rescued from separate desert islands. Lipsticks and combs were whipped out of tiny silver purses, and hairspray hung in the room like low-lying fog.

"Your date is . . . really *tall*!" Cindy said, her eyes wide and startled-looking. "Who is he?" The room got quiet just like *that*, but it might have been my imagination.

"Will Harding," I said. "Upper Ojala." Let her eat that, I said to myself. Upper Ojala meant money, no matter that the Hardings were caretakers. Their blood was as blue as anyone's.

"Ooooo . . ." said Cindy, turning away to bat her eyelashes in the mirror. "Do you like this eyeshadow? It's dark, don't you think?"

"Oooh, no . . . !" chimed a half-dozen voices all at once. Cindy and her reflection smiled as if they'd just been introduced.

With the garters and all the crinolines, peeing was a real chore. I giggled as I perched, balancing on my tiny spike heels, and Lanie said from the next stall, "You okay?"

"I feel like I'm going to lay an egg," I said.

"Don't make me laugh," she said. "Or I'll piss all over my nylons!" And then we started giggling for real and couldn't stop till we came out of our stalls and saw each other's raccoon eyes. "Oh, shit," Lanie said. "Now we'll have to do our eyes all over again!"

When we got back to our table, Jimbo was crouched over like he was having an appendix attack, but he was only pouring booze surreptitiously into a paper cup. Lanie frowned, but the look on her face said, Well, that's Jimbo for you. "Let's blow this joint," Jimbo said. The more he drank, the more he tried to sound like Al Capone.

"Do you mind?" Lanie said to Will and me. "Nobody stays till the end anyway. Only the weird kids."

It was cold enough outside for the rabbit fur jacket. "Looks like something you might have shot, huh?" I whispered to Will.

"Yeah," he whispered back. "Except I don't shoot rabbits."

"Deer?"

"Nope."

"Rattlesnakes?"

"Not if I can help it. Well, sometimes . . ."

"Aha!"

"Aha, what?"

"You *do* shoot living things."

Will rolled his eyes. Before getting into the Jeep, he opened a storage box in the back and took out the holster, strapping it on.

"Well, if it ain't Hopalong Cassidy," Jimbo said. "Look at that, Lanie. We got us a armed guard."

Will buttoned his jacket and slid into the Jeep as if he hadn't heard, which is how you learned to deal with Jimbo. Jimbo had something to say about everything, but none of it was worthwhile.

We drove toward the Callahans', Jimbo barking directions from the back. Already he was tilting a little sideways against Lanie, and his comments had a decidedly nasty edge to them. Lanie ignored him for a while, but finally she couldn't stand it anymore. "Shut up, Jimmy," she said. The slap came out of the blue like a crack of summer thunder. I turned to see Lanie holding the side of her face. "Damn it, Jimmy," she said. "Don't start in. Not tonight."

I didn't realize that Will had stopped the Jeep and that he'd turned in time to see Jimbo rear back and smash into the other side of Lanie's face. Lanie's head snapped to the left. Then Will's gun was in Jimbo's left ear. "Stop," Will said quietly. And everything stopped, even the tree frogs that had been singing along to something going on high above us, and everything was still.

Jimbo froze. Just his eyes slid toward Will. "You crazy

bastard," he said, but there was something like awe in his voice and the air had gone right out of him. Lanie's eyes were wide. She looked from me to Will and back to me.

"Which one of us is crazy is a matter of opinion," Will said, and took the gun out of Jimbo's ear. We all watched the .45 slide back into its holster.

"Jesus H. Christ," Jimbo said. He leaned forward like an anxious dog and barked into Will's ear. "This is none of your goddamned business, you know. This is my friggin' wife. *My* goddamned friggin' wife." I'd never heard him so angry, so frustrated, so embarrassed. That was the worst of it. Nobody got away with embarrassing Jimbo. Like an elephant, he never forgot. It might take him a while, but he'd get even eventually. "Eye for a eye," he'd declare.

"Well, that's her business," Will said. He and Lanie shared a long look, and then Will said, "But what goes on in this car is my business."

"Mr. Six-gun," Jimbo said. "Mr. friggin' Six-gun. You're gonna get yourself in trouble with that thing one of these days if you're not careful."

"If *you're* not careful." Will patted my hand, like we were Ma and Pa Kettle in the movies. Then he started the engine.

Lanie repaired her makeup on the way to the Callahans'. She didn't seem very rattled this time. I thought maybe she was getting used to being slapped around, the way I got used to scrubbing tables. It made me want to cry. I hung on to Will's hand with both of mine and I hung on to my tears.

The Callahans were so gracious. You'd have thought our Junior Prom was the social event of the season. I'd been at the Callahans once or twice, but never at night. At night the front room, designed, it appeared, for important social occasions, seemed larger, more impressive, the marble fire-place grander, the chandelier bigger. Everything glowed. A tiny dark lady in a black waitress uniform and a little white crown served champagne on a silver tray. The glasses were lighter than air, and I knew if I pinged one with my finger-nail, its eerie song would fill the room. The champagne was good, but it evaporated before you could get a good taste of it, and there was the lady right there with another glass.

The dining room table, the one that had been in the family for generations and around which the Callahans *actually sat down to dinner*, was covered with trays of bite-sized sandwiches and things with dollops of cream cheese and olives and pink curls of shrimp. I could picture Lanie at that table, belonging to that table, even though she herself could not.

I introduced Will to Mrs. Callahan and then wondered if I'd done it wrong and should have introduced *her* to *him*.

Mrs. Callahan knew Mrs. Harding from the Women's Auxiliary (of course), so she and Will had things they could talk about, how-was-the-family kinds of things. I tried my best to look charmed and bored in exactly the right combination. That was a Lauren Bacall thing, that look of sulky half-interest. I sipped my champagne, each sip equalizing the social distance between me and the Callahans and Hardings of the world.

And there was J.C. leaning against the mantel, a curved marble affair bedecked with pictures of the family in silver frames and a cut-glass vase of lilies, but J.C. didn't look a bit debonair or even very comfortable. This wasn't his kind of world any more than it was mine. "Hey, racer," he drawled as I walked over.

"Do you go to all the proms?" I said, downing the dregs of my second glass. The silver tray took my empty glass and a full one appeared in my hand. I was getting more comfortable by the sip. "Aren't you guys a little old for Junior Proms?" I felt mean-spirited, like I had to get him back for something, for not waiting until *I* asked him.

"Hey, I graduated in '56. Give me a break!" He'd pulled the knot out of his bow tie, and the ends hung loose down the front of his pleated white shirt. I counted the tiny black buttons that stopped at the cummerbund. Eight. The cummerbund was royal blue and matched Saundra's dress. They'd planned it. They matched. Nothing could have broken my heart more.

"Still hanging out in Santa Maria?" I said. When I got this close to J.C., something went wrong with me. My stomach began muttering strange things to whoever would listen. My heart did alarming flips and stalls. All this kept me from saying the things you should say, the things that Saundra would probably say. I tried to sip my champagne the way you were supposed to, but mostly I seemed to be gulping at it.

"Sure," he said, and shrugged, as if to say all that didn't matter one way or the other to him. "When you gonna race that car of yours? Sticks has been asking after you."

"Really?"

"Naw, just teasing," he said. His eyes kept traveling to my chest, and I kept trying to bring them back. "But, hey," he said as if he'd just gotten the world's greatest idea. "You could beat her in that little car. You're used to that car. Sticks wouldn't have a chance." His look was half-mocking, half-serious, always, and he drove me crazy with it.

"Well, maybe I will," I said.

J.C. gave me an up-and-down look then that seemed to last forever. "Nice stuff," he said.

"Huh?"

(210)

"You heard me."

I wobbled away.

By midnight nearly everyone had left and Mrs. Callahan's polite little yawns began to look a tad less polite. Mr. Callahan was dead asleep in a straight-backed chair, not a hair out of place, not a wrinkle in his dark gray suit. Lanie and Jimbo had gone up to bed. J.C. and Saundra were in the rec room playing pool. Now and then a trill of laughter or the crack of pool balls would filter into the front room. I was about to suggest Will and I join them when Will said, "Thank you for having us, Mrs. Callahan," and stood, extending his hand.

Mrs. Callahan's smile was both gracious and grateful. "Remember me to your mother, dear," she said to Will. The door closed quietly but firmly behind us. Will took the champagne glass from my hand and set it on the porch rail. The sky was full of double stars, each one a little blurred. Looking up, trying to decide which was the real one and which the fake, I missed the first step and came down on my ankle, landing in a heap on the walk. "Oh, hell," I said, "there goes my image."

Will didn't laugh. He didn't smile. He just put out his hand and helped me to my feet. "You okay?" he said. He held the car door like always, but I felt a little tarnished just the same.

My head fell against his shoulder and we were bumping along a road somewhere in space, and I didn't care much about where we were going, only that we were going somewhere, not stopping to think or to talk, just going. But after a while I felt the Jeep slow almost to a stop, and turn, and then the engine coughed and died. I opened my eyes. Below us like fallen stars were the lights of Ojala. I felt Will's chest under my ear, the quiet rhythm of his heart, the pump

(211)

and swoosh of blood. The cicadas were loud enough to wake the dead and I felt half-dead, my mouth musty, my neck in a cramp from leaning sideways.

"I still can't believe I'm here sometimes," I said. But I was thinking out loud, not really making conversation, and Will seemed to know that. I could feel him listening and I knew if I turned, I'd see that serious profile, the long nose and sharp jaw, and that he'd wait like that, like he'd waited for his family outside the Welsh Kitchen, not expecting anything, for as long as he was needed. But my eyes were pulled toward the lights, as if I'd find my answers there. "I hated this place so much." I kicked off my shoes. I wanted to rake out my curls, climb into my worn-out jeans, be my real self. "I feel like I've been stung by a zillion bees," I said. Across the top of the pink net dress, where cleavage should have been, was an angry red rash.

"Hives," Will pronounced. "Timmy gets them when he has to go to the dentist. I know what we'll do," he said. "Hold on."

He started the Jeep, turned, and charged up the road toward the ranch. The air began to revive me. "Where are we going?"

"You'll see!"

We swerved and began bumping along a narrow dirt road. By the time Will stopped the Jeep we were both covered with dust. "This way," he said. I clambered after him in Lanie's silver sandals, pushing branches aside, extricating net ruffles from brambles carefully so I wouldn't tear the dress. "Great idea," I muttered, but Will charged ahead, full of a little boy's excitement, and I stumbled after him.

The pool was sunk in a pile of smooth rocks that shone silver in the moonlight. Ripples crossed it like schools of silver fish. I'd have jumped in dress and all if it had been my own. I looked at Will. He looked at me. "I'll turn my back and you can get in first," he said.

"I'll tell you when," I said. There was so much to unzip and unsnap and peel off. But finally I was standing as God made me, hugging my skinny chest. I didn't even test the water, just slid in, yelping at the cold. "Okay!" I yelled, but Will slipped in just behind me.

"You cheated," I said, ducking so that my chin just cleared the water. I was goose bumps from where my toenails started, clear up to my hairline.

"I kept my eyes shut," he said, his face solemn as church. And then he grinned and I grinned back and it was okay to be just like that, naked in the cold night water, the goose bumps fading and the water feeling like nothing I'd ever known to be so good. I ducked and felt the water whish away Lanie's cotton-candy hairdo and my own hair coming back, soft and clean.

Will swam toward the far end of the pool, moonlight on his back where the strong long muscles showed through. I couldn't swim but I didn't want him to know that. I was the only teenager, maybe the only person in the state of California, who didn't know how to swim. I figured they'd lock me up for my own safety if they knew. In Jersey the nearest public pool had been a half-day's bus ride away, and once, on a church outing, I'd nearly drowned when a fat girl stepped on me. I was better on skates.

I bobbed around on my tippy-toes, turning circles. "Are there any snakes in here?"

"Nope," Will said from the opposite end of the pool.

"No snakes?"

"Most snakes don't like to swim," he said.

And then Will came up behind and his arms came around my ribs. It felt natural to turn and be against him, our skin cool as fish. And then he was hard like I knew he would be and that was all right, too, because he let that be, like his penis was just another part of him, another part of what we made together in the water. He kissed my neck and licked the water off my chin and then he pushed back through the water, leaving me standing, my body still singing, calling after his.

I ducked and let the water cool my face. My ears drummed. Why had he pulled away? Could I ask? I couldn't ask. You didn't do that. The boy was supposed to push at you until you made him stop. But Will had stopped first. I still felt his penis like a warm ghost against my inner thigh. What would I have done if he'd pushed? I didn't know.

I watched him pull himself up and out of the water, turning all in one smooth motion to sit on the rocks. He held out a hand and, after a minute, I let him pull me out. By now he must have figured that the boobs came with the dress and I was what I was. We sat hip to hip and let the warm air dry us. My mind was on spin. Part of this was so natural and right, as if we were friends, two girls or two guys. But what about sex, what about that? If you were naked, wasn't that the next thing?

Something skittered in the bushes. We both turned. A tiny brown rabbit froze still, then turned and darted back where it came from.

"I really don't kill things if I can help it," Will said. "Except for rattlesnakes . . . well, sometimes you can't help that."

"Why not? What did they ever do to hurt you?"

He shrugged. "Nothing, I guess. Timmy got bit, though. On my watch."

"On your what?"

(214)

"My watch. I was supposed to be keeping an eye on him."

"Oh."

"We were lucky it wasn't a baby that bit him. They're the worst."

"And so now you're going to kill all the snakes in the world, right?"

"Right. It's going to take a while, though." He frowned and made me laugh.

"You're crazy," I said.

"Think so?" It was clear that *he* didn't think he was crazy.

"Tell me about your dad," he said, and I knew he'd been thinking about what I'd said earlier, when we'd left the Welsh Kitchen and my giddy father. Behind us in the valley, a wind kicked up. An owl or a dove, I didn't know which, called out. I wondered where to start, but there was only one place and so I began there. It was an easy thing to tell after all, about running home from the bus stop every day no matter what, clutching my books and lunch box and running fast as I knew how because if I got there in time, my father would be alive, I'd have stopped him in time, and we could go on again with our lives as if that awful thing had never happened. I even told him about being embarrassed that my father would do such a thing, though I hadn't known until that moment, as the water trickled from my wet hair down my back, how important that was. That the embarrassment was equal in measure to my fear and even to the grief I would have felt had he died. Testing that was like touching a sore tooth. The more I talked, the less I liked myself and the worse I felt for my father.

Will put his arm around me and laid his cheek on top of my head. "Poor kid," he said.

"I'm not a kid," I said.

"Not anymore," he said. "Nope, not anymore."

And then I started to cry and couldn't stop. Even when the tears stopped, my ribs kept trying to cough them up. Will just tightened his hold a little and hung on while I coughed away in the cave of his arm. After a while, a forever while, I was through. I dropped my forehead to my knees, exhausted. "I'll get a blanket," Will said.

He came back in his suit pants, pulled me up, and wrapped me in the blanket. It smelled like Millicent. "Better?"

"Yeah," I said. The moon balanced on Will's left shoulder like a huge half lemon. Against the sky, his face was dark, his eyes half-closed as if he, too, had come back from some faraway place. "I'm sorry," I said. "I guess I had too much champagne."

"You guess?"

"Yeah, I guess. Well, I had three glasses. Big deal." I turned away. He'd look you in the eye all the time if you let him. You had to be honest all the time.

"I shouldn't have asked you about your father," he said. "It's my fault. Come here. Please," he said in a quieter voice. "Don't turn away. I can't stand it when you do that."

I turned, but only because I was surprised. "When I do what?"

"When you act like I'm not here."

"I do that?"

"Sometimes. Come here." I went into his arms and something dropped into place, settled, like a plumb bob or a spinning top homing onto center.

"I never cried about all that before. I guess I was saving it up."

"How come?"

"I don't know. I thought I had to, you know, tough it out."

"Like the cars," he said.

"Huh? Oh, racing. . . . No, that's different."

"Hmmm!" he said, and I looked up to see his eyes laughing, and just like that we were apart. How could he know about anything, I thought. He was just a kid like the rest of us. And, besides, he lived a sheltered life, a life of privilege. He could ride a horse, sure, but his Jeep was falling apart and he didn't even know it. I stomped back through the bushes to the Jeep and climbed in, wrapped in my horse blanket like an angry squaw.

He woke me in front of the Welsh Kitchen and insisted on walking me to the door, me in the blanket, dragging the pink net behind like a dead ballerina.

"Thank you," he said at the door, ducking his head a little as if he were embarrassed, his old shy self.

"Oh, yeah, right. You had a great time. Come on, Will. . . ."

"No, I mean it," he said. "Up there," he said, nodding his head back toward the mountains. "I felt like, I don't know, like you were trusting me with, well, with your life. Is that nuts? I mean, what you told me. I know it wasn't easy and . . ." He looked anguished with trying to spell out exactly what he was feeling. I couldn't help. I was just beginning to understand things. "And I feel . . . grateful, I guess. Honored or something, you know?"

"Sure," I said. "I guess. . . ."

"Well, good-night," he said, and leaned down to kiss

me lightly on the lips, just as if we'd come straight from the prom, prim and proper from the prom.

I hugged him around the neck, pulling his head down, clutching the blanket to my chest with my other arm. "Thank *you*," I said.

I lay in bed looking out my moon window, trying to put into perspective all that I was feeling about being with Will.

It had been my first time. In a funny way that I hadn't at all intended, it had been my first time. Not to have sex, which I'd always thought might be the end-all and be-all of anyone's real life, but to cry, mourn about what had happened that night years before, when I was thirteen and still a child.

My mother called out in her dreams, "Side of fries!" For a moment the room was quiet. Then the rumbling train of my father's snoring began again. I fell asleep to the rhythm of it, easy as that.

20

I EXPECTED WILL to call the next day and the day after that, but he didn't. He should have. If he thought I was so special he'd have called every day. That's how you knew you were going with somebody. You got joined by telephone wires. Everybody knew that, even boys from prestigious private schools. I knew he worked hard. He'd told me what an ordinary day was like at the ranch, sunup to sundown. And then there was school. As the eldest son, Will, it seemed, was responsible for everything. As if he were Adelaide Harding's husband, not simply her eldest son. I resented her for riding herd on him, for having the kind of manners and grace one got only by birth. I resented her owning a Steinway she herself couldn't play.

Because Will didn't seem to be able to do it for himself, I resented her for him. How dare she dictate his whole life. But I blamed him, too. Didn't he have the guts to confront her? He was so passive, so unresistant. He seemed to understand everything, forgive everyone. And finally I said to myself, in the way you do when you need an excuse to do something you're not quite sure about, that Will had no will of his own. And so I was free.

J.C. played me on a long line. One moment attentive, electrically tuned in, the next moment he would literally disappear, leaving me breathless and empty as if knocked clean of wind. Always that mocking look, a kind of dare. We'd pass on the Avenue. He'd wink and, after, I'd feel my face burn. "He likes you," Buddy said one Saturday afternoon when I'd taken him cruising. "J.C.'s your boyfriend, J.C.'s your boyfriend," he sang, hoping to rile me up.

"Where did you hear that?"

"What?" Already he'd lost interest, sucking up the last of his malt with slurps that rattled the paper cup.

"That he likes me. You make that up?"

"Can I steer?"

"Only if you tell me the truth. If I find out you're making it up, you'll never drive this car."

"I'm not making it up. Hey, there's Chick!" Buddy climbed half out his window and sat on the ledge to wave.

"Get your ass back in here! Buddy! What do you think you're doing?"

He slid back in. A chocolate malt mustache lined his upper lip.

"So tell me."

"What?"

"Damn it, Buddy. You know what. About J.C."

"Oh, him. Well, he said you were a cool chick."

"He did? He *did*? Who'd he say it to? You heard him?"

"Yeah. So what's the big deal? Can I steer now?"

I let him wriggle into my lap. He could steer as well as anybody. It was the thing he liked to do best in the

(220)

world, and I could get just about anything I wanted by letting him do it. I made him use both hands, though. "So tell me. . . ."

"Well, him and Chick, they were working on the Deuce. J.C. has this new tachometer." "Taco-meter," Buddy said in imitation of J.C. "They were putting it in. Chick said something about Johnny, about how he used to race Silver and beat everybody, and J.C. said, well, you could do that, too, if you wanted to, that you were cool."

"That I was cool? Or that I was a cool chick?"

"What's the difference?"

"Tell me!"

"He said, 'She's a cool chick.' Just like I said." A warm buzz shot straight through me and I smiled right at J.C. the next time he passed, a Monroe smile, with all the teeth. He was chewing his gum. Peppermint gum. I remembered from being in his car at Santa Maria. I could almost smell it. And he smiled back.

"J.C.'s your boyfriend," Buddy sang. "J.C.'s your boyfriend!"

"Shut up," I hissed between closed teeth.

SILVER LET ME DOWN just once. I think she wanted to get J.C. and me together, or maybe she had an eye on the Deuce. All I know for sure is that she stopped dead, stone cold dead, in the middle of an afternoon cruise, right in front of Our Lady of Sorrows, and that I was stranded. I turned her key and pushed her starter again and again, but nothing happened, not a peep out of her.

"C'mon, Silver," I coaxed. "C'mon, girl!" Nothing. Cars detoured around us, no one I knew. I got out and tried to push Silver to the side of the road, but she was too heavy for me and too stubborn. Someone would come along eventually, I thought. I couldn't just leave her there. But the most I got from anybody was a curious stare. "Silver, damn it! What are you doing to me?" I cranked her key again, pushed her starter. I thought I knew her, but I'd just been fooling myself. If I opened her up, I'd see nothing but wires and hoses and parts I couldn't name. I thought, If I can do nothing to cure her, I don't deserve her. Maybe that's what she was telling me.

A priest appeared at Our Lady's narrow iron gate, took a short sharp look at my predicament, and came over, his long black robes kicking out from his ankles. He was young and surprisingly strong for a priest, with twinkling amber eyes. "What a pretty little car!" he exclaimed. "Did you run out of gas?" Together we pushed Silver into the dirt lot across from the church. I was so grateful I almost went down on my knees. I thought about asking him to pray for Silver, but I didn't think, nice as he was, that he'd understand. I watched him kick back through the dust and head toward town. Was this God working in one of His mysterious ways?

I was stranded. The Welsh Kitchen was two blocks up the Avenue, but that wasn't the point. The point was that I'd lost my wheels, my wings, my freedom. I sat on Silver's hood, watching the cars that passed. Sooner or later, I thought, sooner or later.

From a distance you could mistake the Deuce for a hundred other cars, but never up close. I watched J.C. slow down and turn onto the dirt lot, clouds of dust gathering. Here comes the cavalry, I sang to myself, and my heart started knocking that strange rhythm it did whenever J.C. came around. He bumped to a stop inches from my bare knee. "Hey, little one," he said, stretching his right arm back over the seat. "What's happening?" The Deuce rumbled softly, nose to nose with Silver.

"Nothing," I said. "And I mean nothing." I slid from the hood, under J.C.'s eyes, which were quick and appraising. "Silver broke down. She won't turn over."

J.C. cut the engine and got out of his car, a frown deep between his eyes, the frown of a doctor to whom you've reported "just this little lump. . . ." He stepped up to Silver and lifted her hood, stepping past me and leaving something in the air you could almost taste. He reached down into Silver and began pushing and poking at things. How could he always look like he'd stepped straight from the shower? His hair was even a little wet, with comb lines running through it. I wanted to touch his back, just touch it, where his white T-shirt lay stretched and smooth, then disappeared into the waistband of his Levi's.

"Change her oil?" he said.

"Huh?"

He came out and said directly to me, as if I were deaf, "Do you change the oil in this car?"

"Uh, yeah," I said. I did, or Chick did, once.

"How often?"

"Um, I don't know." I shrugged. "Is she out of oil?"

He gave me a disgusted look. "Not out, but the oil is filthy!" he said, showing me Silver's dipstick and the grimy liquid stuck there like mud. I burned with shame. He could have been waving my dirty underpants in public.

"But that's not why she won't start," he said. "Try her again."

I slid in and pushed Silver's starter. She coughed once, discreetly, and started up. My heart did the same.

"Bring her over to my place," J.C. said, still frowning.

(223)

He'd gotten a mechanic's rag from the Deuce to wipe his fingers on.

"Huh?" I never could understand him on the first try.

"I'll change her oil," he said.

I followed the Deuce through Ojala's back streets to a small beige adobe with a chain-link fence and a half-dozen scraggly rosebushes hanging on for what was left of life. I hadn't imagined in all my fantasies that J.C. lived in a real house, much less an ordinary one. He always seemed apart from the rest of us, feeding on air and energy the rest of us had no access to. He hopped out of the Deuce and headed for the garage. I didn't know whether to follow or stay where I was, but when he didn't come straight out I wandered in after him.

The garage was as neat as a chef's kitchen, with tools hung on a long pegboard or laid clean and shining inside the drawers of a tall red metal chest. There was a long workman's bench on which a carburetor had been dismantled. There were parts soaking in a bowl of kerosene. There were folded mechanic's rags, clean as kitchen towels. On the wall over the bench was a Miss Rheingold calendar. April Miss Rheingold was decked in skimpy buckskin. She had one leg lifted so that you could see her matching buckskin boots, but also her inner thigh where the pink panties started. There was a long shelf of different kinds of oil from which J.C. took down three yellow cans. "Always use Pennzoil," he said as if imparting all the wisdom of a lifetime.

I said, "Okay."

He stripped off his T-shirt and put on one that was smudged with grease. He was thin. You could see all his ribs in perfect outline as he stretched into the grease-covered shirt. You had to think of a snake, the way he moved.

The oil got changed in no time, J.C. skinnying in under

Silver, then out again. "How 'bout a beer?" he said, and turned to go into the house. I hung out by the fence until he said, "C'mon in." And so I did.

Inside the adobe the ceiling was so low you felt like ducking. The living room was as neat as the garage, with starched doilies spread on the arms of a green plaid couch and matching chair. Across the walls, men on horseback wearing red coats chased an orange fox. All the lampshades had ruffles like the ones on square dancers' skirts, and on every available surface was a ballerina bending and stretching or up on the points of her toe shoes, arms in a graceful circle and caught in the moment of turning. It was the kind of room that made you forget to breathe.

J.C. came from the kitchen with two perspiring cans of Oly and handed one over to me. "If my ma was here, we'd be drinking out of glasses. Here's to ya!" He lifted the can in a toast and took a long swallow. He didn't look so squeaky-clean now. There was dust on his neck and perspiration under his nose and a streak of grease under one green eye that made you want to reach up and wipe it away. I wanted to ask if his mother was dead or just working. What he said could have meant either one. In any case, it explained the ballerinas and the doilies. I took a swallow of my beer.

"You could have made me change my own oil," I said. "I would have done it." Somewhere a dog began to bark, then another, then a whole pack started up, some with deep throaty barks, one with high-pitched hysterical little yaps. A plane passed overhead. A car horn sounded. Somebody yelled, "Angie, god damn it. Get out here!"

"You want to do everything yourself?" J.C. didn't look at you much, but when he did, you got his whole attention. His eyes would home in, clear and green, and you wouldn't think to look away.

"Most things. Are those your dogs?"

"The pound," he said. "It's right down the street."

"Oh." I wanted to say, "Just the facts, ma'am." That's how much we sounded like *Dragnet*. It was hard to breathe right up next to him and with no one else in the house, just the refrigerator humming and those damned dogs.

"Hungry?"

"Huh?"

"Don't do that," he said.

"What?"

"That."

"Oh. No, I'm not hungry."

"Well, I'm gonna make me a sandwich." He went into the kitchen. I stared at the gray face of the television set. The TV had a place of honor in the living room that TVs usually had. This one was like a shrine, except instead of the Virgin Mary there were all these ballerinas. "Well, I guess I'll go," I said. "Thanks for changing my oil."

J.C. ducked his head out of the kitchen. "My pleasure," he said. "That's two."

"Two what?"

"You owe me two."

I knew better than to ask two what.

I was halfway down the walk when he stuck his face out the door. "Santa Maria on the eighteenth," he said. "Bring the car over here the day before and we'll tune 'er up."

WILL WAS SITTING on the porch steps talking to Frieda when I got home. His legs were so long that his knees nearly knocked into his chin. I guessed there was no lunch business or Frieda would be inside. Inside, sitting at a table-for-two, staring morosely out the window, my father would

(226)

be crying into his coffee cup, and his coffee cup would be laced with Old Crow. My mother would be hanging over him saying all the things she said when life wasn't working the way it was supposed to: "It's just a matter of time . . . it's too soon to worry . . . yes, but remember that we've got our health and that's the main thing!" I didn't want to hear it.

Will stood as I came up the walk. I thought he might stick out his hand. I wanted to ask why he didn't call first, why he never called at all, but I was still full of J.C. and I was thinking forward to Santa Maria and that was all that seemed to matter right then.

"Another slow one." Frieda sighed, letting me know I should be concerned, that there was more to life than running around in my car. All that she could say in a single look. "We did four lunches. Four lunches!" Her eyebrows came up as if to say, "Why, God?" She rattled the change in her apron pocket and went inside.

"You look like you again," Will said.

"Ever go to a drag race?" I said. I knew he'd say no.

"Nope, can't say I have. Why?"

"Just wondered. I'm going to race Silver at Santa Maria on the eighteenth."

"You are? That's great! I'll be your cheering section. I'll wave a flag or whatever they do."

I looked at him like he was crazy. He couldn't go. He couldn't be there. "I, um, go with this bunch of kids . . ." I said, and watched his face close a little.

"Oh," he said. Then he tried to pretend that it didn't really matter that he wasn't being invited. "Will you get a trophy or something?"

"I don't think so. It's the women's race. I don't think they have a trophy for that."

(227)

"Why not?"

I shrugged and dropped to sit on the steps. What did it matter? What mattered was that J.C. thought Silver and I had a chance to beat Sticks, that was all that mattered. More than that was the chance to win J.C. He was the trophy.

Will reached for my hand, but mine was restive inside his, and after a few minutes, on the pretense of scratching my knee, I took it back.

"You've got to see the wildflowers," Will said.

"Oh. . . ." Wildflowers.

"But that's okay, we could go another time. . . ."

My father came out, frowning at Will as if trying to remember who he might be. "Don't ever open a restaurant, young man," he said. "A restaurant is just like a woman. Just when you think you can trust her, off she goes. . . ."

"Daddy!"

"Oh, not your mother. A woman, a not-so-nice woman, that kind." He eased himself down on the steps next to Will. A deep sigh came out of him. "Four lunches," he said. "For crying into a bag!" He shook his head. "I knock myself out trying to please these people. Got the best meat loaf in three counties. The mayor himself told me. But where is he? Where's that SOB when you need a little business?"

"Daddy . . ." I shot him Mother's evil eye to shut him up. Will just nodded his head to whatever my father said, as if he understood how it was to run a failing business.

"Another month like this and we'll be out on the street," my father said. The more he complained, the farther his neck seemed to sink into his shoulders. The sparkle had gone from his eyes and from his hair like a circus that had overnight left town. Only empty ground remained.

My mother ducked her head out and frowned. She closed the door and slid the CLOSED sign into place.

"Have you and Mrs. Lewis seen the wildflowers?" Will asked. Will and his damned wildflowers. "I came down to get Bron so that she could see them while they're at their best. Would you and Mrs. Lewis like to come along? It's really beautiful this time of year."

"They don't have time for—" I started to say.

"You don't say," my father said, perking up. "Well, maybe we'll just do that, young man. Helen!" he bellowed. "Helen!" He leaned toward Will with a conspiratorial look and said, "Before she married me, her name was Helen Frye."

"Daddy!"

"She only married me because she got tired of people saying, 'Go to Helen Frye!' Get it?"

My mother stuck her head out the window. "You don't have to yell, I'm right here."

"We're going with the kids, here," my father announced. "Going off to see the daisies bloomin'!"

I gave Will a poisonous stare. His returning gaze was serene, a smile behind his eyes. He knew he had me. What could I say?

My mother came out smiling. "A ride!" she said. "How lovely!" I knew she was remembering Sunday mornings in New Jersey when a "ride" meant hopping in the car and going who-knew-where, leaving behind cups of unfinished coffee and the comics spread across the floor, she protesting that the dishes needed doing but letting my father pull her along, leaving more than dishes . . . leaving the specter of the night before deflated in the corner sulking, Buddy propped up on pillows in the backseat so that he could see, and me clinging to the back of the seat where my parents sat like two slightly older overly excited children.

WILL HELD THE JEEP door for my mother, and she climbed into the back.

"Are you sure you don't want to sit up front, Mrs. Lewis?" Will was really laying it on now. He was the perfect gentleman without even trying but even worse when he tried.

"She'll sit in back with me," my father said. "And we'll neck, just like old times, huh, lass?" My father got into the Jeep. My mother smiled and laid her head on his shoulder.

I folded my arms and slumped as far down in the front seat as I could get. Neck, my father said, *neck*! I could feel Will's eyes daring mine to meet his. I'd never look at him or speak to him again. Passing the Frostee, he slowed to a crawl. "Look," he said. "There's your friend Chuck." He waved and Chick kind of waved back, not exactly committing himself, squinting into the sun at us as if at a band of Gypsies passing.

"Oh, God . . ." I muttered.

Halfway through town my mother, in her warbling falsetto, began singing "Bye, Bye, Blackbird." My father joined right in. Will's smile only got wider.

We left town and began climbing, my parents having done "Down in the Valley," "On Top of Old Smoky" (Will joining in on the chorus), and "Summertime." It was a beautiful day. I hated it. The sun was shining in a flawless blue sky. The hills were alive and we were making our own corny music. Then my father, in a soft voice, almost as if he were singing to himself, began singing "All through the Night." Nobody could sing that song like he could, not

(230)

even the guy who sang it on the records. "Sleep, my child, and peace attend thee. . . ." I tried to hold out against it, but I never could. My father's tenor wound in around us and even the engine's throb seemed to still, as if it, too, were listening. Tears sprang into my eyes and I looked away from everyone, out into the rough terrain, the tumbled rocks and spindly bushes clinging.

There was quiet after that, as if a line had been drawn. Will took my hand. We climbed into the Topa Topas, winding up through a flood of orange poppies stretched right and left as far as you could see.

21

ORNING CAME a bird at a time, a long trill from the eucalyptus outside my window and an answer from somewhere across the road. Then, as if waiting until that very moment for permission, a dozen birds began yakking all at once and the morning light began to lift like stage lights, just beneath my window-sill. My eyes were itchy and raw, my muscles cramped. All through the night I'd prodded myself again and again out of a deep sleep, knowing I'd have to be up and ready at six, that J.C. would be waiting—waiting for me!—and that I'd better be on time. I couldn't use my alarm. Not even Buddy would know I was going this time. This time, it would be just J.C. and me. Alone. All the miles to Santa Maria and all the miles back.

I rolled off my mattress and into the clothes I'd laid on my chair the night before. Always I seemed to be sneaking somewhere. Otherwise somebody's feelings would be hurt, somebody else would be angry. This time it would be

Buddy's feelings. I'd have to explain it to him somehow, make it up to him. "Better not bring the kid," J.C. had said. So he wanted it to be just the two of us. Buddy would get over it. I sneaked past him with the phantom of my guilt dogging my steps and tiptoed down the stairs. He was such a good kid and never asked for much.

The streets were empty, damp with dew, washed clean and ready for new things, surprises. I drove toward J.C.'s, heart high and singing. J.C.'s house, like all the others, was dormant, still encased in the night. I pulled up against the fence. Should I knock? Should I just wait? I turned off the key and then he came out, pulling on that red satin jacket. His hair gleamed wet. "Slide over," he said. "I'll drive." I did what he said. It didn't occur to me to do anything else. He turned the key and Silver started up. "Sweet," J.C. said. "Sweet, isn't she?" And just like that the sun was up.

I didn't know exactly where to sit. Right next to the door was saying one thing; next to him was saying another. I sat halfway between, perched like an alert squirrel.

J.C. drove Silver like he'd had her all her life, smooth and easy, one hand on the wheel, flipping her through her gears with a nonchalant confidence. Sometimes he'd spin her by her steering knob, something I never did. She seemed to be performing for him, shooting away from stop signs, anticipating turns, and then taking them solid on all four of her wheels. How fast she could give her heart away.

"Too bad Chick and Angela couldn't make it," J.C. said as we left the light and headed up the Maricopa Highway. "Told them they could ride with us, but she's got him out looking at couches or something. Poor son of a bitch. . . ."

"Maybe he wants to look at couches." So J.C. didn't plan for us to be alone after all. He just didn't want Buddy along.

"You're kidding."

"I don't know. . . . Would you want to spend your life on a couch that somebody else picked out?" J.C.'s mother's horrid green plaid couch made you want to leap straight up the minute your bottom touched. "I mean, if it's your own couch—"

"Chick's just whipped," J.C. said. "Angela's got him by the short hairs. First girl he ever laid and he thinks he's gotta marry her. Jesus!"

"Really? First one?"

"Swear to God." J.C. raised his hand as if he were on the witness stand. "Don't tell her I told you, though. She'd kill me."

Silver purred along at seventy-five. When J.C. passed cars in places I never would, I just closed my eyes. The day before, I'd buffed Silver till my arms ached and now the sun shot across her hood in bolts like lightning. J.C.'s satin jacket shone, too, and so did his teeth when he smiled. He offered me a stick of peppermint. We didn't talk much. It didn't matter. Elvis sang "Are You Lonesome Tonight?" I closed my eyes. This is as good as it gets, my heart said. This is it.

We were there almost before I knew it and long before I was ready. We sped across the airport, then the field that led to the track, dust gathered into clouds in our wake. We sped past the hot dog stand and the portable johns. In the distance stretched the green-and-white banner. J.C. pulled right up beside the Delaneys and hopped out. "Got a live one for ya, Sticks," he said.

"Nice little rod," Harv said, giving Silver the once-over. "What's she got?"

"That's for us to know and for you to find out, right, Bron?" J.C. winked and patted Silver's hood. Then Harv and

J.C. dropped deep into engine talk, heads bowed, foreheads furrowed. You had to laugh at the way they looked then, nearly identical, hands deep into pockets, shoulders slumped.

Sticks and I looked each other over without letting on. In her denim shirt with the ripped-out sleeves, her crossed arms were white and thin as bones. On her upper right one was a tattooed *D* with yellow wings. A flying *D*, like a brand. I could pretty much guess what she thought of my white blouse with the Peter Pan collar.

"This your car?" Sticks jutted her chin toward Silver and I nodded. "She as fast as she is pretty?"

"Guess so. J.C. says—"

"What do *you* say? I thought you said it was your car."

"It is. She is. But I've never raced her, I mean not for real. . . ."

Sticks leaned over and pulled a pack of cigarettes from the visor of the green Ford and shook a couple halfway out, offering me one. We lit up. "Well, so we'll do it again, you and me."

"Guess so."

We took a drag of our cigarettes at the same time and watched the smoke commingle in the air. Sticks had little-girl hands. Every finger had a different kind of silver ring on it, the one on her right thumb made out of a nail. We watched the cars drive in. Sometimes Sticks would tell me who was who. Sometimes she'd just jut her chin toward someone and say, "Asshole," or, "That's the numbnut beat my old man."

I'd say, "Uh-huh," or, "Oh." Finally I said, just to say something, "You been racing long?" It was hard to tell how old she was. From the side, she looked no more than nineteen, but when she turned her pale eyes on you, she could have been thirty-five, maybe more.

"Too long," she said, scuffing the toe of her boot over the butt of the cigarette till nothing was left but a shred of white paper. "Too friggin' long. And I'm getting real sick of it, too." She squinted at me as if it could be my fault, even if I didn't know it yet.

"You don't like it anymore?"

She laughed, one short sharp laugh like a punch. "No," she said in a mimic of my voice, only higher. "I don't like it anymore!"

"Then why do you do it?"

"Listen, shit-for-brains, you don't know anything about it. Just mind your own business and I'll mind mine, okay with you?"

"Sure. I just wondered, that's all."

Our hips were inches apart as we leaned on the fender of the Ford, but when we talked it was out into the air. I thought about walking off, in a huff like my mother would say, but I knew somehow that Sticks wasn't really angry. Everything she said was in that same flat tone. "Pisses me off," she said.

I knew better than to ask what.

"Look ..." she said, turning toward me for the first time, her arms crossed, elbow bones jutting. "My old man, he doesn't take it too good when I lose."

"Yeah?"

"And, what I thought was—aw, forget it!" She slumped back against the fender.

"What? Hey, tell me!" She held herself back so much you looked for any opening.

She turned again and this time seemed to be sizing me up in a serious way. "How much do you need to win?" she said.

I shrugged. "Well, sure I want to win—"

"No, I said how much do you *need* to win!" Her pointy chin was cocked, and she looked at me through lidded eyes.

"As much as you do, I guess. Why?"

She looked down at the toe of her boot, shaking her head. "Oh, no you don't."

The men came strolling back, one of Harv's greasy paws on J.C.'s shoulder. He was a head shorter than J.C. but thick through the neck and shoulders. Short and square and bolted to the ground. I thought, He can kill somebody with a single swing of that arm. That was the way it was with men. They had that power. The good ones wouldn't use it, but they had it all the same.

J.C. dropped to his knees and began prying off Silver's hubcaps. "See what's in the trunk, Bron," he said. I knew it was empty, except for the spare tire and the stuff it took to change it. Before I'd washed and polished Silver I'd stuffed two boxes full of things I'd thought were forever lost, library books, Lanie's red sweater, two pairs of shoes, not to mention all the moldy peanut butter sandwiches and apples turned to brown mush. I popped the trunk, hoisted out the tire, and then the jack and tire iron.

"You can race her if you want," I said, but it came out like a kid offering gum with one arm twisted behind her back.

J.C. squinted up at me, then he said, "Just came along for the ride, kid." He *knew*. He knew I wanted to be the first with Silver. My heart spilled over with dumb quiet gratitude. I was learning to read him, to find the way through the dark places, like a miner, to his heart.

We watched some heats, and in between he'd pull me along from car to car. We'd lean into the engines and he'd point things out. For me, all the heat was in being next to him. Crazy things would happen inside my head. I'd want to pull him on like a coat or roll with him inside a rug. I'd wonder about his belly button. Was it an innie or an outie? Did he eat cornflakes for breakfast? Did he kiss his mother? What color was his toothbrush? Did he ever dream about Angela? And was she naked? All this time he's talking amps and cams, piston speed. I was one of the guys. Maybe it was my flat chest. When I leaned over, nothing.

The loudspeaker crackled and a voice with an Okie drawl came over the wires. "Okay, y'all get ready. Delaney's old lady is heating up for a grudge match. The little lady she's runnin' against . . ." A hand covered the microphone and static came over the wire. My heart stopped. "Bonnie Lewis her name is . . . all the way from beautiful downtown Ojala . . . didn't quite let Sticks get away last time but this time, Sticks says, she's gonna wipe the little lady's puss all over the track. That'll be three heats from now, don't miss it." The blood pounded in my face. I didn't dare turn my head to see who might have spotted me, Bonnie Lewis, in the crowd.

"She thinks she's gonna take you, Bron," J.C. goaded.

"Bonnie," I said. "Don't you mean Bonnie?"

He raised astonished eyebrows and I knew he'd set the whole thing up, talked to the announcer. I stomped away, losing myself in the crowd, counting off heats. I kept half expecting Buddy to pop up somewhere. I missed him. There were times when I thought Buddy was the only person in the world who knew who I really was. And then I'd know how dumb that was. How could he know what I didn't?

I set off across the broken asphalt, the adobe like solid rock with weeds somehow poking through. Haze like a layer of soot lay on the horizon. The sun glared orange through it. I felt weightless. How you feel sometimes when you've had too much to drink the night before. Only I'd had nothing to drink and very little sleep. I wanted something. J.C. But I didn't know what I wanted from him, not really. My fantasies always stopped short just where, if he had any for me, they probably began for him. I thought about Will then and how easy it had been to slide against him naked in the water.

A car horn stuck. Someone cursed. The announcer called, "Ladies' Heat, five minutes. . . ." I stalled long enough to make J.C. sweat, then wandered over as if I had nothing further from my mind than hurling a two-ton bomb through space.

"Where the hell have you been?" J.C. dropped Silver's hood and threw his rag to a kid who'd been hanging on his heels. "Part of all this is, you know"—he tapped his forehead—"mental. You gotta psych yourself up. You don't just hop in the damned car and take off!"

"You don't?"

"Get in the damned car," he said. "Now, do you remember everything I told you?"

"Stomp the gas, pop the clutch. What's so hard about that?" I was beginning to see how to rattle J.C.

His eyes darted left and right, his lips were pinched in a tight, white line. His fingers tapped Silver's roof like spiteful rain. "Okay, Miss Smartass, let's see what you can do." He whipped away and disappeared into the crowd.

Alone, I felt the thin veneer of my bravado vanish. I knew just what to expect next. Fear crept up through my legs and settled in the cradle of my stomach. My knees began to knock. *You can do it,* I told myself. *You can do it. You've done it before.* I ticked off J.C.'s advice, all that I could remember. There *was* more to racing than stomping the gas—I just couldn't remember what it was. I searched the crowd for a red satin jacket. Nowhere in sight. Not a familiar face.

Sticks gunned her engine. I turned. Our eyes caught. *How much do you need it?* I gunned Silver's engine, heard her scream, and remembered: None of that kid stuff. *Sorry, girl*, I said, and took her down to a high smooth idle. People crowded in, their interest peaked by the announcement of a grudge match, by two skinny girls who thought they could be men. "Give her hell, Sticks!" someone yelled. Sticks let her engine answer, three quick snarls like a cat in heat, then she settled into the place where I was. *How much do you need it?*

A quarter mile down the track through heat waves that made the letters dance and shimmer was the Castrol banner. When we sailed under that, it would be over. Nothing different from before, except for Silver, and I knew that with her I could win. It would be over in no time. Twelve, thirteen seconds, no more. And then what?

Along the track, behind yellow barricades, were hundreds of people I'd never know. *How much do you need it?* No one cared whether or not I took this race. Maybe not even J.C., wherever he was. If Silver went up in a ball of gasoline and me with her, I'd be something to talk about for a week or so. They'd pull me out of Silver like an overcooked french fry and say, See? I told you women shouldn't race. Sticks would lick her paws, curl herself up for a nap in the sun.

"Ladies and gentlemen, our final heat of the afternoon, the *Ladies'* Heat." Some hoots and scattered applause. "Now, these ladies met once before, pushed the pedal to the metal, and came out even, tail to tail. Today, they tell me, that isn't gonna be the way this race ends. Today we'll get our ladies' champ*een*." More applause from the crowd, a wash of faces and colors. "Are you ready, ladies?" I half expected Sticks to answer, to throw a fist out the window or stomp the gas, but her chin was set, her eyes far away. "Okay, this is it, then! Give her hell! May the best lady win."

The flagman took his place. He pointed the tip of his flag at Sticks. She nodded once, just a jerk of her pointy chin. I did the same when it came my turn. The flag came up, slow, slow, as if through water, and then it came down and we were off the line, Silver against the Delaney Ford, Sticks and Bonnie Lewis. Somehow I knew there'd be no tie this time. Inside Silver, inside me, nothing but engine, no sound but that, filling me up. We had Sticks in low gear by half a fender, but when she shifted into second, the Ford leaped ahead. Down into second, *Go, Silver!* So quick she was, so light. But Sticks came on, her hair flying every which way, as if she'd taken hold of a live wire and been shocked. I watched her hand come up and jam the gearshift into third, and as the Ford ripped ahead, I saw the way Sticks screamed, the cords in her neck stretched taut, her head bent back, a silent cry in the rush and scream of engine, and I watched her pull away. The green Ford sailed under the Castrol banner and then we were under, too, Silver and I. *It's okay, girl,* I said, and patted her dash like you'd pat a horse's mane.

We drove back, Silver humming quiet now. The warm breeze blew cool onto my damp neck. The crowd came apart like marbles sent rolling, and there in the center was the red satin jacket. I idled toward it and cut the engine. J.C. stood where he was for a minute, his fingers pushed into the pockets of his jeans. On his face was a look I couldn't decipher. Then he sauntered on over, leaning in on his crossed arms, ducked to scratch the back of his head, looked up again. People passed on both sides, couples arm in arm, a man with a two-year-old stuck on his shoulders. "So?" Idling back, I'd tried to guess what J.C. would say, or wouldn't say. How I would answer. How I would explain. Close up, his eyes weren't so much green as shades of color blending and changing. "So?"

"So why did you let her have it?"

Why was I surprised? Of course he knew. Through the gears he was that much ahead of me, shifting just a second before. When Sticks came out of third, he was there with her. But I wasn't. "She needed it," I said.

"Shit!" The flat of J.C.'s hand came down on the ledge of the door. He turned and disappeared into the crowd. I thought about driving off, about leaving him there. That would show him. Wouldn't it? I got out and made my way to the soft drink stand, stopping short when I saw J.C. talking to Sticks and Harv Delaney. Harv had slung his arm over Sticks's narrow shoulder blades and she was laughing, her head thrown back against his arm.

We drove in silence, J.C. behind the wheel again. I fiddled with the radio. Things were all wrong. The sky had turned orange, the orange of fire. We drove straight into it. "Got any gum?" "Nope." "A cig?" I lit two cigarettes, passing him one. And then somehow it was dark, pitch-dark, with a moon like a comma and stars all around.

"Sticks will do just about anything to win," J.C. said into the dark. "Don't feel bad about it. I heard she let the air out of somebody's tires one time. What'd she tell you? That old Harv would beat the hell out of her if she didn't win?"

I didn't answer.

"Aw, Bron, you fell for that?"

We drove on through the dark, oncoming headlights piercing the windshield, illuminating J.C.'s face in a flash, then fading past. I laid my head against the seat and closed my eyes, no longer able to fight the suck of exhaustion. Sticks needed that win, no matter what anybody thought. In her crude way, she'd let me know things she'd never have the words for. She'd touched some place in me deeper than I knew, except in music. I'd begun to sense that there was something as important to me as that race was to Sticks, only I couldn't yet say what it was. It wasn't drag racing.

Sticks didn't win that race because I gave it to her. She won it because she knew what she wanted. It was as simple as that. She decided what she wanted and that made her who she was.

After a while I half woke. My head had dropped against J.C.'s shoulder. Too tired to care what he thought, I settled my head in his lap, Silver's engine around me like a lullaby.

And then there was no engine, no sound, my face on the seat in a little puddle of spit and J.C. gone. I propped myself up and blinked over the edge of the open window. VACANCY, a yellow neon sign said. TV. COMPLIMENTARY COFFEE. A neon horse bucked and disappeared, bucked again. *Bucking Bronco Motel* in looping yellow letters. J.C. came out of the office, crunched across the lot, and opened the door. "Come on," he said.

"Where are we? Why are we here?" I stepped out onto the gravel, my hand in J.C.'s, my head still fuzzy with sleep.

The number on the door was 4. I didn't think my mother would call it lucky. J.C. fitted the key into the lock. When the door opened, he turned and kissed me, a flat kiss half-open. I expected the director to leap out and yell, *Cut!* but no one came. J.C. pushed a button over a mirror stuck next to the door, and the room came half-alive in the weak gray-blue fluorescent light. Shapes of things loomed forward, a hanging lamp like a flying saucer, a painting of a child with haunted eyes the size of grapefruits, a double bed with a double sag, as if two people had lain dead side by side for as long as it took for the springs to give out beneath them.

J.C. dropped spread-eagled onto the bed, hands beneath his head. "Come on over here," he said.

I sat on the edge of the bed, knees together. "I gotta get home," I said. "My folks wait up."

J.C. rolled onto one elbow and smirked. "Yeah, right." He ran a finger down my thigh and back up again. "You think I don't know how you spend your time? You think I don't know you're out there cruising, you and Lanie, half the night? Come on, Bron, you're a big girl. You make your own decisions, don't you?"

"Yes."

"So make one."

"Huh?"

"Don't do that."

"Oh."

"You gonna kiss me or aren't you?"

"*That's* my decision? Like ending up here in this room. My decision, right?" The lights buzzed like a bad headache.

"Hey, we were both knocked out. I could hardly keep my eyes open." He sat up abruptly. "But you say the word, we're on the road." Now it was his whole hand that ran slowly up and down my thigh, then up my ribs as far as the edge of my bra and my breath coming faster than I wanted it to. I watched his lips until I couldn't see them anymore, until my eyes crossed. I thought, I'm kissing J.C. Clearheaded, not like I thought it would be, but standing outside myself as if I were my own twin sister. What are you doing? she said. She watched me bend beneath J.C.'s

(244)

weight down onto the bedspread, watched the blouse come out of my jeans, watched J.C.'s leg come over mine.

"Hey, no . . ." I said when I could get my mouth free.

I pushed his hands and he rolled away, fast as if he'd been bitten. He wasn't breathing hard. There was nothing out of place, not a hair. "What's wrong?" Eyebrows lifted and on his face that mocking grin.

"I wanna go home," I said.

"That's your decision?"

"That's it." Was it?

He rolled off the bed. "Let's go," he said, swiping up the car keys. He opened the door and stood in the yellow light, waiting. A moth flew in, surveyed the room, and flew out again. I hadn't moved from where I sat on the edge of the bed.

"Well, come on," he said.

I crossed the room like a chastened child.

"Here you go," he said, dangling Silver's keys. "I'm bushed. Turn left at the stop sign and head for 101. Can't miss it." He climbed into the backseat, and before we found the freeway he was snoring.

22

WITH JUST TWO WEEKS until West Point summer, Will seemed suddenly to wake up. He'd appear at strange hours, five-thirty in the morning, and wait in the Jeep while I slept. Sometimes he'd be sitting at a table-for-two at lunch, just like a regular customer. He just wanted to watch me, he said. As if he'd been born before the invention of the telephone, he never called, not once. He simply appeared. If I had to work or had some other plans, he'd take off with a smile that said that, too, was okay. He'd be back another time.

He showed me every place he knew, pulling me behind him up the sides of mountains, or else we'd ride the horses, hour after lazy hour through meadows where the wildflowers faded. I knew all there was to know about the Chumash Indians, whose spirit still owned the land. I could name most plants, tell the scent of a nearby fox from a coyote. Will had been a fine teacher, one who sneaks up behind to lay a whole world in your lap. For some reason this had been vital to him, that I know all that he did. The closer we got to his leaving, the more he needed to tell me. I began to kid him. When would he give me my exam? He'd laugh at himself but kept right on. I began to see just how much he loved the backcountry and how hard it would be for him to leave it.

It wasn't easy for Will to get away from the ranch. He'd have to start long before sunrise to get his work done and get to school. Sometimes he'd fall asleep with his head in my lap, exhausted. I'd study his face, the freckles like mine only smaller, like specks of pepper, surprised that I knew his face so well. Sometimes he felt like an older brother to me, sometimes like a best friend. We kissed easy and long. He held my hands against his chest so I could feel how his heart raced. Once he took my hands to his penis. My cheeks beat with blood, but he wouldn't let me look away. This is part of me, too, his eyes said. And soon we had nothing to hide, not with bodies or with words. That we had not "done it" seemed beside the point, at least when I was with him.

Once, he said that we were "intimate," for me a word emblazoned in crimson on the cover of *True Confessions*, only now the word was different. Intimate. My thesaurus said joined, united, wedded. . . . I'd roll the word over in my mind and try to understand how Will meant it. But there was no way to do that. You had to know it, like the Chumash knew the earth, like a hawk knows air. It was deeper somehow than love, and yet it was love.

A week before he was to leave we rode for miles along the dry creek bed that ran the length of the adjoining ranch. Securing the horses, we began a zigzag climb that brought us eventually to the summit beneath the flat stone expanse of Hurricane Deck. The Hardings' small ranch and the extended range to which it was appended like a poor relative

(247)

stretched out below us. Will stood with the toes of his boots just over the edge of a flat boulder looking down through a thousand feet of space, thumbs hooked into his belt loops, Stetson low on his forehead, for him an unaffected posture. "From here," he said, "it all makes sense, doesn't it?" I knew he'd had to fight free of his mother. Her hold on him was so strong. You could see it in the way she followed him with her eyes.

He stood looking at his toes for a while, then, as if he'd just realized how unnecessary they were, he began removing his clothes, shucking his boots, stepping out of his jeans, dropping his plaid shirt and jockey shorts all in a single, smooth motion. Then, beginning with the top button of my blouse, he undressed me, too. "Old Indian tradition," he said.

There was nothing frantic in this, no heavy breathing, the silly backseat rustling that I knew. We lay on the warm rock, holding hands. Pressed against each other, we kissed like ancient lovers. When Will rolled away and lay on his back, his erection looked to me like some exotic plant, a sun-seeking mushroom. Overhead, hawks traced wide looping circles in the sky. In the quiet, you could hear their wings play the air. Sharp-eyed lizards shot fast across exposed rock into the protecting red-veined fingers of manzanita. We watched the birds, named clouds, and after a while curled into each other and, innocent, slept.

WITH JUST three days left, Will said he had a surprise. We were going to a "very special place" for dinner. It was formal, he said. He would wear his dinner jacket, but no pink net was allowed. There were few places we could go without driving out of town, the Country Club and Harriman's, a place my father had walked us out of after tasting the soup. I didn't think Will had either one in mind. Maybe we'd drive to Santa Barbara, to Joe's, where some kids went on prom night. I began to catch his excitement. I'd wear something really special, something to light up his eyes though they lit up every time he saw me no matter what I wore.

J.C. had disappeared again. In his absence I would create alternative scenarios for the last time I'd been with him. I would transform the ghastly motel room in the blink of an eye, whip away the leering mirror with its rusted edges, rip up the smelly carpet, haul out the sagging bed. Instead we would lie together inside something pink and light as the underlining of a shell. J.C. would whisper irresistible things in my ear (what things exactly I was not sure, except for the words *darling* and *my love*). We would kiss very tenderly and for a very long time. At last he'd slip a bra strap from my shoulder and lean into the cave of my shoulder to touch the skin with light lips. The word *caress* wove through these daydreams. J.C. would caress, somehow, certain parts of me. Never very specific parts and never in very specific ways. We were always more ethereal than real flesh.

I called Lanie. She was cooking up a mess of fried chicken, she said. She and Jimbo had their own trailer now and she was having "the family" (meaning only the Callahans) over for dinner. Her voice was light and bubbly, like the voice of a TV wife. She said we could meet the next day, that she'd love helping me shop for a dress. She liked Will. He didn't "take any shit," she said, and yet he was a gentleman. She sighed after that. What could you do with a Jimbo except take him as he was? She thought Will and I were a perfect couple. Too bad Will was leaving so soon. They'd have had us over to dinner. We each knew how far from reality that was.

(249)

Lanie and I shopped and chatted just like old times. We might have been prom shopping, only Lanie didn't try anything on. "I just hang out in these now," she said, indicating her faded jeans and one of Jimbo's shirts knotted at the waist. "I mean, who am I trying to impress? Jimbo wouldn't notice if I wore a bag over my head!"

"Are you guys . . . all right?" I said. I had to know.

"Sure!" she said too fast, with that too bright smile. I let it go. We couldn't put into words and maybe didn't fully know how the act of her marriage had separated us, girl from woman. Now there were certain things I could no longer understand, things that went on between men and women when they became man and wife. It was fiction for the most part, her life had not changed, but we lived it because it was all we knew.

Lanie lifted a black dress from the rack, one I'd have chosen for her but never for myself. "Here, try this," she said, and led me toward the dressing room.

"It's not my type," I protested. The dressing room was the size of a closet, but Lanie wriggled in after me.

"Here," she said when I'd shucked my jeans and shirt. The black dress slid over my head and down over my shoulders like rain. Had it not been for the sheer black nylon across the chest, it would have been strapless and I'd have never held it up. This way, it was perfect.

"Sex-y!" Lanie pronounced. And it was. From the neck down, I was Sophia Loren with Debbie Reynolds's waist. "You can borrow my four-inch black patents. He won't be able to keep his hands off you!"

"Oh, yeah, he can," I said before I even thought about it. It wasn't fair or even very accurate but once it was out, it was out.

Lanie frowned. "You guys never . . . you . . . ?" She

waved her hand to fill in the words we never would say right out.

"Well, we come close. I mean we fool around a lot, only . . ." My face burned with shame. Did I emit some horrid substance that held them at bay? Even J.C. leaped away with incredible ease. What was wrong with me?

Lanie's hands went to her mouth and her eyes widened. "He can't do it? Does he get, you know, does his thingie get . . . ?"

"Oh, sure," I said, slipping the dress back over my head; $32.98, the price tag read. A lot, but I could afford it out of the tips I'd saved. After all, I wasn't going to have to buy shoes. "There's nothing wrong with him. It's just that he, I don't know, he just doesn't seem like he's in any hurry, you know?"

It was clear that Lanie didn't know. I didn't either. We'd fought *them* off for as long as we could remember, boys with speedy little fingers and wheedling promises. "Just let me touch you with it. I won't come in, I promise. . . ." "Second base, just second base! Please, please, *please* . . ."

"He isn't like other guys," I said lamely. "He's, I don't know, *older*. He acts as if we have the rest of our lives."

"Maybe he thinks you do," she said, thoughtfully now.

"Huh?" I pulled on my jeans, brushed my hair into place, just a kid again. But it was nice to know the femme fatale was lurking in there somewhere. It was true what the magazines said. All you needed was the right clothes, the right eyeshadow, accessories, an alluring perfume. If only J.C. could see me in that dress. His eyes would give him away. That's the way he spoke, with his eyes, or so I told myself. He certainly didn't do it in words. The words were only in my daydreams. *Darling . . . my love . . .*

"Will sounds serious," Lanie said. "I mean serious.

He's thinking long term, Bron. That's why he's in no hurry. He thinks you're going to be around for the rest of his life!"

"Oh, don't be silly," I said. But she had struck home. There were times with Will that felt like we'd met in another life, a life before this, and that we were simply continuing on. The excitement, the charge, all the risk and danger—what I felt with J.C.—had happened long ago with Will in that other life. What we lived now was deeper than that. All this I knew instinctively but could not understand, could not translate. Something akin to it passed sometimes between my parents, some ineffable thing that joined them, and so I did not trust it. I knew the love they had went deep and held fast. And yet I knew my father capable of weakness and betrayal.

Over chocolate Cokes at the pharmacy I told Lanie about J.C., right down to the horrid blood-red spread at the Bucking Bronco Motel.

"You did the absolute right thing," Lanie said. For the first time, I noticed the dark circles under her eyes and that her skin had coarsened as if toughening up inside had made its way finally to her beautiful face. "He wouldn't have respected you. You know that!"

"I guess. . . ."

"What do you mean, you guess!"

I sipped my Coke. "You sound like my mother."

"Yeah? Well, in this case she'd be right. J.C.'s a bird dog. He'll sniff up any backside that's stuck in his face."

"Lanie! That's disgusting!"

"Yeah? Well, it's the truth. I should know." She whipped her chocolate bubbles to a froth.

My heart fell. So, like every boy over the age of twelve,

J.C., too, had had the hots for Lanie. Why was that such a surprise?

"You went out with J.C.?" There was a squeak in my voice like I'd run out of oil.

"Me? Hell no. But he's made enough passes, let me tell you." She poked a cigarette between her lips and went fishing in her bag for matches. Frieda came over with our chicken salad sandwiches. "So, how's married life treatin' ya?" she said.

"Fine!" Lanie said with that quick punch of breath.

"Who's working lunch?" Frieda asked me. If she and I were both here, that left my mother. She knew that. She just wanted to make a point.

"I had to get this dress . . ." I said.

"Oh, of course," Frieda said. "One has to have one's dresses." She turned and, grabbing a coffeepot, sailed off, orange curls bouncing indignantly.

"What's biting her?" Lanie said.

"How should I know? On the rag probably. Lanie . . . ?"

"Hmmm?"

"Maybe I should have let him. I mean, where is he now if he respects me so much?"

"J.C. . . ." Lanie said with a sigh.

"J.C.," I said.

"What about Will?"

"What about him?"

"Bron, Will and J.C.—it's like comparing, I don't know, steak and hamburger. No. Champagne and beer. Peaches and spinach. Oh, you know what I mean. J.C.'s nothing but a good time, a *short* good time. Will's for keeps."

I chomped into my chicken salad sandwich. "Someday, maybe. . . ."

"Yeah, well, you're young," Lanie said, like we weren't exactly the same age. "There's time."

Will made use of the telephone at last. He was packed and ready, he said. The next morning his mother would drive him to the plane. He'd pick me up at seven. Our reservations were for seven-fifteen. So I knew we wouldn't be going out of town. The Country Club probably. I hoped it wouldn't be Harriman's, though I knew they'd let Will keep his gun. You could get away with anything at Harriman's. You could haul your unfaithful wife out by the hair and beat her up in the parking lot. As long as you didn't go too far, nobody interfered.

I locked myself in the bathroom for an hour, trying my hair all ways and finally giving up, letting it fall like it would anyway whether I set it or not. I knew that's what Will preferred. "You're naturally beautiful," he said once, tilting my chin toward the sun. But cactus was naturally beautiful. So were lizards in their way. I wanted more than that. I wanted heads to turn. What was naturally beautiful to drop-dead gorgeous? I smeared shadow on my eyelids, rubbed rouge into my cheeks, curled my eyelashes, lined my lips and filled them in with Persian Melon. I took a step back, shrieked, and scrubbed it all off with Noxzema.

"You all right in there?"

"I'm fine, Dad. I'll be out in a minute."

"Your prince awaits," he said.

"Will's here?"

"You were expecting Clark Gable?"

I slipped into black panties and hooked on a new black garter belt. Carefully I rolled on a pair of transparent black stockings with a seam up the back. Finally I stepped into Lanie's black stiletto heels. I barely made it down the stairs.

"Hubba hubba, zing zing!" my father yelped, as I knew he would, but there were no customers to show me off to.

My mother looked dazzled as well. "So grown-up!" she cried, and wrapped her arms around her middle as if I were still in there, and she could keep me there, safe.

Will jumped up and cleared his throat, looked quickly at my father, then back at me. "Well, um, I guess we'd better get going. . . ."

I pecked my father on the cheek. "Good-bye, Papa!" I said. I touched my mother's cheek to mine the way they did in Paris. "Good-bye, Mama!"

The night was as dramatic as my dress, full moon in a sky blacker than black and swept clean even of its stars. From time to time, catching you by surprise, a wind from the north blew in and up went the dry leaves like startled birds. The Jeep played tag with a tangle of tumbleweed as it careened down Ojala Avenue. Will reached for my hand. When I turned, his eyes were dark and sad and I felt my throat catch in dumbfounded surprise that someone else's sadness could hurt as much as my own. It was time to lighten things up or I'd be crying. "About this dress," I said, turning to Will, fists on my hips.

He grinned like a guilty cat. "You threw me," he said. "I didn't know what to say!"

"So say it now. How do I look?"

Will pulled the Jeep to the side of the road and cut the engine. He threw his head back and closed his eyes. He was smiling, maybe praying. Turning toward me, he opened one eye, then the other. He took hold of both my hands. Oh, boy, I said to myself, this is going to be great. His shirt cuffs dazzled. The cuff links had been his father's with his father's initials, and of course Will's, scrolled into them. The moon flooded the open car like a spotlight. "You look so . . . pretty," he said.

"Pretty," I repeated.

He rolled his eyes skyward and tried again. "More than pretty . . . beautiful, really. . . ."

"Beautiful. *Really*." I had him on the run.

"Aw, Bron. You look, damn it, like some movie star. Like, I don't know . . . Piper Laurie. What would Piper Laurie be doing with me?" He scratched his head, shrugged his shoulders. "You look . . . magnificent. How's that?"

"Gorgeous," I supplied.

"Gorgeous," he agreed.

"Striking. Exotic. Sexy!"

"Sexy. Yes. Sexy." We giggled. I began to wonder if the heroes and heroines of my romance novels wouldn't giggle, too, given the chance.

Will started the car and I snuggled against him, close as I could get with the gearshift in between. "We'll be late if we don't hurry," he said, glancing at his watch, also his father's.

We drove out toward the hills past the Country Club and, happily, past Harriman's. Will took several turns I wasn't familiar with, down narrow dark roads lined with eucalyptus trees spaced like giant soldiers at attention. As the trees whipped by and blotted out the moonlight, Will's face came in and out of shadow. How familiar that face had become in so short a time. I could close my eyes and every detail, every freckle, would be there.

I almost knew that for the miracle it was.

And then we were on a familiar road and I began to worry. Surely this "special" dinner could not be at the

Hardings', his mother in attendance like Dracula's widow draped in black silk. I bit my tongue. After tomorrow, there would be no Mrs. Harding as far as I was concerned. No Will either, but I wasn't going to think about that yet. But we sailed past the gate to the ranch. I breathed again as the Jeep climbed roads I now knew well and the moon floated just inches from the peaks of mountains I'd come to love. "Will Harding, where in hell are we going?"

"Will's café," he said. "Your dad would really love this!"

The Jeep bounced down the narrow dirt road and came to a stop at the line of aspen that bordered the river. Will hopped out and came around to my side, offering his arm. "Madame," he said.

I stepped out in Lanie's spikes and sunk to my heels. "You should have told me to wear my hiking boots," I said. "The gold lamé ones, of course."

"Of course," he said. "Would Madame care for a lift?"

"Madame better have a lift or she's going to have to crawl all the way to the river in her sexy black dress."

"The management wouldn't stand for it," Will said, and I went up into his arms like I'd dropped ten pounds back on the road. His strength surprised me and shouldn't have. Ranch work had made a man of Will before his years caught up. "We'll go over the threshold like this someday," he said in that same light tone, and I felt my heart stop. He must have felt me tense against his arms and so he set me down carefully, as if parts of me might break off. "I mean . . . someday. You know, when we're ready."

I leaned down to slip off my shoes, taking longer than I needed to. *For keeps*, Lanie said. *Will's for keeps.*

"Would Madame care to hobble this way," he said, and the mood was light again and fun.

We pushed through the trees and there in a flood of moonlight, perched on the flat rocks, was a card table and two folding chairs. The wind teased the skirt of a linen tablecloth and had already upended the napkins that had been folded, as I'd taught Will, into upside-down ice-cream cones. There were champagne glasses, a bottle of champagne in a silver bucket, and china that matched the tea set from which we'd drunk our tea in the Hardings' parlor. How much did Will's mother know about all this?

"Is Madame pleased?" Will said. He was having trouble keeping a straight face. I imagined him putting this together, first planning it, then running back and forth until he had it all right, sneaking out the china and the crystal glasses. . . .

"Madame is delighted," I said. Will pulled, or rather scraped, my chair out. It wobbled a bit on the rock but sat all right. But when Will took his seat and reached for the champagne bucket, a gust of wind hit head on, sending our glasses flying. They shattered in two quick, light shots on the rock and twinkled there like evil stars. Will was caught by surprise, the champagne half lifted from the silver bucket, and for a moment he looked almost frightened. Then it passed. "Shall we drink from your shoe?" he said, struggling with the cork.

I'd opened dozens of champagne bottles by that time and couldn't bear Will's valiant struggle. I reached for the bottle and he relinquished it without a fight. "This isn't going exactly as I planned it," he said. "In case you couldn't tell."

The wind got more serious, blowing my hair across my face, but the cork slid out with a gentle pop and I offered the bottle to Will for the first sip, bubbles running down my arm. "Here's to your first year as an officer and a gentleman. You're already a gentleman, so you can just work on the other part. And always keep your head down."

"Well, I won't be an officer for a while. They make you wait for that. It's a long time. . . ."

"But you'll be home summers, right?"

"You bet." He took a swig of champagne and passed it over to me. "Hungry?"

"There's food?" Will dragged a metal chest out from behind a manzanita bush. Inside, neatly packed in Mrs. Harding's Tupperware were shrimp cocktails (heavy on the catsup), mostly cooked cold fried chicken, and Wonder bread, already buttered. "All my very favorite things!" I exclaimed.

"Madame is too kind," he said. "It'll go down pretty well, I think, with enough champagne."

"I'm going to miss you," I said, and the words made it true, deeply true, for the first time. It occurred to me then in the moonlight as wind rippled the surface of the water that I'd taken Will, Will's kindness and thoughtfulness, his quirkiness and good humor, all for granted. He was precious in that moment and rare, a gift I hadn't been ready for and didn't quite know what to do with. I wanted to tell him that, but the words wouldn't come, not the right ones.

"I love you, you know," he said. My tears came so fast I couldn't think to stop them. "Bron, no . . ." he said. "Don't. . . ." He got up to reach for me and the table went over, Mrs. Harding's fine china clattering across the gravel. One plate made it intact to the stream and floated there like a fallen moon. Will had me in his arms then and held me, apologizing over and over. "I didn't mean it. I mean, I did. I *do* love you, but I didn't mean to upset you. It's okay . . . it's okay . . . shhhh. . . ."

Why was I blubbering? I didn't know. Was I in love, too? If so, was it supposed to feel like this? And why, for no good reason, did I think of J.C.? "Your mother will kill you," I said, and blew my nose in my linen napkin. We righted the table, gathered the dishes and pieces of dishes. We laughed and found our balance. The wind came from way off, from the mouths of enormous dark caves, and it talked or sang, mournfully, like a train whistle long after it's left the station. We sat together on the rocks, both Will's arms around me, inches from the water. I thought about my parents, about Watchung Lake, about life transformed into a simple love story. What would my story be? A coyote bayed and another answered. Once a sound like that would have spooked me. Now I'd become part of what had seemed so strange just months before.

"What I said doesn't mean . . . doesn't mean . . . I know you're going to be a senior and you've got to do all the things that seniors do. I'll try to make it back for some of that. If you want me to. But I don't want you to sit home, Bron. It's not like we're, you know, going steady or whatever. . . ."

"No," I said.

"So you're free. And so am I. Not that I'll have time for . . . but I think that's the way it should be when somebody goes away, don't you?" He sounded like he was reading from a script.

"Oh, absolutely," I said. Why couldn't he just grab me, throw me down, and brand me for his own? What was all this fairness stuff?

"Well, good, then. That's settled. No more tears."

A run went up one nylon stocking straight to my garter belt. How alluring I had tried to be. $32.98 and we sat like

(260)

diplomats at the bargaining table. Half of Albania for you, half of Yugoslavia for me. Well, then, that's settled. . . .

"Will?"

"Mmmm?"

"The last time we were here. You know, after the prom. When we swam . . ."

"Uh-huh." He'd snuggled his cheek into my hair.

"I just wondered why you . . . why we didn't, you know . . ."

Will pulled back to look at me. He said nothing for what seemed a long time. "Did you want to?" he said. He brushed the hair from my eyes, leaning toward me so that his eyes were level almost with mine.

I shrugged. "I dunno. . . ." I looked down at my hands, somebody's hands, they looked like mine, but he waited, and so finally I had to meet his eyes again. "I just didn't know if *you* wanted to. I mean, if you really cared about me or if we were, you know, just friends. . . ."

"We *are* friends," he said, gripping my shoulders. "We are. And more. And you thought I didn't want you? Good Lord, girl," he said, throwing his hands in the air. "You don't know what goes on in a guy's mind, do you?"

"I thought I did."

"Yeah, well, it's beyond your imagination, believe me. If I told you what I think the minute I wake up, how I picture you. . . ."

I began to squirm. "Well, you had your chance," I said.

"Why didn't you let me know?"

"Me?"

"Who else?"

"The girl isn't supposed to—"

"Bullshit, Bron," he said in a quick flash of anger.

"We're the same, you and I. We have the same drives, the same feelings. Why do you want to pretend there are different rules for you than there are for me?"

"Because there are," I said.

"Only if you want there to be," he said. "Only if you buy them."

Clouds zipped across the moon, casting ragged shadows on the rocks. Very small and busy things clicked and skittered in the bushes. "We've been making love all this time, silly. Didn't you know that?"

On the porch of the Welsh Kitchen Will's last kiss felt strangely like his first, brand-new, and when I opened my eyes I seemed to be seeing the whole of him for the very first time all over again, the serious face and long sharp nose, the scars cut in along his jaw, the dark eyes so quick and intelligent, eyes that hid nothing because they couldn't, or because they never tried. I remembered the stubborn boy who stood on this porch, hands behind his back, and looked off into the dark at something only he could see. I'd gotten used to the gun. It lay against his leg now, just as it always did. I'd probably never know why. Maybe he didn't either. Or, if he did, it was the one thing he never told me.

"You'll write, won't you?" he said.

"One for one," I said. "Even Stephen."

"Deal," he said, and held out his hand just the way he did when meeting someone for the very first time. A firm grip, chin forward.

"Deal," I said.

23

THREE FIRES FLARED UP in late August, the first two easily extinguished but low in the hills, near homes, one very close to Lanie's trailer park. My parents were appalled and frightened, though no one else seemed to be. August was always "fire month," they said. At the first hint of smoke in the hills, every able-bodied male hit the road as if an internal alarm had sounded in each of them, and, almost always, the fire was beaten back. Once, when the town consisted of a dozen homes and businesses, Ojala burned straight to the ground. But that was long ago, before the bombers. Now fires were doused with clouds of magic chemicals. There wasn't anything to worry about. Anyway, as with earthquakes, you got used to it.

"Nobody worries about anything in California," my father said. "Except you, Helen."

"Well, somebody's got to do it," my mother said.

"Well, you do a great job, sweetheart," my father said, patting her hand. "I'm sure everyone is properly grateful."

The third fire woke everybody up. Not literally, since it began in the lull of an afternoon too hot for napping, but no one ever talked about fire in the same way again, not after that one. Never again would anyone relax until after the heat and the winds of August passed on. Someone would always be watching. A good fire was sneaky, Mr. Alvarez said later. It could get a lot of business done before anybody caught on. You had to get to a fire like that almost before it started, and of course that wasn't possible. So you had to keep your eyes open. If you didn't, well, you were asking to lose it all.

The third fire was one of those fires, a "good" one, and it nearly finished Ojala off.

We were clearing the last two tables when we heard the siren. My mother lifted the bus tray and headed for the kitchen. "I wonder where that is," she said.

My father took the tray and set it on the sink. "Why do you insist on carrying those, Helen?"

"Where's Buddy?" my mother said. "Buddy?" She opened the door to the attic and yelled up the stairs. "Buddy! Where are you?"

"Up here!" Buddy said. "You can see smoke. There's a fire in the mountains!"

We went out onto the porch. People came from all directions to gather at the corner, where they could get the best view of the curling plume of smoke in the distance. A few brought binoculars. "Oh, dear," my mother said. "I hope it isn't bad." We joined the others. "See how the wind has started to pull that smoke?" one of the older women said. The skin had closed in around her eyes as if to shield them from the many awful things she'd seen. "That's no good. If the wind picks up, we're in for it. Ain't seen one this close in a good while. . . ."

"Not since, when was it? '46, '47, when the Baptist church went up. Now, that was a fire!" A man who might or might not have been the woman's husband sucked hard on a dry pipe and his own spittle.

I kept looking up, expecting bombers to streak past at any moment. "You don't want your fires late in the afternoon, no sir," said the old man. "That's when them Santa Anny winds come down. Your wind and your fire, that's a deadly combination, yes sir." His eyes had a dreamy faraway look as if he'd passed to the other side of being afraid of fire and now just had a scholarly interest in it.

The Avenue was quiet. No cars passed. As if a war had suddenly begun, the town had been cleared of its young men. Shops were closed. Two priests stood at the gate to Our Lady and looked out toward the smoke. I hoped they were praying. "Where are the bombers?" I asked.

"Not bad enough yet," the old man said. "Besides, there's a fire down in Glendale. I hear they're all down there."

We went back in to check on Buddy, who was hanging out the attic window, and that's when we saw the first lick of flame, just a single orange lick like a ribbon in the smoke. And then there were several.

"I think we should pack some things in the car," my mother said, going from window to window, peering out. "Buddy? Buddy! Get down here."

"Now, let's not get excited," my father said. "That fire's still a ways off."

"There's only one road out of here, Tom," my mother said.

"She's right, Daddy," I said, realizing how seldom I

ever took her side. "It'll be like a fire in a movie theater, everybody running for the door at the same time."

"I'm not going anywhere," my father said.

My mother frowned. "Tom, this isn't a time to be stubborn."

He let that pass. "It wouldn't hurt to hose things down. Bron, grab the hose. I'm going up on the roof."

"You can see real good from upstairs," Buddy yelled, clambering down the stairs. "There's nobody at the Frostee. Did you see old Jimbo take off out of the Frostee? J.C. was in the back with Chick and some other guys. They all had shovels and stuff!"

"You're doing nothing of the kind," my mother said to my father. "Have you lost your mind? What's in here anyway but a ... but a few pots and pans, a bunch of old tables. . . ."

My father stopped and turned. His head was cocked as if listening to someone whisper in his ear. "A bunch of old tables, is it? Is it, lass? Is that what it is?" My mother looked ready to cry. If she had heaved a chair at him, she could not have hurt him more. "Well, I see something else here. Always have. Funny, isn't it?" He said this quietly, as if he were testing the strength of the words, seeing if they would fall through. Then he turned and went outside. Our Afghani customers had hung a string of bells on the back of the door, and when he left, they jangled gaily as if a pack of camels trailed behind.

"Don't let him climb up there, Bron," she said. She'd sent me after him before. At ten I'd slam into any bar she named and hold my ground until I could see in the dark which man of the dozen lined up along the counter was my father. That was when I thought that what I did made a difference.

"He's probably right," I said. "It's an old roof. It'll go up like dry hay."

"That's not the point," she said. "We don't own this place. It isn't ours."

"Could have fooled me," I said. "The way you guys were acting, I figured you'd pump in your last pint of blood before you gave up." How tired she looked. She'd always kept her hair in a neat roll at the base of her neck. Now she gathered it without much thought and stuffed it through a rubber band. The shorter hairs worked their way out by the end of the day and hung in her eyes. She'd push at them with the back of her hand, hands full of flour or suds or catsup. And when had she stopped wearing makeup? I wanted to say, "Buy a new dress, Ma. We can afford one decent dress, can't we? That one's popping at the seams!" Instead I said, "Don't worry. I'll keep him off the roof." When Buddy tried to follow, she grabbed him by the arm and held him in a vise grip.

Outside, a haze hung low in the air. The sky had turned a forbidding mustard color and the air smelled acrid. Flakes of ash floated like fish through a tank. I found my father on the side of the house trying to steady the ladder against the eaves. "You got the hose?" he said.

"Why don't I go up there?" I said. "You can anchor the ladder."

"Man's job," he said. "Get the hose."

"I'm not supposed to let you climb up there," I said, flinging my arm across the ladder.

My father raised an eyebrow, thought about saying something. Then he brushed my arm away and began to climb. I watched his boots with the traces of Sicilian Spaghetti, Chicken Marengo, pot roast, gain one step and then the next. There were knobs of arthritis on his fingers and brown splotches, the kind old people get. The ladder creaked and swayed. I sat on the bottom rung to steady it. If he was going to fall, I wasn't going to watch. "Okay, pass me the hose," he said when he had gone halfway.

I fed him the hose, leaning into the ladder to steady it as he climbed. "Be careful," I said, and then he was standing on the peak of the roof, a foot on either side. I heard him cough several times. Then he turned and said, "What are you doing down there, picking your nose? Turn the water on!"

I flipped the faucet on and scrambled up the ladder, not thinking much about it. My father turned with a look of pleased dismay as I climbed on the roof and stood up beside him. Water splashed lazily from the hose onto the worn gray shingles. A muffled cry of sirens found its way through the smoke, engines heading our way from Ventura, perhaps farther south. But still no bombers.

My father's face was bathed in a greasy sweat. He looked so determined that I began to wonder if he wouldn't go down with the ship. His own place, my mother had said. It had nothing to do with a deed. It was his all right, and I could see that he meant to keep it.

He leaned over in a racking cough and came up holding his apron to his mouth. "Daddy, this is nuts. Mom's right. I think the whole town's going up. Listen to all those cars on the Avenue. People are getting out of here."

He fished in his shirt pocket for his Camels and stuck one in his mouth. He rummaged around in his pants pocket. "Got a match?" he said, straight-faced, eyes twinkling with all the old mischief. He could almost have caught a spark in the air and lit that cigarette. He pulled a pack of matches from his pocket and lit up. I didn't dare ask him for a cigarette. He inhaled deeply, coughed, and exhaled. "Go down and get your mother and Buddy. Pack both cars. Your mother can probably drive Bess if she puts her mind to it, but take Buddy with you."

For a minute I didn't know what to do or to say.

"Go on, now," he said.

"What are you talking about, Dad? You think you're going to stay up here? Fight this thing by yourself?" The smoke was thick now and you couldn't see the sky. Three in the afternoon and it looked like the middle of the night. "I'm going down but I'll be right back," I said. I scrambled down the ladder.

Mother had packed a suitcase too heavy to lift. She bumped it down the stairs behind her. "Can we take my bike, huh? Can we?" Buddy pleaded.

"I can't get Dad to come down," I said. I grabbed two napkins and ran them under the faucet.

"You tell that man to get down here right now or . . . or . . . !" She gave up.

I scrambled back up the ladder and handed my father one of the napkins. He pulled it across his face and I helped him tie it on. "Stick 'em up, pahdnah!" he said. The roof was wet and he told me to be careful.

Somewhere in the smoke someone yelled, "Anybody there?"

"Up here on the roof," my father said.

"The fire's reached the Avenue," the voice yelled. "They don't think they can contain it. You'd better clear out!"

"Pansies," my father muttered. "They should see a mine fire. Now, that's a fire!" He gazed off into the smoke. "I ever tell you about—"

"Yup."

"You don't even know what I was going to say!" my father protested.

"Yes, I do. You wouldn't even be here right now if it wasn't for your uncle Em, who dragged you out of the shaft. . . ."

"By my hair," my father said.

"By your hair," I said.

"Well, that wasn't the one," he said. "That wasn't the one I was going to tell you."

"Sure it was."

"Was not." My father sniffed, insulted.

We heard my mother at the base of the ladder arguing with Buddy. "Come down here this minute, you two! Tom? Bron?" Her voice rose disembodied through the smoke.

"Lass?" my father said, and even then, in all the danger and craziness of the moment, his eyes lit up at the sound of her voice.

"Tom?" a plaintive cry, as if she were wounded.

"Get whatever you think you'll need and put it in Bron's car. She'll drive you and Buddy out of town."

"I'm not going," I said.

"Helen? You have to do it right now, sweetheart."

"Bron?" my mother called.

"I'm staying here," I said.

"Don't be a stubborn ass," he said.

"Like somebody we know?"

Our eyes met over the edge of our wet napkins. I saw the anger rise in his and watched it fade. "Touché," he said. "Lass?"

"Tom?" Hysteria edged that single word.

"Do you think you can drive Bess? Do you remember how, my darling?"

She didn't answer. Many years before, she had left whatever car we had then in the middle of a busy intersection and walked home. The clutch pedal slipped off again, she said. She'd had it with cars. If they couldn't make them to work right, she wasn't going to drive one.

"Helen? You're going to have to drive the car."

"Oh, Tom...." She had begun to cry. My father would give in now. He'd turn and climb down the ladder and I would follow. Tears always worked with him.

"Helen, go in the house and get the car keys from the dresser. Are you listening, Helen?"

"Yes...."

"Take the keys and Buddy and drive ... do you hear me, Helen? Drive the car to Ventura."

"Bron?"

"I'm staying with Dad," I said.

"Oh, Lord ..." my mother cried.

We heard the bombers then, two of them. "Like London during the blitz," my father said, scanning the sky. But you couldn't see them. All we could see were our own hands and each other's, each other's frightened eyes. But something else, too. I'd never fought alongside my father before. I'd always fought against him. Even when I thought we were on the same side, his, we weren't. I'd always been on mine.

"C'mon, Mom," Buddy coaxed. We heard their voices drift away, his encouraging, hers defeated. My father and I sat side by side on the peak of the roof.

"I'll bet you never expected this when you decided to come to California," I said.

"I didn't know what to expect," he said. "We just took a chance. Sometimes you have to," he said. "Take a chance." He was quiet for a few minutes and then he said, "Have we told you how proud we are of you?"—blinking at me through the smoke.

"Huh?"

"The way you came through, making this adjustment and all, finding friends. I know it wasn't easy."

"No. . . ." Once I would have had something barbed and nasty, ready to toss. Now for some reason, I had no words.

So my parents were proud. How could that be? Proud of what? Of whom? I wasn't exactly an honor student. I'd ditch a class on the slightest provocation. My friends, all except for Will, were going nowhere, had no plans. Half were alcoholics. I was no better. I could polish off a six-pack with the best of them. I had no dreams, no ambitions. I no longer played piano. And what did I do for them? for my family? Sure, I'd put my hours in at the restaurant, but that was for me, to buy clothes and gasoline.

I thought about the day, almost a year ago, that we landed in Ojala and stood in front of the pharmacy looking out into our future like pioneers. Well, this is what happened to pioneers. They got burned out. They moved on. They got punished for having ambition, for dreaming too hard. Sirens screamed as three engines raced through town, their red lights eerie and muted in the smoke. And then the water cut off. My father threw the hose. "Bah!" he said.

We heard my mother grinding Bess to a start, stalling her several times. "We're going, Dad!" Buddy cried. "Bye, Bron!" His voice was bright with excited fear.

"Take care of your mother," my father called. "And sit in the backseat. Buddy?"

"Yeah, Dad?"

"Are you in the back?"

After a minute: "Yeah, Dad."

"Tom!" my mother cried. "I'll never forgive you for this, god damn it!"

It was the first time we'd ever heard her, as she would put it, "take the Lord's name in vain."

"I think she means it," my father said, his eyes wide with wonder.

There were three pops, like gunshots, in the distance. "It's those trees," my father said. "The eucalyptus. They're like torches ready to light. You'd think God could have made a smarter tree for a place dry as this. Strange place, this. Like the desert. I thought we were going to live on the beach. Dig for clams. Hang our hammocks from the palm trees." He shook his head. "But it's a good place. There are good people here."

The planes came back, one, then the other, and the sky was quiet again. "They'll be back," my father said. We seemed to be the last two people left on a gaseous planet, floating in space. "Maybe we should write a will," I said.

"That's a good one." My father laughed. "What shall I leave you, my girl? Would you like my best cooking pot? The one I stew the lamb shanks in? Or Bess, maybe. She's got some life left in her."

"The Great Books!" I cried.

"Ah, yes, the Great Books," my father agreed. We shared a good laugh, remembering how adamant Mom had been that the entire set (uncracked) be packed in the California or Bust box tied on the top of Bess.

"And, let me see, what family heirloom shall I leave Buddy?"

"Your razor," I said, words before thought. I bit my tongue, too late. My father's breath caught, and then it was as if I were all alone on that gray planet, my father evaporated into the mist. Something hard like a knuckle had worked its way under my ribs, and I thought how easy it would be to let myself slide down the glassy wet shingles and be gone.

The air began to clear, in patches at first, and then there were lights like glowing jewels on a broken string and the swirling red beams from fire trucks. My father reached for my hand, patting it as he often patted my mother's, to comfort her when he didn't know what else to do or say. "It's over," he said. "We're all right now. There's nothing more to worry about." It wasn't just the fire that he meant.

A pickup barreled down the street, in the bed a half-dozen men leaning on shovels or tipping cold beers. "How's it going?" my father yelled.

"We got the worst of it," called the driver. "It's just mopping up now. Thank the Lord."

"Thank the Lord," my father said, no longer a religious man but always an agreeable one. "Let's get the coffee on, Bronwyn."

While I brewed pots of coffee, my father scrawled "Ojala is saved! Free coffee!" in dripping red letters on the back of the OPEN FOR LUNCH sign and stuck it on the porch.

They came like soldiers back from the front, with hair-raising stories and bottles of whiskey. Their faces and arms were soot-blackened, smeared by sweat. My father and I poured endless cups of coffee, he trading stories from the mines for stories from the fire. "Hell, yes!" I'd hear him cry from somewhere in the crowd. "You *want* to run, by God you do, but you stand your ground." His voice had a ring to it I'd never heard before.

Whiskey bottles clanked as someone proposed a toast, then another. "To Ojala!" "To Chevrolet!" "Long live Jack Daniel's!" The Afghani bells clattered as more and more men clomped in, their heavy boots scuffing the floor. "I could use a cup of that coffee!" "And one here!" I poured

(274)

till I thought my arm would fall off. Some faces I recognized, a few. And then I was looking straight into the eerie green glow of J.C.'s eyes, greener than ever against the bright white and the soot. "Gentlemen," he said in a whiskey slur. "This here"—he grabbed my arm—"this'ere's the only gal in the entire shitty, whoops! excuse me, *city* of Ojala that will not give me the time of day!" A few laughs. "A woman of good sense," someone said. "A rarity."

"I fix her car, I change her oil, I take her to the races, and what? Nothing!" I slid from his grasp. The coffeepot shook as I poured. I moved on to the next table. I hated how my heart kicked over at the sound of his voice. It was independent of me, it didn't care what I thought. It didn't care what a sensible girl would do. It was the most confused and fickle of hearts, and I was stuck with it.

Then my mother appeared, coffeepot in hand. She looked a bit shell-shocked but poured with a steady hand and a quick smile. Buddy made a beeline for J.C.'s table, leaning there on his elbows, drinking in everything J.C. said.

They stumbled out just after midnight, the last of them, full of booze-laden gratitude, buoyant and weary. My father was sober, bright-eyed, high on nothing but the sweet taste of adventure. J.C. hung back at the door. "Coming?" he said.

"Where?"

"In my traveling motel," he said, running a sooty finger down my nose.

"Stuff it," I said.

"Ooooo, harsh words!"

I slammed the door behind him, sending the bells flying. "He makes me soooo mad!" I said, slamming into the kitchen. The kitchen air was charged with something that prickled my neck, my parents' faces familiar, yet strange, too, in the yellowish glare of a naked lightbulb. My mother, taller than she should have been, looked predatory; my mother, yet someone else besides. My father, backed against his stove, glanced quickly at me and back at my mother. His eyes never left her face again.

"Do not *ever*," this mother said in a voice I'd never heard before, "*do not ever* risk the life of one of my children again. Do you hear me, Thomas Lewis?" Not a muscle twitched in my father's face. I waited for the joke that would break the tension, his arms to reach out and halve the distance between them so that she could come in, surrender. But neither of them moved. There was only her voice, this voice with a life all its own, a voice that might have dictated the terms of surrender to Hirohito or parted the Red Sea. "I mean this, Tom. Your life's your own. You may do any fool thing with it that you will. But not with Bron and Buddy. Not with my children."

"He didn't make me stay . . ." I said from half in, half out of the kitchen. She shot me a menacing glance.

"We were lucky this time," she said, softer now. "And we were lucky once before. God smiles on fools for His own good reason, and He's smiled twice on us. Don't push Him, Tom."

My father's smile was lopsided. I waited for him to fall apart, to crack at our feet like Humpty Dumpty, to quiver while we pasted him back together again. Instead, he straightened, and in his kitchen as the last of the bombers flew overhead, he grew tall as my mother. "I'll not be pushing Him again, lass," he said. "You have my word on that."

24

*n*O ONE TALKED about anything but the fire for several weeks. What else was there to talk about? Not a single teenager had wrecked his car, not one disgruntled spouse had shot another. And if there were unresolved angers or traces of bitterness at the culmination of a parched dry summer, the fire purged them. On the side of the mountain was an ugly black scar to remind the town how close disaster had licked.

Miraculously, just three homes had gone up, and a fund had been established at the bank to help the families get back on their feet. People gathered in all the usual places, Ojala Lanes, the bar at the Roundup, the Flying A, or stayed overlong in the checkout line at Bailey's Market or in the bank endlessly recounting what *they* had thought that night, what *they* (or their husband or neighbor) had done. How close to disaster they had come, how lucky we all were. You wanted to be a part of it, to hug close that feeling of camaraderie, of a whole town pulling together.

At the Frostee, Chick and J.C. were treated like heroes. I'd catch J.C. looking over at me as if to say, *See? They like me. What's the matter with you?*

The *Sun* announced a citywide celebration party to be held at the rec center. We shunned the rec center as a rule. It was too pitiful the way the city tried so hard to provide healthy diversions for us, softball games, ice-cream "socials," stitch-and-chats. Cold beer on ice and we'd have been there in droves. But we wouldn't miss this party. Everybody would be there.

I wrote Will, telling him all about the fire and the upcoming celebration. I wished that he could be there, I said. I knew he'd be sorry to have missed all the excitement. Had his family been evacuated? I was sure they had, though theirs wasn't one of the homes listed as destroyed. Already I'd gotten three letters from him, one written on the plane. In written words he sounded less sure of what he was doing. Despite the prestige of West Point, the food was appalling, they made you stand at attention till your feet grew numb. The instructors vied for the honor of dreaming up the best humiliation of the day. He hid his Robinson Jeffers under his mattress like a dirty book. He was a duck out of water, he said. In the night, just before sleep, he'd whisper my name and send it across all the space between us. Did I hear?

The rec center was brightly lit and jammed with people by the time I arrived with Lanie and Jimbo. Jimbo and I spoke to the left and right of each other. Or, if he said something straight into my face, the old way, it would be some nasty slur about Will.

A banner had been strung clear across the patio. THANKS, FIREFIGHTERS! it said in bright blue letters. Someone had attempted to draw a hose spurting water but it looked more like a penis, which drew a lot of laughs. Chunks of marinated beef sizzled on barbecues, and beer flowed from several kegs stuck into ice. Strains of a badly executed "Rock Around the Clock" blared out of the brightly lit rec room, strung with crepe paper and balloons left over from the previous year's Centennial Celebration.

"I'm gonna get me a beer," Jimbo announced, and pushed off into the crowd.

"He's got to find his buddies so they can swap more war stories," Lanie said fondly. "It's all he talks about." Lanie looked like her old self again. Her white dress was a copy of the one Marilyn Monroe wore to get her skirt blown up, and it looked just as great on Lanie as it did on Marilyn. "Don't you ever tell a soul, but I wasn't really all that worried about Jimmy that night," she said in a voice only I would hear. "You know how he is. All talk. But when I heard how he'd waded right in there . . . ! Whew! I swear I fell in love all over again." She rolled her eyes, then poked me with her elbow. She really did look happy.

We walked into the rec room just as the lights went out. "Hey!" several people yelled. "Aw, leave them off!" someone else cried, so they were left off. The light from the kitchen was enough to dance by and not bump into anyone else. The band slid pretty nicely into "Earth Angel," sending a flood of old memories my way, sock hops in Plainfield, Joe Panucci, whose ring I finally returned. Another life. I felt a hand touch my shoulder and turned into J.C.'s arms.

"I've been looking all over for you," he said.

"You have?" Coy, like Kim Novak in *Picnic*.

His eyebrows went up. "You don't believe me?"

He slid his hand down my back to draw me in. His ribs were hard against mine, his cheek smooth and smelling of

(279)

some after-shave that only he seemed to know about, a private stash. He moved with me or me with him, not a foot or a toe out of place. I closed my eyes and listened to the hum inside. The slightest pressure of a finger, the side of a palm, and I would move just right. He knew just what to do. Then he nibbled lightly on the crest of my right ear and I pulled away, tingles everyplace, like the feeling after a fever breaks, or just before one begins.

The song ended and I turned away like a zombie, toward the door to catch my breath. Where was Lanie? I felt pulled to leave, pulled to stay. I could sense J.C. somewhere behind me, daring me to turn. Daring me toward him. He knew I couldn't refuse a dare. It would be the same with him as it was with cars, that was what he knew, and so he drew me like a magnet, as a spark leaps from plug to piston. A soft mood had come over the crowd now as the band slid into "Moonglow." Couples nestled against each other in a common cocoon, drifting lazily through the dark.

Somehow I was in J.C.'s arms again, and aching. A good ache or a bad ache, what was the difference, all the same thing. . . . He could read me, that was his gift. He could read women, girls. That's what all the warnings were about. "Warm in here," he said against my ear. A tickle of sweat ran down the back of my neck. "Let's go outside."

He guided me through the crowd, across the grass, and there was the Deuce, grinning in the trees like a panther. Reaching in, J.C. pulled out a bottle. "Cold Duck," he said. "Good for what ails ya." He twisted the cap off and passed it to me. It was sweet, and sharp with bubbles. "Come on," he said, and opened the door.

"Where? What's wrong with this place?"

"You still don't like me, do you?" His green eyes teased the words to my lips.

"Sure I do."

"C'mon," he said. "Let's go for a ride."

I sat by the door, letting the wind dry the perspiration from my hair, from under my arms. My cotton skirt lifted in puffs as the air came through the vents. I knew without knowing where we were going. The Deuce sailed, singing. It was a sweet car.

"I've been thinking a lot about you," J.C. said.

"What have you been thinking?" About turning him away at the Bucking Bronco, that's what. I tipped the Cold Duck, letting the sweet liquid burn its way down.

"Huh?"

"*What* have you been thinking about me?"

"Oh, you know, just thinking. . . ." He grinned like the bearer of a well-guarded secret. "C'mon over here. Sit by Papa. I'm not going to bite you." He put his hand on my knee and I slid over. In the headlights of a car headed toward us, I glanced up at his profile, half expecting a sharp nose and serious dark eyes, but J.C.'s nose was like mine, small, a kind of snub nose. He had high cheekbones, a chiseled chin, skin smooth as a baby's. Where our arms touched, there was heat.

He swung the Deuce into the trees, just where I'd thought, only halfway through the dark orchard he turned again. "No one knows about this but me," he said with a wink. When he cut the engine a relentless sawing buzz of a zillion cicadas set in.

"So?" he said, turning, left arm over the steering wheel, the right one free, somewhere behind my shoulder. "It's your call," he said.

I wanted to kiss and run, that's all I wanted. A taste, no more, but I wanted that taste. He took my fingers between his lips and nibbled on the tips. He kissed the inside

(281)

of my arm. I wanted to jump toward him, away from him, as you do with a snake, all in one piece. I tilted up my face and his was right there. His lips were thin, like I remembered, and so sure, and this time I didn't pull away. He tugged gently at my blouse where it met my skirt. Phrases from romance novels leaped into my mind: *sensuous caress . . . her limbs in flames . . . the blaze of desire.* . . . I was shaking all over from the inside out, but J.C. was strangely still, calm, moving slowly as if through a field picking cotton. His hand slid up under my blouse to the edge of my bra and crept inside and I thought, That's where he'll stop, rear back, and laugh. Not a woman after all, a little boy, but when his fingers touched I felt my nipple swell and push into his hand. And something said, something reckless said, Why not? Sometime it's got to happen and why not now.

He fumbled with the button on my skirt, giving up, pushing the skirt instead up to my waist, peeling away the cotton panties, not the black silk ones, not the garter belt. Oh no, I said, pushing his hand away, then letting it find where the center of me throbbed and the panties came away and his breath came fast now, the zipper down, penis like a rubber thing I didn't want but too late, couldn't do it again, couldn't say no, and what the hell, it had to happen sometime.

"Hey," he said after, softly, brushing the tears away. "Why didn't you tell me you'd never done this before? I'd've, I don't know, been more careful." Careful. Wasn't it too late for careful? Did he think I had protection? "Hey, it wasn't too bad, was it?"

I blew my nose on the hem of my skirt and shook my head.

"You sure had me fooled," he said. "I said to myself,

Hey, this is one that really gets around. Know what I mean?"

I rode within his arm all the way back, head on his shoulder, but I was someone else looking on, detached. In a way, fascinated. As if I'd successfully completed a project in the biology lab. It wasn't going to blow up the world, my project. No big deal. Was it? It'd go into the back of a closet with all the others. Only I would know it was there.

And then I would think of Will.

The Welsh Kitchen was dark when J.C. dropped me off. He'd call, he said. Walking the walk of the ex-virgins, I went around to the back, opened the screen door, and pulled my father's old green sweater off its hook, slipping into it as if into the shelter of a cave. I tried hard not to think of Will, and the harder I tried, the harder it became not to. I couldn't cry. Not for Will, whom I was trying not to think about, and certainly not for myself. I wasn't worth the salt. All I could do was count. In four days, maybe five, I'd have my period. And so I was safe. Wasn't I? No one would ever have to know. Not Will (I'd been told you could hide these things), not my mom and dad. I wasn't even sure that I'd tell Lanie.

I got up and tiptoed through the kitchen, smelling of cold grease and Clorox, worn linoleum creaking underfoot. A smoke trail filtered toward me. In the darkness of the dining room, a pinpoint of orange light. "Daddy?"

"No, it's me," my mother said.

I could barely see her face in the dark, except when she inhaled and the burning tip of the cigarette caught the glaze of her eyes. "Can't sleep," she said with a little shrug. "Thought a smoke might settle me down. Don't you dare tell your father." I was grateful for the dark. A mother could certainly see if you returned in some condition other than the solid state in which she'd made you. "How was the party?"

"Good. The whole town was there. You and Daddy should have come."

"Well, there's this little thing called work, the business. . . ."

"I'll bet you didn't have a half-dozen customers."

"Ten, twelve." She sighed.

"Ma . . ."

"Hmmm?" She sucked the smoke in like a pro, funneling it out through her nose. Her fingers were slim and graceful, made for ebony cigarette holders, artist's brushes, not for fluting the edge of piecrusts. How could she stand it day after day, the same pies, the same tired complaints from customers, eighteen hours on her feet?

"Do you think there's just one person for one person? You know, like people are destined for each other, to find each other? And then you just *know*?"

All the tables had antennae made from the legs of upended chairs. I could feel my mother thinking. After a while she said, "Sometimes I think that's true. Sometimes I think your daddy and I would have found each other some other way if it hadn't happened at camp. . . . I don't know."

"Well, how do you know? What happened that day on the dock after he kissed you that first time?"

She laughed. "I couldn't stand him."

"But then when did you know?"

"Are you asking me how you know when you're in love?"

"Yeah, I guess. . . . How do you know that?"

"Oh, a little voice inside tells you. That's what I always heard."

"And then you'd know for sure, right? And you'd never look at anybody else. You'd stay true no matter what, right?"

"Well, your dad didn't give me a chance. He followed me home from camp, and there wasn't a day I didn't spend with him right up till the day we got married." She sounded less than pleased with him. "Wasn't taking any chances, I guess."

The house creaked and settled. Sometimes it seemed you could still smell smoke leaking from the rafters. I reached for a cigarette. Her hand came across the table as if to snatch it back, but instead I heard the scratch of a match and a flame met the end of my cigarette. We smoked like sisters in the darkness. After a while she said, "It's Will, isn't it? You love him."

"I think I always did."

"Then you know," she said.

Tears slid down my face, and as I inhaled I saw my mother's eyes squinting through the dark into mine. "What? What is it?" she said. "Tell me."

But I couldn't. There were things you didn't tell your mother. And, besides, to tell would make it real, something I could never take back.

"Why did you drag us out here anyway?" I said instead, opening an old wound.

"Oh, Bron, not that again. You know why. Your father was dying." She heard me start to say something and pushed on, "No, not just that awful thing he did. That was physical. It could be patched, taped up. It would heal. The other . . . dying . . . that was inside. I had to risk it, don't you see?"

She grabbed my free hand, squeezing the words into me. "I had to risk what we had to keep him alive."

"It was just a threat," I said bitterly. "A spit in the eye. He didn't really want to die, or he'd have done it right."

"Bron . . . Bron. . . ." I felt rather than saw the shake of her head, the croon of my name like a balm. "You talk about love," she said. "About how you know you're in love. Well, that's how. I'd have done anything to help your father come alive, to breathe life into him. No, he didn't cut deep enough, not then. He didn't even have the heart to do himself in."

She tapped a half-smoked cigarette against the ashtray several times, then ground it out. "You don't know," she said. "You don't know what it's like to do something you can't take back, an irreparable thing, something you have to spend the rest of your life regretting."

I sucked smoke to numb the ache in my throat.

"How would you feel if every day of your life you had to earn, *earn* someone's forgiveness?"

I NEVER WROTE Will again. Each time I tried, the words stuck like dead flies to the paper. One part of me would say, So you made a little mistake, so what? If he knew, he'd understand. He'd forgive you. That's the way he is. The other part said, You made your bed, girl, now lie in it.

I'd ponder for hours the age-old question of why things were different for boys from the way they were for girls. When Tommy Nyro lost his virginity (at thirteen, he said, but you had to wonder), he ran outside and bayed at the moon. He was a *man*! He'd finally wet his dipstick and couldn't wait to do it again. Why didn't Lanie feel that way when she lost her virginity? Why did *Seventeen* ask *Will He Still Love You Tomorrow? Six Good Reasons to Say No*. No self-respecting boy would ever read *Seventeen*. How could he know about the six good reasons? It was all up to us girls to fight them off and fight down our own feelings as well. It wasn't fair. If God had meant us all to be virgins, wouldn't He have set the start-up button closer to twenty than twelve?

I'd get angry and the anger would make me strong. The racetrack wasn't made for girls either, but that didn't stop me. Why was this any different? It was God's fault, that's what! Or if not God, then America. But that never worked for long. What it came down to in the end was Will. Just a boy and a girl. Will and me. He'd been saving up for something special. I'd cashed in early.

Sure I could pretend, lie if I had to. But Will didn't deserve that. He was too good for that.

Will continued to write. He began to sound puzzled: "I hope my letters aren't getting lost in the mail. . . ." Then worried. "Are you okay? Is everything okay?" Then I stopped reading. I stopped reading his letters.

I did not see myself as cruel. I had simply become someone else, someone he would not have written to had he known who she really was.

J.C. was surprisingly attentive. He'd phone on a whim with some amusing little story. He always took me out on Saturday night. He wasn't a bad guy. In fact, he was quite ordinary. I'd test his knowledge of literature, of classical music by dropping names, like stones, into the dull water of an ordinary conversation. He'd flunk every time. And smile. It didn't matter to him, and he would have been surprised to know that it mattered to me. We communicated according to a formula I should have recognized before, half oil, half water. We were best in a crowd where we didn't have to make real conversation. We hung out at the

Frostee or else on the porch of the Welsh Kitchen in the slow hours of the afternoon between lunch and dinner. We'd get on each other's nerves. "What's the matter with you?"

"Nothing. What's the matter with you?"

"Nothing."

I was sitting with my back to the street one afternoon late in November, legs propped up on J.C.'s chair, when I heard the Jeep. It had an unmistakable miss in the engine every third stroke that my heart took up like an old song. I turned and saw Will hop out and amble up the walk. He had the beginning traces of a smile on his face, the kind of smile a fond husband might allow himself returning home after a hard day's work. The presence, the outdoors, the rightness of him hit me like something solid in the chest.

"You know this guy?" J.C. said. We both stood. J.C.'s left hand moved proprietarily to the back of my neck. He extended his right. "Hi, I'm J.C." Big smile.

Will hesitated for a fraction of a second, looked at me, then took J.C.'s hand.

"This is Will," I said, lips numb. "Will Harding."

Will slipped off his hat, scratched the back of his head, all in one motion. "You doing okay?" he said. His look took all of me in as if, for the moment, J.C. had never been there.

"Okay," I said, a hollow sound.

"Just here for the weekend," he said. "You know, checking up." His face reddened. "I mean, the ranch and all. . . ."

"Nice boots," J.C. said with a smirk.

Will looked at him as if he couldn't remember who he was and looked back over at me. I shucked J.C.'s hand off the back of my neck.

"Well, I just thought I'd drop by," he said. "I'll, uh, give you a call."

We both smiled, an old joke. "Give me a call once in a while," I'd chided him. If you were a couple, the guy was supposed to call. That's the way it was. He'd curl his hands around his mouth like a megaphone. "Bron!" he'd cry. "Bronwyn! Can Bron come out and play?"

I watched him read my eyes. "It's okay," he said at last as if to himself, very quietly, then maybe to me: "It's okay." Then he settled his hat back on and turned. We watched him hop into the Jeep. He made a U-turn, waved, and was gone.

"Where'd'ja know that shitkicker from?" J.C. said.

Will didn't call. We both knew it was up to me, but I was stuck, floating behind a dam I'd begun to build after the night in the orchard with J.C. I didn't know how to get out from behind it. And finally it was easier not to.

I saw the Jeep pass the house one afternoon and my heart grabbed hard, but it was David Harding at the wheel with Timmy beside him. Had Will gone back to school, then? My days settled into a pattern as familiar as Lanie's in that trailer at the edge of town. There was work; there was school. At the end of the day, there'd be J.C. with the after-shave that was already wearing thin.

AND THEN ONE MORNING I awoke to find my father sitting on the end of my bed, head down as if he were sleeping sitting up, or maybe praying.

"Daddy?"

"Will had an accident, honey," he said. "With the gun."

THERE IS A CERTAIN THING in people that will not accept accident. That weaves and spins and forces, and finds at last some fit between event and cause, between a person and the thing that was done. It is merciless. It does not rest until the pieces fit, the guilty party or parties indicted, the world made rational again and safe, the lid back on Pandora's box. After all, what kind of a world would it be if, stepping out into the sunlight of an ordinary day, you had to carry with you the knowledge that you might never return? and that you, yourself, would have nothing whatever to do with that. What kind of a God would maim a child or take the life of a loved one for whatever mysterious reason? You had to be able to explain away accident or it would always be there, like a beggar at the door.

On the other hand, if you needed to absolve yourself or someone else from blame, that's exactly what you said. It was an accident (silly, tragic, fatal . . .). And so my father had had his little "accident." Only with ourselves and with those we love are we ever that kind. In all other cases, there has to be a reason, a line leading back to the powder keg.

No one who knew Will, knew what kind of boy he was, believed the rumors that licked their way across town toward the Hardings' ranch. But Will was not well known. He was a rancher, a boy who wore a gun. Drove that old Army Jeep, you know the one. Strange family, kept to themselves. . . . Couldn't be an accident, they said, that boy knew guns, couldn't be an accident. The kid was making a statement, the way they do sometimes when they're young. Tragic. What's happening with kids these days?

YOUTH FOUND SHOT the *Sun's* banner read, and then the facts: William Harding IV, 19, had gone to visit his grandmother the previous afternoon, and when he didn't arrive, the grandmother, Mrs. T. E. Davidson of Pasadena, called Harding's mother, who went out in search of him. Mrs. Harding found her son's body in his car on the old ranch road. She found the gun on the floor. The county coroner located the small hole in the boy's femoral artery through which his life spilled, it was said, in less than eight minutes.

My father closed the restaurant for the day. "We'll go for a ride," he said. "Up the coast." I knew the sacrifice he was making, but I was too numb to argue or to be grateful. My mother went in search of her purse. I followed her like a sleepwalker. She put her arms around me. She rocked me like a child, but I was stiff inside with horror. Something had happened to tear the fabric of my life; what was it? Will was gone. Was gone. But there was a shield between me and what that meant. Objects had an unreal quality to them as if they could be walked through. Voices had a hollow ring, even my own, as if we were talking in a tunnel.

Buddy and I sat together in the backseat, as if we were setting out across the country all over again. In a year he had grown so much that he didn't have to reach to look out the window. He watched me with worried eyes as if I were ticking and might blow any second.

We went out the mouth that had sucked us in, the long curving road through the ring of mountains, and there suddenly was the sea and out beyond, like humpback whales, a string of gray islands. There were people strolling along the edge of the water, a few in bathing suits though the air had a decided chill to it. Boys balanced six-foot-long surfboards on three-foot waves. A red kite danced in an updraft. A flock of pelicans playing Simon Says sailed inches from the water and up again. It was all so exotic. We might have lived hundreds of miles away for all we knew of this California.

We stopped for fish and chips on the Ventura pier. My mother and father did their usual critique: "The batter's pre-made," my father said. "Tch, tch," my mother said. "Bottled dressing on the coleslaw, too." My fries grew cold. My father and mother watched me with haunted eyes. Suddenly I'd have done anything to make them happy. "It's not bad," I said. "The fish." And then, in imitation of my father: "What were you expecting? Sturgeon roe?"

My father barked. My mother's eyes filled. Buddy picked his nose.

"Well, it's good to get away," my father pronounced. "Just like old times. Just the family."

My mother insisted I take Buddy to the memorial service. "That way I know you'll drive carefully," she said, wiser than I sometimes gave her credit for. He had to have a new suit, since he'd outgrown his old one. It was dark gray with knife-edged creases in the pants and wide lapels. He looked like an underaged undertaker. "You may take off the jacket in the car," she said, brushing imaginary lint from his shoulder. "Bron, make sure his shirt is tucked in and his tie is straight." Buddy and I set off on the curving back road to Santa Barbara, sailing past avocado orchards, Buddy stiff and awkward in his new suit, his hair stuck in clumps from too much Brylcreem. Clouds like the kind on our Welsh posters hung in a deep blue sky. Crows called from high in the eucalyptus trees. It was a day no one could die on. Still, because of Buddy, I took the turns sensibly. "Sanitary driving," J.C. called it.

I didn't know why Mrs. Harding had chosen Santa Barbara for the service until I saw the church. It was set within a stand of immense pine trees, a small wooden church that seemed, in its natural setting, to intentionally efface itself. Its one vanity was a glorious stained glass window, a kaleidoscope on the verge of sudden change with chips of red and blue and gold and green like emeralds.

(292)

It was dark inside, cool, and smelled slightly of floor polish. A scatter of people in pews faced a simple altar and two banks of lilies. I'd expected a coffin. Had steeled myself for a coffin. She would not have had it open, I'd been certain of that. She was far too private for that. Only now did I understand just how private she was. She would share as little as possible of her son with the rest of us. If not buried already, he would be soon, next to his father, where he'd always known he'd be. When he was an old man. When people were supposed to die. I saw her in the front row, a son on each side.

As Buddy and I crept into a pew at the back, the organist did a soft run of notes sliding, minor, then a hymn that sounded familiar, though the words wouldn't come. I'd heard of services where they expected you to stand up and say something about the deceased, and felt I might slide right under the pew if anyone looked my way. Fine wires and string held me together for I didn't know how long. When Buddy slipped his hand out of mine I realized I'd been cutting off his circulation. I'd be expected to say something, wouldn't I? The girlfriend who used to be. The one, you know . . .

The service was brief. A minister took the podium and began talking about somebody named William Harding (Bill, he said at one point), a fine student, a dutiful son. He said nothing about his integrity (couldn't his mother have told him about that?), about his love for Robinson Jeffers's poetry, or that he knew everything there was to know about the Chumash. He might have been talking about someone very ordinary, a nice kid. I wanted to stand up then. I wanted to say, "Stop this nonsense!" Will would have laughed at all this. We should be standing all together, those who loved him, on Hurricane Deck. We should be watching hawks glide, listening to the wind, to the things that carried on after we were gone.

Outside again in the brilliant afternoon sunshine, I joined the line that inched its way to where Mrs. Harding and the boys stood. Mrs. Harding stood ramrod straight, shaking hands, accepting condolences with a firm nod of the chin. Moving toward her, I began to crumble, and when I was facing her, my hand in both of hers, I began to babble, "I'm sorry, I'm sorry. . . ." Tears choked back whatever else I might have thought to say.

She held me up with her two thin hands and said, "It couldn't be helped, my dear. You mustn't go on so." The brothers gazed on with well-bred scorn.

She passed me on, leaning over to shake Buddy's hand. "Will was a good guy," Buddy said.

Mrs. Harding smiled from a long way off. "Yes, dear, he was," she said.

I spent whole days on Hurricane Deck, leaving Silver below in the shade and climbing up the dusty trail in my sandals, like a pilgrim. I knew what Will would have to say about all this, how gentle he would be. I even knew that at some point he would have laughed.

I would talk to myself or to him, trying to figure things out. Sometimes I'd pound my fist in the dust and yell, as if he were in the sky looking down, like the God of my childhood. "Damn you and your gun! Damn you and your damned gun!" And then I'd be stricken with a terrible guilt and sob that I had betrayed some understanding I should have had but didn't.

The *Sun* reported an ongoing investigation into the incident. There was evidence of foul play, they said, a beer bottle, though Will had never been known to drink beer, a tear in his shirt at the collar as if he'd been grabbed. But he'd been found with his wallet in his pocket and his father's expensive watch still on his wrist. Who would have shot him except in a robbery attempt? He hadn't an enemy in the world.

J.C. came around just like he always did, but I couldn't talk to him. He grew angry, then sullen. He called less often and finally stopped coming around. I couldn't blame him. He was trying to understand, but I wouldn't let him in. It would be the final violation, I thought, of what I'd once had with Will. Will's letters were in a cigar box next to my bed. Opening the box, seeing the spikes of his words as they grew more anxious would destroy me, I thought, and so I didn't open it. But the letters and Jeffers's poems were all I had left of him. The only thing I could touch that he had touched. I would never throw them away. In the isolation and blind self-centeredness of my youth, I was certain that I would never recover. I fully intended to die of a broken heart. No one had ever suffered more, felt such pain. I would never let it go.

From Hurricane Deck I'd look down at the Hardings' ranch and pretend Will would come out of the barn at any moment, turn and wave up at me. I wanted to crawl beneath the covers of Will's bed, touch his books, sit at his desk, stick my feet in his old boots, bury my face in his clothes. I needed to be close to something besides the letters in the box.

And, much as I despised myself for giving in to doubt, I had to find out for sure. I had to hear from someone who knew him at least as well as I did that he'd never do the thing they said, never take his own life. Only his mother would know that.

I called her on the telephone, fingers damp, voice jittery. Of course I could see her, she said. Any afternoon. Wednesday would be fine. I should come for tea.

On Wednesday, appropriately, the sky cracked open and it began to rain. Fat drops pelted Silver's hood and spattered up like grease. Her wipers, cracked and ineffectual from months of baking in the heat, thwack-thwacked across the windshield, leaving traces of mud in their wake. There were branches in the road I had to steer around, scattered wet leaves. This was country that never got used to rain. There were no gutters. Ditches would fill and overflow, sending waves of water across the road. People drowned in senseless ways, driving across swollen streams, saving cattle that had spooked and stood up to their withers in what had been the dry bed of a river, bawling.

I felt steadier, warmer as I neared the ranch, as if a part of me allowed itself to be deceived. Will would be there after all. It was all a mistake, a case of mistaken identity. He would come to the door, he'd be laughing like he'd really pulled one over this time. I'd be furious with him, but what was my fury to the flesh of him again?

I wondered, when you lost somebody, how long it would be before the feeling of him against you faded. Was there some force field, some lingering thread of energy that held on for just so long while you, and the spirit of the person you loved, learned to let go? Because I could feel him sometimes, as if he had just been with me. Will. Not my imagination of what Will would feel like but the real person. If that stopped, I didn't know how I could go on.

Will's mother appeared like a gray ghost behind the screen door. It opened with a familiar screech and she held it as I stepped in. "You're right on time," she said, as if I'd been trusted with a special responsibility and been a very good girl about it. "The tea's just ready. Make yourself comfortable." She disappeared into the kitchen.

I slipped out of my rain jacket and hung it on the peg next to Will's sheepherder's jacket. I glanced toward the kitchen and, because I couldn't help myself, buried my face in the sleeve. It smelled like smoke and hay. It made my throat ache. When I pulled my face away, I saw that Mrs. Harding had been watching. Despite the weight of the tray it was quite clear that she would have stood until I'd finished my barbaric little ritual, however long it took, and come to my senses. "Shall we go into the parlor?" she said.

Rain beat against the french doors. Opposite, over the rose bower couch, raindrops slid in a shadow show down the wall. The pendulum on the grandfather clock rocked back and forth, but you couldn't hear it for the rain. There was dust on the piano, a sign that not all was well.

Mrs. Harding's hand shook as she poured the tea. The cup she passed me clattered lightly in its saucer. "Forgive me, I've run out of cream," she said. "I hope milk will do." Her smile was weary. Had she been that impossibly thin all along? Except for prominent blue veins and age spots like my father's, her hands were as small as a child's. She wore the same long skirt she'd had on the day we met and an olive green blouse, silk or something equally elegant. Her hair was in a neat bun. There were deep shadows beneath her gray eyes.

"I don't know why I'm here exactly . . ." I said.

"Of course you do, my dear," she said smoothly. "You want to be near Will." She smiled as if she'd caught me with my hand in the cookie jar. "And that you know is not possible." Rain pelted the glass door. She lifted her cup halfway to her lips, then replaced it in its saucer. My eyes went inadvertently toward Will's room.

"And," she continued smoothly, "you want to know that it wasn't your fault." Her eyes called mine back. My mouth was dry. I could not manage the tea. Was I supposed to speak? "I can assure you that it wasn't." There was kindness there, behind the pain. I'd recognized it before but had not needed it then. It had been easier to make her unapproachable, less than fully human.

She stirred a quarter teaspoon of sugar into her tea, raised the cup to her lips and took a small sip, frowned, and returned the cup to its saucer. She gave me time to speak, but I couldn't. Finally, because I could see that she wasn't going on, I said, "I don't think I can stand it."

Our eyes locked. Who was I to own a grief beyond a mother's? "Of course you can," she said. "You can because you have to. For Will, if not for yourself. Anything less would be a betrayal of your feelings for him, don't you see." It wasn't a question.

"I hurt him," I said. Betrayal, she'd said. How much did she know?

She said nothing more for a long time. She stirred her tea. I watched the slide of the raindrops. Finally she said, "We hurt each other in a thousand ways over a lifetime. You and Will didn't have a lifetime, that was the only difference. He cared a great deal for you. You must know that."

"Yes . . ."

"But he would never have taken his own life, Bron. You mustn't listen when that sort of thing is said. Ojala has all the need for drama of a two-bit saloon."

"I didn't think . . . I didn't believe . . ."

"No, of course not. You knew him. One only had to know what kind of young man he was. Now," she said. I put down my saucer. I was being dismissed. "I'd like you to play for me if you would."

I glanced quickly at the piano. She couldn't be serious. "If you'd do me the honor," she said. I wondered if she'd ever been refused anything in her life. If that was the case, how did she deal with God? How could she manage the loss of a son?

I went to the piano and sat on the cool bench. I lifted the lid. My fingers, independent of any thoughts my mind might have had, any decisions about what might be appropriate, found Mozart's Twenty-first Concerto. The notes rose in a kind of incantation, clear and bell-like over the sound of the rain. I closed my eyes and it was as if that great belly of a Steinway were playing itself. What had I to do with any of it? But when I began really to listen and allowed myself to feel, I found that place where notes are born, in sinew and brain and tendon and something else less tangible we call soul. The notes carried me free, free for the moment that I played them even from Will. They delivered me across the river of overwhelming self-pity in which I had been drowning and deposited me on another shore.

I felt her hand on my shoulder, a light pressure, when the piece ended. "Go on, please," she said. And so we went on, Mrs. Harding and Bronwyn Lewis, in the rain. With Chopin and then Schumann and Bach. I wondered how I could have forgotten how exquisite each piece was, how each answered in its own way whatever was asked and ended in the resolution of a prayer.

I stopped at last and felt her hand leave my shoulder. "Thank you, my dear," she said quietly. I think she might have been crying and I didn't dare look.

(299)

I'd played well. As well as I'd ever played in my life. And I knew for the first time what promise was, and how I'd shucked it off like an ill-fitting coat, one more thing to be sorry about. If ever I was going to do something right in my life, I'd better start soon.

Epilogue

NEAR THE END of my stay at the music academy, my mother called to say that the investigation into the death of Will Harding had been dropped. Tests were done and they'd re-created the death scene in various ways. Jimbo had been interrogated, but no one believed, not even I, that he would ever go that far. Officially, Will died as a result of an accident with a handgun. In the room I shared with a roommate, I sat staring out the window into the courtyard below. It was spring and a line of daffodils edged the walk, their bright faces to the sun. I had just written Mrs. Harding, as I did every few weeks. I found it easy for some reason to talk with her on paper, to tell her how I was getting on. It was more than the fact that her money, the money she'd saved for Will's future, made a dream I'd once had into a reality. We'd connected that day in her parlor. There were things she expected of me, beyond the expectations of my own parents, whom I'd always pleased no matter what.

(301)

There were times when I resented those expectations, chafed under them. For a time, when things were particularly hard, I thought she might be punishing me for having loved her son. Why else would she pay my tuition? What else could move her to walk into the restaurant one afternoon and offer this new life? She'd stunned us all. But she knew, didn't she? how hard it would be and that I would fail. That's how she'd get even. The more illogical my reasoning, the harder I fought through practice, the harder I tried. That she, beneath the quiet chilly demeanor, could simply be a woman of great generosity and goodness was beyond my understanding.

The academy was a serious place. Only serious students of music were invited to attend. Only the very serious remained. I don't remember much laughter, though it was a beautiful place to be, cloistered within the trees. I'd been close enough to live at home, of course, but it was a condition of the scholarship, Mrs. Harding insisted, that I live on campus. She was wise enough to know that I should not be tempted unnecessarily by those who would not understand why someone would ever want to master a fugue.

She told me that day in the little parlor, after I played for her, about finding Will in the Jeep. It was not easy to hear, but it gave me the answer I needed just then.

It was the turkey buzzards, she said. She was not a half-dozen steps from the back door when she saw them circling. "I told myself," she said, "that it was a cow, some other large animal. I hoped not one of the horses." She looked out through the rain-streaked window as she spoke, and after a while I could not be sure which were the shadows of raindrops and which were her tears. "And of course it was Will and he was dead. There was no doubt that he was dead." Her eyes shifted to the hands clasped in her lap. "I climbed into that old Jeep"—she looked at me then and smiled almost shyly, eyes brimming with tears—"and I took his hand. And I said to myself, You don't know this boy, you never knew this boy." She pulled a handkerchief from the pocket of her skirt and gave her nose one good hard blow. "Because, you see, it seemed so clear that he'd taken his own life. Yes," she said to my stricken face. "Even I, who should certainly have known better, entertained that awful notion." She tucked the handkerchief back in her pocket and her eyes came suddenly alive. Her shoulders straightened. She was her old self again. "It was then that I remembered the snakes." I must have looked puzzled. "Surely you know how it happened, Bronwyn, the way he'd whip that damned gun out and shoot on the run, right out the side of the car before you could even think to catch your breath." And suddenly I saw it, and it was just as she said. Only this time the gun didn't slide free of the holster, it caught on a buckle or a button and went off. An accident. "Damned cowboy," she muttered through her tears.

I let that be. I even thought for a time that by accepting her version of things, I was protecting her. From a horrible senseless reality. The way my mother had tried to protect us that morning in the kitchen long ago when she said, "Your father has had an accident." Of course I knew better. I knew it was my fault, that as surely as if I'd taken Will's gun in my own hand, I'd killed him. He was a romantic, even a little naïve. His heart had broken that day on the porch. That was what I should have known. He was a boy whose heart could be broken. *That* was his essential nature.

And then I began to think, What if it were the other way around? What if Will's mother had been protecting me? Would she have done that? Wouldn't she, that afternoon in her little parlor, for practicality's sake if nothing else, do what she could to avoid destroying another young life? She'd known all along that he'd killed himself. Of course he had. But she was the only one who would ever know that. A last intimacy with her eldest son. There must have been a note, I decided, some kind of suicide note. Had she saved it? I chewed long and hard on that, resenting her knowing something I would never know. At least she had certainty; I would have to live without the answer to what had become the central question of my life.

And finally I had to accept that she knew nothing more than I did. There was no simple answer to what could never be answered simply. Perhaps what had happened to Will was an accident; perhaps it wasn't. Perhaps it was and also wasn't, a terrible ambiguity but one closer to the way things really are in life.

Suppose that in reaching for the gun as he always did, Will thought for just a fraction of a second about the girl on the porch, about the boy she had chosen in his place. Wouldn't that have done it? Veered the mind and hand just far enough off center? My fault, pure and simply. But Will had chosen guns as I had chosen cars, as my father chose alcohol. Will carried a loaded gun everywhere. The gun had a hair trigger. He used it irresponsibly, even recklessly. What if, instead of me, he was thinking about school? Thinking about the fact that a choice had been made for him, one he'd not have made for himself. Was the act that took his life then, at least in part, his mother's fault? I needed an answer so desperately that I'd have laid the blame in God's lap if I could have. I'd have laid my burden down, gratefully.

Two months before I left for Juilliard, Lanie had a baby girl. They named her April, for the month and because "April Love" had been one of *their* songs. Lanie left Jimbo when April was just six weeks old. He'd grabbed the baby, she said, grabbed her and tossed her like a dish towel across the kitchen floor because she wouldn't stop crying. That was what it took finally to leave him for good. Lanie could never have done it for herself. I left that June, afraid to find in every letter she wrote that she had given in, gone back again, but she never did. Instead she began to take accounting classes at City College. "I'm pretty good at this stuff," she wrote. "There's a brain in the old skull after all! (Don't count the words I spelled wrong, okay?)" The following June she married the police chief's son, who was himself a policeman. "The nicest guy in the entire state of California," she said. "And here he was the whole time, just waiting!" I flew home to be her maid of honor. They married, at my suggestion, in the redwood church where Will's memorial service had been.

ARLINGTON NATIONAL CEMETERY is as beautiful a place as I've ever seen, no matter that it's filled with gravestones, reminders that life comes, expected or unexpected, always to an end. In my trips there I'd pass the Kennedy graves, the flame that never dies. Will's grave is far more modest, of course. There's just a small bronze plaque next to his father's, identical except for two things, the numeral after the name and Robinson Jeffers's words:

> *Life is grown sweeter and lonelier,*
> *And death is no evil.*

Each time when I was there, I'd feel as if I'd completed some loop begun that day when Will said, "You should go to the music academy, Bron." After a while I no longer mourned for what might have been, and I never rose to that exquisite place where one is grateful for having known "such a wonderful person." I would have given it all up, every last note of music, to have Will back.

There are musicians, my favorite teacher said, and there are those who play instruments. "One must have felt great pain," he said in that thick Russian accent, "in here." He tapped his chest dramatically. It took years to acknowledge that I had become a musician in part because I had known Will at that time when life came hard and fast and impressions went deep; that I had become a fine musician—and this has always been more difficult—because I no longer had him in my life.

VALERIE HOBBS teaches writing at UC Santa Barbara. She has published many short stories in literary and commercial magazines. This is her first novel.

She and her husband, a high school teacher, live in Santa Barbara, California.